The House of the Prophet

Also by
Louis Auchincloss

Fiction
The Indifferent Children
The Injustice Collectors
Sybil
A Law for the Lion
The Romantic Egoists
The Great World and Timothy Colt
Venus in Sparta
Pursuit of the Prodigal
The House of Five Talents
Portrait in Brownstone
Powers of Attorney
The Rector of Justin
The Embezzler
Tales of Manhattan
A World of Profit
Second Chance
I Come as a Thief
The Partners
The Winthrop Covenant
The Dark Lady
The Country Cousin

Nonfiction
Reflections of a Jacobite
Pioneers and Caretakers
Motiveless Malignity
Edith Wharton
Richelieu
A Writer's Capital
Reading Henry James
Life, Law and Letters
Persons of Consequence: Queen Victoria
and her Circle

The House
of the
Prophet

Louis Auchincloss

Houghton Mifflin Company
BOSTON 1980

Library of Congress Cataloging in Publication Data

Auchincloss, Louis.
The house of the prophet.

I. Title.
PZ3.A898Hp   [PS3501.U25]   813'.5'4   79-21382
ISBN 0-395-29084-8

Printed in the United States of America

s 10 9 8 7 6 5 4 3 2 1

For Adele

A prophet is not without honor,
save in his own country and
in his own house.

— *Matthew 13:57*

The House of the Prophet

Roger Cutter (1)

NOTHING is more shocking about old age than the speed with which even the most famous persons are isolated and forgotten. Felix Leitner had been a friend of presidents, of chiefs of state; his books and columns had been read by millions and taught in schools and colleges; his name had been mentioned in cartoon captions, in plays and even musicals, as the very symbol of the intellectual commentator, the detached political philosopher; and yet, in his eighty-third year, a "guest" at Mrs. Corliss's small but select nursing home in McLean, Virginia, he was largely dependent on me for his books, his papers, his company and the management of such affairs as he had left.

I do not mean to imply that Felix's isolation was entirely the result of the world's hardness or shortness of memory. Most of his old friends were dead or in similar condition. His daughter, Felicia, came dutifully, if rather noisily, once a month to call; the thinness of their relationship was as much his fault as hers. He had no wife, but then he had been twice divorced. And younger friends were put off by his sudden irrationalities. Some were secretly repelled; others wondered if it was worth their while to call, if he would even remember that they had. And McLean is a half hour's drive from Washington.

He had made a considerable recovery from the stroke that had for a month paralyzed his left side. He could walk again, though laboriously, and he had fair use of his arms. His speech was usually clear, though the wrong word sometimes emerged. But his brain was given to curious twists. Sometimes he would be rational for as much as fifteen minutes at a time, a strange shrill ghost of the old Felix; at others, he would take complete leave of reality. The alteration would come without warning, as in this interchange:

"Roger, do you remember my address book?"

"The red leather one? It's with your other things in storage. Do you want me to get it out?"

"No, but I want you to do something for me. It has an invaluable list of people who do things and fix things: you know, tailors, cleaners, upholsterers, caterers, and the like. I couldn't get on without it. I want you to speak to my lawyer about putting it in my will."

"For what purpose?"

"I want to leave it to Harvard."

It never ceased to seem strange to me that I should be the person in the world closest to Felix. All of my life I had seen him through a barrier of older, more privileged people. As a boy, in Seal Cove, Maine, he had been the revered friend of my parents, the star of their circle. When as a young man I had been favored with his friendship, there had been nothing like intimacy. It had been the relationship of master and disciple. And even in the last years, when as his principal research assistant I had come to play a major role in his personal life, running his household, paying the bills and so forth, the factor of employment had placed a certain distance between us. But now, suddenly, I was "in charge of" Felix Leitner. And it was a position, too, that nobody disputed, nobody envied me.

Except perhaps Julie Pryor. She had been the closest of his woman friends in the last years and had acted as his hostess at the little parties in Q Street. It had been she who had persuaded me that Felix should be moved to a nursing home.

"It's really not safe to have him at home, Roger, no matter how well you set it up. When the next stroke comes, he should be in a spot where there's every sort of help available. I know just the place, too — Mrs. Corliss's in McLean. It isn't like a nursing home at all. Very comfortable, with only a few distinguished patients. Justice Kent went there, and old Senator Blandford. We can see him all the time and take him out for drives and meals. He might even come home if he gets better!"

Of course, we both knew that Felix wasn't going to get better. But I felt sick after this conversation with Julie. I had prayed that Felix would die before so drastic a step should become necessary. What I found hardest to bear was the speed with which one became accustomed to his present state. It was as if he had died and we had buried him and placed a crazy barber's pole instead of a tombstone on the site. Sometimes, when I sat by him in his wheelchair, watching him stare at some inane family comedy on the television screen, I would almost shriek under my breath, "Die, can't you! Die now!"

But when he was moved to the nursing home, he seemed to improve, and I had to concede that Julie had been right.

Mrs. Corliss was of Virginian origin, very distinguished, if one were to credit all she claimed. She was a little chirping bird of a woman, with raven-black dyed hair, a sharp knife of a nose and two plump hands that she was always clapping or clasping. Her establishment, a former private house, was all on one story with little oblong wings that protruded into a pretty garden and lawn. It had been "modern" when built in 1920. She could take six inmates, each of whom had a bedroom and living room. Meals were served on trays, but there was a large parlor and a dining room for those who were sufficiently "ambulatory" to use them. The furnishing was comfortable, miscellaneous, Victorian. The walls were covered with large bad landscapes and prints of historical scenes. The service was excellent, and the nurses did not wear uniforms. The "guests" did not see each other unless they wanted to. It was not unlike a small summer hotel.

Felix seemed calmer after a few weeks in the place, and his mind was distinctly improved. But there were moments, perhaps when he sensed that he was never going to get out of there, that he had terrible tantrums. I happened to be present when he threw a glass of tomato juice at the girl who brought him his tray. He had wanted some other aperitif. Mrs. Corliss appeared almost at once, as if she had anticipated the incident.

"Now, Mr. Leitner," she said in a firm but kindly tone, tapping the tips of her fingers together, "I think I had better explain to you one of our house rules. We are all ladies and gentlemen here, and we try to get on. Mary is going to have to change her dress, which will mean that Mrs. Lydig next door will have to wait another fifteen minutes for her lunch. Now we don't want that to happen again, do we?"

Felix stared at her with his mouth half open as if he did not understand. But when he spoke, he was perfectly docile.

"It was an accident," he said bleakly.

And this was the great Felix Leitner!

It was the time of Watergate. The funeral pyre of our presidency, providing as it did a flickering background for the decline of Felix, gave me a lurid sense of national conflagration. Although I had never been an admirer of Nixon, I found that for some curious psychological reason I tended to identify myself in his plight. As the months passed with their increasingly scandalous revelations, I felt some of the agony of our chief executive, twisting and turning, doubling back in his tracks, increasingly tangled in the mesh of his lies, an Emperor Jones alone in the fetid jungle of his misgovernment, listening to the ineluctable approach of the drums. Then I would imagine the president impeached, indicted, convicted, even jailed, standing, pale and haggard, in the corner of a prison yard while a circle of convicts mocked him. I fancied that there might be a kind of masochistic ecstasy in the sheer scale of such humiliation. The fall would be so awesome as to dwarf the crime.

On Felix's eighty-third birthday I arranged a little party in Mrs. Corliss's parlor, with champagne and a cake, for some of the old Washington friends. There were only about a dozen there, including Gladys Leitner — Felix's second wife — the faithful Julie and a nice young man from the *Washington Post*. Mrs. Corliss, very gracious, with an orchid pinned to her shoulder, glanced about among the elderly, perhaps in search of new recruits. Felix, neat and brushed, looked oddly young in his wheelchair. His snow-white hair was almost regal, and his long pale face and once so luminous skin seemed less blotched than ordinarily in these sad days. But when he rolled his large eyes you could see how bloodshot they were.

The conversation was desultory, constrained. We talked, of course, of Watergate. Gladys Leitner took the lead.

"Everyone seems to be so moral these days. I've never known anything like it! People who don't hesitate to cheat on their spouses or their income taxes, people who can't cross a border without smuggling something or fill in the simplest form without telling a lie, are suddenly very stern indeed about what goes on in the White House. It seems that in America only the president must obey the rules! But I fail to see why we should throw out an efficient administration for something that hasn't cost us a single penny or a single drop of blood. What is it they say? 'Nobody drowned at Watergate!'"

Gladys had shriveled with age, yet you could see that she had been a handsome woman. She was dyed and wrinkled and bony, but there was still a distinct air of chic, a whiff of the daring twenties, in her high heels, her jangling bracelets, her husky voice. It was notorious that she had always regretted having left Felix, but he had never given her the chance to come back. Now she seemed to be challenging the precedence of Julie Pryor, who was talking to the *Post* reporter. Julie, nearing seventy, was still blonde, with a faded, lovely elegance, the very opposite of her rival. It might have been a diplomatic question between them: who ranked whom? The divorced spouse or the "friend"?

"Did you hear that, Julie?" Felix demanded shrilly. "Did you hear what Gladys said?"

"No. What, dear?" Julie responded in that gentle voice that seemed to make every relationship intimate.

"She thinks Nixon shouldn't be impeached!"

"Oh, Gladys, how can you defend that terrible man? He's disgraced us in the eyes of the whole world!"

"Stuff and nonsense, Julie. You should spend more time away from Washington. Why, in Paris, where I've just been, everyone was asking me what 'Monsieur Neexon' had really done. They can't believe a great nation would seriously consider cashiering its chief executive for spying on a rival political party. 'Who doesn't do *that*?' they ask."

"It's not the spying, Gladys. You can tell your Gallic friends it's the cover-up."

"But if you spy, don't you *have* to cover up?"

"I'm afraid I find you very cynical."

"Perhaps Gladys finds *you* naive, my dear." This was from Felix, who seemed to be playing his old game of setting one admirer against the other.

"I do, Felix, I do!" Gladys affirmed.

"What do *you* think, Mr. Leitner?" the man from the *Post* asked, to break the impasse.

"Well, I can't help having some friendly feeling for a man who has been so appreciative of my columns. I should hate to see him shot."

A nervous titter spread through the listening group.

"Surely they won't go that far!" Mrs. Corliss exclaimed.

"Oh, but they will. You'll see. They'll back him up against a wall and riddle him with bullets, just the way they do in banana republics. Once Congress gets the bit in its teeth, you can't stop them. They've always wanted to kill a president. Now they'll do it." Felix glared about the silent half circle. "But they'll find they won't like his successor any better."

"You don't care for Mr. Ford?" the *Post* reporter asked.

"Ford? Why should I care about Ford? I'm talking about that Greek fellow. What's his name?"

"Agnew?" The reporter relaxed, as one who recognizes that he is dealing with a lunatic. "We thought he had resigned his office. To escape indictment."

"What if he did? The act regulating the devolution of the presidency provides that if the chief executive be impeached for high crimes and misdemeanors, his successor shall be the vice-president elected to serve with him, *if* that vice-president be living and competent. Certainly your man Agnew meets those qualifications. Now, whether or not a previous resignation of office will bar his claim is a matter for the Supreme Court, but I suggest their decision in U. S. versus Elder is controlling."

The *Post* reporter turned to me, gaping, and whispered: "Is that so? I never heard it. What the hell is this Elder case?"

I was happy to wrap another cloud over his misted vision. "Mr. Leitner is a great constitutional expert, you know," I whispered back.

His stare was followed after a moment by a little snort. "Come off it, Cutter. Who's loony now?"

Gladys Leitner sought to regain her lead. "It's the Duke of Windsor all over again," she opined. "Except there it was the conservatives who wanted to get rid of the king because of his socialist views. With Nixon it's just the opposite."

I wondered if I could read contempt in Felix's steady stare. He had always considered his ex-wife a goose.

"I thought it was the religious issue," Julie put in. "Surely if Mrs. Simpson hadn't been a divorcée, he wouldn't have had to abdicate."

Mrs. Corliss suggested that it might have been because the duchess was an American. She went on to say that if this were so, it was most unjust, as Wallis Warfield had been very well born — even, it was hinted, a distant relative of Mrs. Corliss.

"You're all wet!" Felix exclaimed with sudden loudness, and we all stared at him in surprise. "Mrs. Simpson could never have been an acceptable queen to the English," he continued in something like his old clear, faintly grating tone. "They could never have stomached the fact that there were two living men who would have been privileged to state, even in the sacred precincts of a gentlemen's club and without risk of being called out or expelled: 'I've fucked the Queen of England!' "

The effect on the listening circle was as if somebody had broken wind. Never had I heard that word from Felix's tongue. When it was necessary to be explicit, he had always used a more exact term.

"Two men?" Julie asked. "What two men?"

"Her first two husbands." I explained.

"But surely there have been queens who were widows," she protested. "What about Catherine Parr? And queens who had lovers. Yes, there was that poor woman who married George the Fourth. What about her?"

"No, no. I see it!" the *Post* reporter exclaimed with enthusiasm. "A widow would have been acceptable because her husband was dead. And if a queen had a lover who was crazy enough to make that boast in a club, he could be beaten up. Mr. Leitner is quite right. It's the fact that those two men were *entitled* to say it! That a gentleman would have had to take it from them." He turned to me and murmured, "It completely explains that whole abdication crisis. The old boy's as much on the ball as ever!"

I thought it was a good moment to tell Gladys Leitner that I wanted to ask her a favor. She nodded, and we moved to a corner of the room.

"I'm going to write a book about Felix."

"You always were," she said, with a sniff of hostility.

"I'm going to write two, as a matter of fact. The first will be a university press kind of thing, a history of his thinking. The second will be much more personal, a picture of Felix Leitner, the man. It will be . . ."

"A best seller, of course. A sensation! I suggest you get Warren Beatty for the film."

But I was determined to be patient. "It will be a serious book. Perhaps even more serious than the first. I want to tell the whole story. I want conversations, letters, everything. I want to reconstruct him, as best I can."

"And does Felix know this?"

"He's always known it. Ever since I became his principal assistant, back in nineteen fifty. He wants the whole truth told."

There was a gleam of malevolence in her black eyes. "Of course, it's convenient that he's no longer in a mental state to deny that."

"That would be true if I were lying. But I am not lying. I never lie about Felix. You should know that, Gladys. You were willing enough to make use of me in the old days when you wanted to get close to him. And the only reason you've disliked me since is that I was loyal to him, not you. That should be a sign to you that I'm truthful."

"Of course, I know that Felix has been your whole life. I suppose it's only natural that you should want to write about him, no matter what the cost to the feelings of his family and friends."

"I don't believe that great men belong to their families or friends. They belong to the ages."

"That sounds very well, but it's often just an excuse to make a best seller out of their bad breath and body odor. Phooey! Would you put in the crazy things he said this afternoon?"

"Yes. In the proper context. With the proper explanation. To my mind they have a certain relevance to his former thinking, like King Lear's raving on the heath. I would put in nothing that was not relevant to his mind and soul, but I would put in everything that was."

"Well, that leaves me out. I was only relevant to his body. Surely you won't ask me to expose this ancient carcass to your lewd gaze?"

"I'd be only too happy to gaze at it," I replied, knowing that, with her, no flattery could be excessive. "But that is not precisely what I'm after. You were immensely relevant to Felix's soul. His leaving Frances and his family for you was the single most important emotional and moral event of his lifetime. I want you to write it up for me in your own lively words. I know you can do it. Felix always said that nobody could write letters like you. I want you to put aside all trumpery inhibitions and recreate for my book exactly what happened in the summer of 1938."

Gladys was speechless for a moment. I could see that I had struck home. "Well!" she breathed. Then she resumed her suspicious air. "I suppose you're asking every Tom, Dick and Harry to do the same."

"How many Toms, Dicks and Harrys do you think there are left? It's appalling how rapidly the past falls away. Lila Nickerson is dead."

"Oh, no! I hadn't seen."

"On Sunday, in New Mexico. It's not in the paper yet. And Aleck is a vegetable. And Frances is long gone. And so is Felix's old law partner, Grant Stowe. And Felicia's never known anything about her father. All the real characters of the drama have faded away. Except you and me."

"And Heyward. Heyward's still alive, you know."

"Yes, but he'd never talk to me. I doubt he'd even allow Felix's name to be mentioned in his presence."

Gladys appeared less sure of this. "You could try him," she suggested. "Time is a great healer. And Heyward has more ego than people think. He might even like to appear in your book. God knows what else the poor devil will have to show for his long life."

I suspected that in speaking so of her first husband, she was speaking of herself. For all her professed respect for privacy, she, too, wanted to be in my book.

"Will you think it over, anyway?"

"What else have I to do at seventy-seven but think things over?"

I chuckled silently to myself. I knew she was seventy-eight.

Our little party was breaking up. I saw Julie rise and go over to Felix. Apparently in response to an appeal from him, she leaned down and listened to something that he whispered in her ear. Then I saw him reach a hand into his coat pocket to give her a piece of paper which she slipped, rather furtively, I thought, in her handbag.

The *Post* reporter was taking his leave. I escorted him to the door.

"Of course, there's nothing in that Agnew business," I assured him. "I know you'll be kind in your write-up."

He did not want me to think that he had been taken in, even for an instant. "He's wonderfully convincing, isn't he? You begin to wonder which is the visitor to the loony bin, you or he?"

When the last guest had gone, I went to say good night to Felix, but he appeared to have gone to sleep in his wheelchair. I had the distinct impression that he was shamming. Mrs. Corliss and I had a brief colloquy in the front hall. I congratulated her on the party, and she simpered a bit.

"We must give him all the pleasure we can," she said. "Dr. Levy says that he's subject to continual little strokes now. Sometimes he is not even aware of them. But it can't be long before there's a bigger one."

Because she loved clichés, I supplied her with one. "When it comes, it will be a release."

"I try to think of it that way."

"Did you find any new recruits among the guests?"

"Oh, Mr. Cutter!" She gave me a little push. "You are terrible!"

The next morning I telephoned Julie from my apartment.

"What was that paper Felix gave you?"

"Oh, Roger, I *knew* you'd see it. You never miss anything. The trouble is, darling, that he made me promise not to tell you. Of course, I know that a promise to a person in his condition is not exactly binding, but, still, when he's so earnest and seems so rational, it's hard not to do as he says."

"Just tell me one thing, Julie. Was it important?"

"Well...no, not anything that concerned Mrs. Corliss or you or any of your arrangements. I think he really appreciates all you do for him. Certainly the rest of us do!"

"That's not the point. Does it concern his career?"

"Well...yes, I suppose it does."

"Was it something that he wants published?"

"Roger, you're a fiend! How did you know?"

"Listen to me, Julie. You and I are in a very delicate position. We are Felix's closest friends — the only real ones he has left. But he is incompetent, at least some of the time, and I have no legal right to be handling his affairs. The bank has been co-operative; so has his lawyer. They've given me the green light. But I'm still sticking my neck out, and one day I may face a lawsuit from darling Felicia and her moron brother. I'll take that risk — fine — but only on condition that I know *everything* that's going on."

There was a long pause. "Very well," Julie said with a sigh. "I have to admit that's fair. We certainly don't want Felicia barging in and taking over. What Felix gave me was a column. He asked me to deliver it to Sam Perkins."

Sam was the Washington editor of *Profiles,* the weekly magazine that had contracted to take a monthly column from Felix shortly before his stroke.

"And you've done that?"

"I've done it."

"Thank you, dear. Good-bye."

I hung up. There was no time to lose. Less than an hour later I was in Sam's office on Connecticut Avenue, to confront his boyish, tousle-haired, disingenuous evasions.

"But what is your authority for asking to see it, Roger?" he persisted.

"I tell you I have none — other than that I'm the spokesman of decency and fair play. Felix Leitner is a lunatic — or an incompetent, if you prefer the word. I do not wish — nor would he, in his right mind — to have the end of his career muddied by the publication of some piece of idiotic drivel!"

"You think I'd publish idiotic drivel?"

"You might. Anyone might. If it was by Felix Leitner."

"Well, then, it's not idiotic drivel."

"Is it perfectly rational?"

"Perfectly rational?" He hesitated. "What is that?"

"You know what I mean, Sam."

"Let me put it this way. It's novel. It's imaginative. It's interesting."

"You confirm my worst fears. It's nutty."

"Well . . . let's say it's unusual."

"Sam Perkins, if you don't give me back that column, I'll tell the whole world you're nothing but a yellow journalist!"

"All right, Roger, all right!" He raised his hands deprecatingly in the air. "I'll give it back to you. But you're going to have to square us with Leitner. Suppose he accuses us of censoring him? I'm not at all sure that he's as far gone as you think. I want Leitner's assurance, in his own writing, that he has withdrawn that column."

"You shall have it."

This gave me no trouble. Felix signed all the correspondence that I set before him without reading it. I took the piece of paper that Sam now handed me and left his office. In the corridor of his building I paused to read the following and to thank my lucky stars that I had taken action.

> America is engaging in one of the most ancient of tribal rituals: the burial of the fisher king. The ailing chief is made responsible for the wasting of the land; the tribe must kill and bury him so that out of his corpse, symbolic of winter, may sprout the redeeming spring. Americans have always loved and hated their presidents. Though they depend on their leadership in time of trouble, they are fretted by it in time of peace. It reminds them that they are never really free. Periodically, the chief must die, that his people may enjoy the illusion of living. Even Washington, the father, had his would-be entombers. Lincoln was buried in the body of Johnson.

Grant and Harding were covered with the ashes of scandal. And now Richard Nixon, for a routine political trick that would never have come to light under a more cautious ruler — a Jackson, a Roosevelt, a Kennedy — must be sacrified to the public's hatred of great men, like a Mayan victim driven up the steep stair of the pyramid to bare his chest to the obsidian knife.

※　※　※

I had no trouble getting Felix to sign the letter to Perkins along with the rest of his mail, and I prayed that he would forget the whole episode, but he did not. After two weeks had passed and two issues of *Profiles* had failed to contain the column, he was very angry. When I arrived at the nursing home (as I did each day at noon) on the morning of the second deficient publication, it was to be greeted by a Felix angrily brandishing the magazine in his hand.

"You will call Perkins immediately," he cried out to me. "You will ask him to explain himself. How dare he presume to decide which columns of mine he will print and which he won't?"

"Oh, you sent him a column?" I rejoined weakly.

"Don't you know that I did?" He had entirely forgotten his subterfuge. "I expect you to take better care of my affairs. Please see that Perkins comes here himself to explain his conduct."

There was nothing to do but confess what I had done. Felix stared at me balefully while I did so.

"And may I ask you to explain this remarkable effrontery?" he demanded in his coldest, most scornful tone.

"Felix, you don't realize how ill you've been," I pleaded. "You're going to get better. You're getting better. It's only a matter of time, but you do need that time. Please let me be your mentor in these matters for just a little bit longer. I can't bear to have you hurt your reputation by something written when you're not at your best and clearest."

"And what is that something, pray?"

"A column that calls Mr. Nixon a great man. That implies he's the victim of a plot."

"And when did I write such a thing as that?" he asked in astonishment.

The very subject of the column had slipped from his mind!

"Felix," I begged him, "you've got to trust me. You've got to try to believe I'm acting in your best interests. You've got to . . ."

"I haven't got to do anything of the sort!" he interrupted me furiously. "And I don't for a minute believe that you're acting in my best interests. Ever since you were a boy, you have had designs upon me. I used to try to think it was a genuine admiration for my work, even a kind of filial affection. I knew of your loneliness, your problems of health. I wanted to be kind to you, to help you. But you have only had one thing in mind from the beginning. To own me! To own Felix Leitner. Because you had no life of your own, you were going to steal somebody's else's. And you aimed high, too, my boy!"

"Oh, Felix!" I cried, looking away in pain. "Don't. I can't bear it."

"You can bear anything. It was you who persuaded the world I was crazy. It was you who locked me up in this so-called nursing home, with the help of your partner, that woman Corliss. It is you who intercept my mail, keep away my friends, give false testimony to my lawyers. And now, by God, you suppress my columns! Well, you will see, Roger Cutter, that I still have ways of getting around you. Don't be too sure you won't be dragged to justice yet. Julie is on to you. Julie will go to the police! You'll see!"

"I'll leave you now. I'll tell Julie to come. I shan't bother you again. I'll say good-bye, Felix."

I went over to his wheelchair to take his hand, but he slapped mine away. I left the nursing home and drove to Rock Creek Park, where I strolled for the rest of that bleak winter afternoon.

I had too much sense to be really hurt by Felix's senile accusations. In the past year I had become too familiar with his irrationalities to take any of them seriously. If a senile Felix hated and feared me today, a senile Felix had wanted to make me his residuary legatee only a week before. No, anyone who loves another person should be prepared for the rejection that may come with the mental ailments that attend our increasing life span. But what made my heart numb and my soul sick, what turned my life to dust and ashes, was the idea that Felix's concept of a Roger Cutter who served him only to serve himself might not be simply the product of a burst blood vessel in the brain but the survival of a picture of myself entertained but never divulged in the time of his reason. If this were so, had I not better die when he died?

When I came home that evening my telephone was ringing. I could hear it through the door as I fumbled desperately with my key. Suddenly it seemed as if my very life depended on answering it. I pushed the door open and ran into the living room, falling on the telephone and grabbing it as if it were some dangerous snarling beast.

"Mr. Cutter?"

It was Mrs. Corliss. Oh, God, may he be dead! Let this agony be over!

"Yes?"

"It's Mr. Leitner . . ."

"He's gone?"

"No. But the stroke has come. I don't think he knows me. He can't speak."

Roger Cutter (2)

D R. LEVY said that Felix might live a year or die any minute. It was difficult, he said, to determine the exact amount of brain damage, as Felix could not speak and could not, or would not, respond to questions by moving his head or his hands, but it seemed fairly sure that there was little comprehension left. For all essential purposes, Felix Leitner was dead. I continued to go to see him, though now only twice a week, to be absolutely sure that he was properly taken care of. I would stay for an hour, telling him news of the world and spicy bits of carefully selected gossip. I had no idea how much of it got through — Dr. Levy thought none — but if the smallest fraction did, it was worth the effort. When I left him, he would press my hand in both of his, and I liked to imagine that he was telling me he had forgiven me. But I am afraid that he made the same gesture to Felicia and Julie, the only other persons admitted to his chamber.

I had come to the end of my role in Felix's life, but not of his in mine. I no longer performed duties or received a salary — the Riggs Bank had been appointed his conservator — but I had an income just adequate for my very simple needs, and I resolved to live for my two books alone. The one on

Felix's work could wait; all the material for that lay in my library. The book on his personality had to receive my initial attention, for I had to scurry about to interview the remaining friends. I had to hound Gladys Leitner to be sure that she wrote what I had asked her to write, and I had to get in touch with her first husband. Also I had to collate and annotate the material I had already collected and check its veracity with the dwindling group of people who were qualified to know.

Felix had said to me, several years before: "Biography is a whole new ball game. It is possible now, even in the lifetimes of our very greatest men, to persuade their friends and acquaintances to record on tape their most intimate impressions of these individuals. All you have to do is wave in their faces the sacred banner of history. The files of our universities are being filled to overflowing with unpublished recordings of the fears, the neuroses, the sexual habits, even the bowel movements of our public figures. Oh, yes, the readers who demanded information about General Eisenhower's stools after his heart attack and who wished to study Adlai Stevenson's income tax return to question the deduction of a dead sheep, will be denied nothing. And perhaps it is not altogether a bad thing. We shall learn too much, but for those who know how to pick and choose, it may be a gold mine. Let my past be an open book, Roger. I can think of things in it of which I'm ashamed, but none of which I'm afraid."

The increase of candor in modern speaking, matched with the decline of reticence and discretion, should go far to ease the task of the biographer. People tend today to be generous and frank with their reminiscences. But he who ventures into the field must always remember that his principal enemy is still the same who afflicted the chroniclers of old: the so-called witness who is really a would-be biographer himself, the person who is giving you not so much a memory as a creation, the man who has his own obsession, loving or hateful, about your subject. This has always been my biggest problem with the men and women in Felix's life.

What did I already have? I had three fine accounts, written by Felix himself after agonies of urging by me, about three periods of his life: his boyhood, his work at the Versailles peace conference, and his first divorce. These alone put me leagues ahead of any other potential biographer, for they were the only writings by Felix about his own life. Then I had — thanks to Felicia (but this was the only thing I ever got from her) — the privately circulated typescript of the first Mrs. Leitner's memoirs, written for her family: two chapters of it dealt, very importantly, with her marriage to Felix. And there were the few rather touching pages from the Paris journal of Felix's crippled stepdaughter, Fiona Satterlee, which she herself had kindly given me.

I also had one other document, a very curious one, which I had unearthed, unknown to Felix, several years before in the files of Dinwiddie Stowe & Whelan, the Wall Street law firm in which he had been briefly a partner. It was the transcript of a tape made by the late Grant Stowe in connection with a history of the firm that he had written in his retirement. Only a small part of it had appeared in the final volume. This document had been supplied by a younger partner who was an old school friend of mine. His authority to do so was questionable, but what was that to a biographer?

And that was all. The rest I had to glean from my own recollection. What I had to do was to put my accounts together and bind them with my own narrative of what they were and how I got them. These would then supply the source material for my book on Felix's character and personality, or if for any reason I should fail or be unable to write such a book, they might constitute a kind of book in themselves.

I was not young — fifty-eight — and I had never been strong. I owed it to history, and I owed it to Felix, to assemble my material in a coherent form and see that one copy at least was safely deposited in the Felix Leitner Papers at Harvard Law School.

Manuscript of Felix Leitner's
"My Youth and Parents,"
Written in 1965 for Roger Cutter

R OGER has been after me for months now to write some account of my life or at least of the events and emotional experiences that most affected me. I have been rather grumpily averse to the idea, and he has finally been reduced to silence, but Roger's silences can be eloquent. The way he drops a letter on my desk, the way he shrugs his shoulders when I put a question that he chooses to regard as rhetorical, even the way he answers the telephone, can serve to remind me of what he has asked for and has not received.

"You have written about everything and everybody under the sun," he told me. "Why is it so difficult to write about yourself?" And then, of course, he underlines it all with a flattering assurance, all the more dangerous for being sincere, that he, Roger, would find me more fascinating than any other subject.

My trouble is not that I do not find myself interesting. I have, God knows, enough ego for that. No, my real trouble is that I hate the idea that I might seem to be writing one of those determinist novels — like Zola's — where it is assumed that if the author correctly sets forth all the determining factors in his hero's childhood and background — domestic, societal, genetic — it must follow logically that the hero will grow up to become a president, or to commit a murder, as the author will have predicted. I reject and abhor the doctrine that removes, or even denigrates, the free will of man — particularly my own!

But what has at last "determined" me to pick up my pen and prepare to compose something about the elements in my life that a modern Zola would select as making me "tick" — that is, my parents, my disillusionment at Versailles, and then my divorce — is the realization, tardy but not perhaps too late, that if I do not do it, some Zola may. And then think of all the tommyrot that will be written about my being ashamed of my Jewish heritage, my denial of my past, my cultivation of Wasp society! Oh, it's too nauseating to think of! Why, in an America that is rapidly approaching classlessness, are our historians and sociologists so obsessed with class distinctions?

But they are. I must accept it. And now let me get on with the job of describing mother and father. Parents. What are they?

James Bryce in his *Holy Roman Empire* described the division of world rule in the medieval mind between a spiritual vicar and a temporal chief. Man's soul on earth was under the aegis of the Pope; his body under that of the Holy Roman Emperor. All creation bowed to the sway of these two forces of church and state. The fact that the Mediterranean swarmed with Moslem fleets, that in Constantinople the claims of Rome were scoffed at, and that half of Europe considered the emperor as nothing but a German king did not in the least affect the theory. The medieval people loved ideals. It pleased them to think of civilization as a unit under the cross and the scepter.

But these opposite yet complementary concepts, this yin and

yang, had a way of coming together, of merging, and then of flying apart again, each having borrowed some of the characteristics of the other. Sometimes the emperor seemed the holier, the more spiritual of the two; sometimes the wearer of the triple crown showed himself in armor on the field of battle. To obey one was by no means to win the approval of the other; indeed, it was usually the opposite.

In some such way did I, an only child, view my father and mother. They represented the opposite poles of power to my infant eyes, and they had the same confusing way of combining and exchanging characteristics. Each had different needs and different expectations, and as soon as I thought I had learned what these were, my parents promptly changed them. What they always had in common, however, at least for me, was the quality of seeming to expect more of me than I could ever reasonably hope to expect of them.

We lived on Riverside Drive in a stone house with a pompous beaux-arts facade much too grand for the meager, three-window frontage that it presented to the water. In winter the winds howled down the west side of Manhattan over the gray, ice-chunked river, but inside, behind closed French windows and heavy, drawn curtains, amid the odor of incense and of hothouse flowers, in chambers cluttered and gleaming with jade and teakwood and bamboo accessories, my mother lived like an odalisque — if that word can be imagined for a woman so strongly built and virtuous. Mother's craving for the exotic, for a dimly lit interior, her satisfaction at staying always home amid the profusion of her camellias, her roses, her lilies, dressed in trailing silks and satins, her red hair piled up and elaborately curled, was perfectly consistent, at least in her own eyes, with an image of herself as zesty, full of plain common sense and downright thinking. So she balanced my father — always in black or sober brown, portly, bald, rather fierce-looking, with the big watch that he was so constantly consulting and his loud *chugarum* of a cough — who seemed, in a house dedicated to epicurean luxury and idleness, a stranger from the world of men's business affairs, yet who nonetheless had mysteries and melancholies that seemed to look askance at truths too easily accepted by his spouse.

Viewed from one point, Mother was thus the symbol of the passive life, the indoors existence, with its emphasis on the sensual, the beautiful, the artistic, while Father was more properly the sign of a male world, all bluster and action, like the sound of his stamping feet in the front hall when he came in out of the snow. But it was not always so simple, for I can remember Mother, though I was only eight at the time, declaiming like a maenad over the sinking of the *Maine* and calling, over the Meissen tea cups, for a crusade against the Spanish despots, while Father, oddly subdued, actually head-shaking, muttered insinuations about the imperialist demon disguised as the angel of rescue. Both sexes were contained in each. Violence lurked in the potted palms, and peace in the eye of the winter storm outside.

My father, Morris Leitner, was the son of a German Jew who had in the 1840s emigrated to escape racial injustice. Grandfather Leitner had made a small fortune in a textile business that had been carried on by his two oldest sons. Uncle Jacob, the third son, became a lawyer. He represented the family firm and also represented my father, the youngest, who had sold his share to the older brothers and invested the proceeds in tenements. Aunt Renata, their only sister, had made what the family considered a brilliant match, to the banker Isidore Adelheimer. Childless, she devoted her life to the embellishment of the Adelheimer collection of European paintings and objects of art now at the Metropolitan Museum. She was my favorite of all the family.

Mother was not Jewish, at least so far as anyone knew. Her mother had been an English actress, married, or so she always maintained, to a Scotsman called Knox. Nobody has ever been able to discover anything about my grandfather Knox or any evidence that my grandmother had married such an individual, and I myself caught her, in her old age, in several inconsistent stories. But whatever the truth, we know that "Mrs. Knox" came to New York in 1888, and, abandoning her own unpromising stage career, had devoted all her considerable energies to pushing that of her only child. Mother had the handsome, stately looks required for heroines of the period and a fine enunciation, but by all accounts she was too wooden in her movements and too mechanical in her interpretations to go very much beyond the very mild success she had enjoyed in two or three parlor comedies. She and my grandmother existed in boarding houses, hoarded newspaper notices, and besieged managers. Without her Cerberus of a mother, the lovely but naive Florine Knox, placid and luxury loving, might well have ended as a stockbroker's mistress.

But Grandma was there, always there. That was the point. When Father, an open-handed, well-to-do bachelor of forty, who had been accustomed to many cash conquests on Broadway, decided to add Mother to his list, he discovered that he could not even take her out to dinner without the chaperoning presence of Mrs. Knox. The only way that he could address a word to her out of earshot of this dragon was by sitting with her at one end of the boarding-house parlor while Mrs. Knox pretended to glance through the newspaper at the other. I do not know if my grandmother consciously intended to inflame the desire of this middle-aged *coureur* by such treatment, but she certainly succeeded, and when Father, after six months of it, actually submitted a written proposal of marriage to the mother of his beloved, he told Uncle Jacob that it had been elicited half by passion and half by a reluctant admiration of the old girl's tenacity. I suppose he had decided that the time had come to marry, if he were ever going to, and that no bridegroom in the city could have had greater assurance of the purity of his future spouse! Florine would be a healthy and virtuous mother for the son and heir he wanted.

I hope there was sufficient sport in my making to compensate poor Father for all he had to pay, but it scarcely seems likely. He had to expand his style of living to include these two women, and his passion could not have survived my birth, for there were no other children, and Uncle Jacob once told me that Father had returned to his "bachelor habits" as soon as my presence had begun to make itself unattractively present in mother's figure. But the extraordinary thing about Morris and Florine Leitner is that they lived together in total amity, without even a quarrel that I could remember, until his death when I was twenty-one.

How did they do it? By leading separate lives, I suppose, and by asking good manners of each other. This may be what is called in fashionable circles a "civilized" marriage, but it is rare, because it is rare that desire and resentment cease simultaneously on both sides. But so it must have been with my parents. Mother, who was probably what is now called frigid, was perfectly happy with her house, her flowers, her interiors, her afternoon drive in a closed car, her few faithful, empty-headed friends. She enjoyed being the star of a tiny but exclaiming world. Even her mother was eclipsed and sank into subservience once her job was done, and she now lived in silent content on an upper story. And Father had his business and his girls, his cards and his horse racing. He had depressions, I now know, but he did not show them in the parlor or dining room.

I was never really close to either of my parents, but I saw

much more of Mother than of Father. I am sure she thought she was as loving a parent as any boy could have found. She was totally complacent about herself, her life and her future, and fate justified her, for she died in her sleep at eighty, still not bored and with all her faculties intact. As a parent, she was kind and mildly interested, but detached. She always treated me as an equal. One of the few serious issues between us was clothes. Of course, at fourteen, I wanted to dress as the other boys at Mr. Driscoll's day school on Central Park West did, and Mother wanted me in a velvet suit like Little Lord Fauntleroy.

"I don't see why boys shouldn't appreciate beautiful things like other people," she said, fixing on me that placid stare that might have expressed all of her interest in the subject or might have been the veil of other preoccupations. "You may find that your suit is actually envied."

"Never!"

"You mustn't be so sure of things, Felix."

"I can be sure of *that*."

"Very well, then, let us assume that the suit will not be popular. Is popularity everything? Can't you stand on your own two feet?"

"Yes, but in shoes, not dancing pumps!"

"I have learned not to consider the opinions of others, unless I believe they know what they're talking about. Your father's family have always disapproved of *my* clothes. They think I'm dressy. They do! They think this house is dressy. Just because I don't choose to live in rooms shrouded with brown cloth wall coverings and filled with black mahogany!"

This was rather beyond me. I was vaguely aware that the Leitners found Mother, to say the least, unaccountable, but I knew there was no real hostility. It was Father of whom they disapproved, because he had abandoned the faith.

"Perhaps you can wear the suit to school *one* day, darling," Mother continued in her tone of sublime expectation. "Then we can see how the boys react. Don't worry. I shan't be unreasonable. If they give you a hard time, I won't ask you to wear it again. Surely that's fair? You and I are both basically reasonable people. There's more Knox in you than Leitner. We don't go batting our heads against stone walls, but then, on the other hand, we'll try anything once. Isn't that so, my darling? Come now. Say it is!"

There was something about Mother that could not be resisted when she appealed to me in this way. What was it? A son's natural gallantry? A son's natural love? Perhaps. But as I look back, it seems to me that I make out a faint quiver of apprehension, of something like alarm, in those wide gray-blue eyes fixed on me over that strained, small smile and those powdered cheeks. Was she appealing to me? Was she, a child at heart, asking me, another child, to confirm her belief that it *was,* after all, a child's world? Did she suspect that there might be terror and loud, rumbling noises in the world that adults made up? And that, if I let her down, she might find out that it was *not* made up?

"I remember when I was afraid to play Juliet on the road because somebody had said that Juliet was only twelve and I was already twenty-one, and Mama said to me that if I tried it once, just once, and it didn't work out, she would never ask me to play it again. And then I remembered how Mama had worked for me and pinched and scraped for me, and of course I could not let her down. It's not, darling, that I have had to pinch or scrape for you, for your father pays all the bills very generously and never complains — not, I suppose, that he really should — but you must know that I *would* have pinched and scraped for you had it been necessary. I really would!" Mother was now looking straight ahead, as if she were reciting something to herself, a creed, perhaps, that *had* to be true. "And so, I think if I ask you to do me a little favor, like wearing that pretty suit to school once, just *once*, it's not unreasonable."

"But, Mummie, *why?* How can it matter to you?"

"I'll tell you why, dear. Because I want Mr. Boldini to paint you and me together, and I want you to be wearing that suit. But Mr. Boldini said that was wrong, because boys don't dress that way any more. So I told him that suit had been worn at the Driscoll School. Now do you see? It *has* to be worn there. Once, anyway!"

What could I do with an argument like that? Of course, I wore the silly suit, and of course I was made cruel fun of and got in a nasty fistfight with Sam Rosen, the class bully. But I was careful to remove the precious jacket before I engaged in strife. And when I went home I told Mother there had been no trouble at all. It was lucky that Rosen had not blacked my eye.

"Well, you see, darling, Mummie is sometimes right. Oh, I know your father has been telling you that I'm hopelessly impractical and otherworldly. He thinks all women are. But I was earning my own living before he even met me. I know something of this great, hard world. And I know that it's not always as great or as hard as it's cracked up to be."

The next day I wore the suit again. Rosen and his little group at once accosted me.

"Is your memory defective?" he asked sneeringly. "Wasn't yesterday enough?"

I removed the jacket, slowly and deliberately, and then struck him in the chin. He jumped on me and might have killed me had not a master intervened.

But the third day when I appeared in the suit, Rosen exchanged a look of confusion with his cohorts. Was I a lunatic? So a Roman procurator in Judea might have felt when the survivors of a persecuted sect turned up at his gate with the same shrill cries, day after day, though he felled whole forests to make crosses for their crucifixion.

He looked away when I went straight up to him and asked him if he liked my suit. He snarled to his friends that I was "nuts." On the fourth day he knocked me down again. On the fifth he admitted, with a half-angry, half-sheepish laugh, that he guessed the suit was all right and walked away from me.

The class was divided. Some thought me a masochist, a term just then coming into vogue. Others thought me a fool. A few admired me. But nobody commented on my suit again. I had converted the privilege of chastisement into an embarrassment and a bore.

Now what was the significance of my bizarre conduct? What was really at stake that I should expose myself to such ridicule and battery? After all, Mother had stipulated only that I should wear the silly suit for a day. I suppose that what I must have seen in it was Mother herself: it was pretty, very expensive, highly individual and totally inappropriate. It had nothing on earth to do with boys or with school or even with Riverside Drive. But the moment I put it on I became a part of Mother, and then there was no further denying it. But why should I have felt this maternal identification so strongly, when I associated myself so little with Father and his family? Perhaps it was because Mother was alone and therefore presumably vulnerable. If I did not protect her, nobody would, and then she might be put down, annihilated, and after that they — whoever "they" might be — would come after me. Oh, Mother, I see you to this day, naive, smiling, unaware, never asking for help!

The reader will ask why she needed help. Perhaps she didn't. But I can still flinch, yes, even now, when I consider how painful it might have been for her to discover that people, including Father, including the Leitners, including the maids, were simply laughing at her. That they found her a pretentious, dressed-up doll. And there had to be a kind of salvation in saving her from that, even a kind of savage joy. It was as if, to return to my Roman image, I had climbed over the railing of my arena box and leaped, my toga flying about me, into the sand below to face the stalking lions and the sudden outraged roar of the watching crowd, alone with Mother.

But she would only say: "Felix, darling, you really *are* a goose. Those lions are perfectly well fed and won't harm a hair of your head. Don't you see the whole thing's a pantomine?"

I hope she died still believing that. Have I explained any part of what I felt about her? It was not so much filial love — although that, of course, was in it — as a funny sense that Mother and I belonged to a race apart, that we were different. And if *she* wouldn't keep her eye on the mob and on those lions, it behooved me to do so.

I never told Mother what I had been through to defend my costume. As I look back on her, it seems to me that she must have had considerable strength of personality. She caused those around her to act as props or stagehands or, at most, supporting members of the cast in a drama of which she was the principal, perhaps the only, star. It was thus that my grandmother's ambition for her had been finally realized.

My relationship with Father was altogether different. If I felt responsible for him, it was not to protect him, but to try to induce him to adhere to higher moral standards. Basically, I think I was ashamed of him. He had paid no attention to me in my childhood, and this may have been my form of revenge. When he finally began to pay me serious attention, it was too late.

I was sixteen before he did so. Because I had always been quiet and reserved, he had not realized that I was intelligent. Perhaps, too, he had found it difficult to imagine that any child of his wife could be blessed with brains. But when he began to take in that I was above average, perhaps even unusual, he started to make plans.

"You're more of a Leitner than I thought," he told me frankly once. "We'd better see what we can make of you."

Father, in his middle and late fifties, was that not uncommon type in American culture, the man who has played hard but aimlessly and suddenly realizes that his active years are ending and that he has wasted considerable talents without even achieving happiness. He felt, I believe, not so much despondent as foolish. He had dissipated his energies revolting against a stiff Jewish orthodox tradition without putting anything in its place.

"I had it all," he told Uncle Jacob when he was dying. "I had it all in the palm of my hand. And what did I do with it? I simply threw it away."

As he grew older he reverted, in outward form anyway, to the image of the Leitners as projected by my uncles. Portly, solid, of a dark complexion, he had a tendency to fur-collared overcoats, to jeweled rings, to walking sticks. The roué, the gambler, the atheist, the cultivator of bohemian and artistic circles, seemed to have been buried alive under the Manhattan burgher. But the curious part of this evolution was that the younger Morris Leitner seemed to have survived and to be witnessing, with an occasional outburst of sarcastic laughter, his own transformation. Father would never, for example, be angry with me when I wanted to be frank about his business. He seemed to have anticipated that, as I approached college age, I should be a bit of a radical.

"You pore over maps of the city," I pointed out to him once, rather loftily. "You keep abreast of proposed buildings. You try to occupy this corner or that corner because you think the city may grow toward it. What's the difference between you and one of those hill-town robber barons of the Middle Ages who lived by exacting tolls from travelers who passed below them?"

"Very little. Had I been born then I might have put together a chain of hill towns!"

"But where is the social purpose, Father? So you make a fortune. But isn't it by exacting rents from all the poor devils whom the city shoves into your lap? What have you contributed?"

"It's business, my boy! And when you've succeeded in business, that's your contribution. Then none dare call it treason."

"I don't think I'd be very proud if I'd spent my life doing that. I'd feel like a kind of highwayman." Oh, yes, I said it. Just that way. Children have no mercy on adults. It does not occur to them that adults may need it.

Father looked at me thoughtfully for a moment and then shrugged. "Perhaps I might answer that I've contributed as much to society as most of my generation. Many of the so-called best people, too. But I don't pretend to be anything I'm not. I don't go about shouting that I'm a philanthropist."

"But don't you ever feel you could do more for people? What about some of those tenements you own? Aunt Renata calls them slums!"

"She doesn't object to her husband taking them as security for his mortgages!" Father exclaimed more hotly now. "But anyway, I'm getting rid of them. At the end of two years I expect to be invested entirely in commercial real estate. There's going to be an awful outcry, sooner or later, about conditions in this city, and I don't want our name associated with it. Your name, anyway."

"But just getting rid of them doesn't help the people who live there. Shouldn't you *improve* them?"

"Where am I going to get the money for that? Besides, there are always going to be slums. The point is not to have them hung around your neck like a stinking albatross!"

I did not argue this further. I had learned early that it was almost impossible to make a grownup change his mind about anything. And besides, getting rid of the slums was at least a step.

Father's occasionally smothering interest in me continued to intensify, and by the time I went off to Yale I was relieved to get away from him. I was beginning to suspect that the role that he planned for me was simply to make up to him what he had missed in life, that I was to enjoy what Morris Leitner had thrown away. That was why the real estate was being cleaned up and why a respectable fortune was being put together. Father had no desire to see me in his business. No, the money was to make me independent so that I might be free to become a politician, a statesman, an ambassador . . . who knows, maybe the president!

"Your Aunt Renata collects art," he told me. "She prefers paintings to human beings. That is quite all right. I don't question her preference. But it's her preference, not mine. Mine is for extraordinary men, not extraordinary art. Renata and I may agree that the mob is not worth much, but we differ about the value of the individual. She can have her gallery. I'd rather have *you!*"

He glared at me almost defiantly at this, and I had the uneasy sense of being, not a beloved son, but a kind of young monster designed by a Frankenstein. And let me insert here at once that he was utterly wrong about Aunt Renata. Father insisted on seeing people in his own, not always lovable image. Aunt Renata was, if anything, his opposite.

She was small and plain and prematurely wrinkled, but she had large beautiful eyes. Gray and green, with a touch of blue, they sparkled in a friendly, sad, reflective way. I used to think of them as her jewels, her real jewels, alive, in contrast to the big rubies and emeralds on the rings that tumbled about on her skinny brown fingers. I was the favorite nephew, and she used to take me with her to art galleries. Uncle Isidore's taste was for objects of art: Renaissance bronzes, Byzantine ivory figures, Chinese jade, medieval reliquaries. Aunt Renata relieved the glinting heaviness of their great dark house on West Seventy-second Street with her lighted canvases, drawn from all periods, so that her collection formed a tiny history of European painting. Her eye was unerring, and it was under her influence that, in my junior year, I decided I would become an art historian. Aunt Renata's paintings had given me the idea of writing a history of France as seen through its art. This may have seemed hardly an original idea, but it was going to be original the way *I* would do it!

Father was thoroughly disgusted with this turn of events and furious with his sister at what he deemed her interference with his plans, but he was too wise to overdo his opposition. Young people, after all, were prone to change their minds, and he contented himself with mild efforts to undermine my admiration of my collecting relatives by poking fun at Uncle Isidore and his habit of stroking the backsides of his bronze nudes. He did not realize that I drew the sharpest distinction between Uncle Isidore and Aunt Renata.

She never encouraged my ambition in art. In fact, she ultimately exploded it. She could say anything she liked to me, because I had absolute confidence, both in her love and in her disinterestedness. In the summer after my junior year I met her and Uncle Isidore in Paris and spent some weeks with them. They were on a buying tour, so we occupied many hours at the dealers', but Aunt Renata and I managed also to fit in several mornings at the Louvre, dedicating each visit to a different century.

On the one that we devoted to the seventeenth we spent a full half hour before the great portrait of Cardinal Richelieu by Philippe de Champaigne. Aunt Renata particularly admired Champaigne.

"He did so many of Richelieu," she said. "I keep hoping I'll find one. There was a portrait for sale in Lisbon, but a poor example. None of them is anything like as good as this. Don't you love that cold stare? Brr!"

In this great portrait the cardinal seems to have been moving from right to left and to have paused, as if he had just noticed you. The right hand, holding the hat, is lowered; the left arm is bent; and the fingers of the left hand, whose palm is up-turned, are twisted in what seems a kind of incipient grasp. The cold gray eyes fix you — just for a moment — and then the mighty minister will proceed on to the king, to a cabinet meeting, to some weighty council. But that glance has been instantly articulate. "Oh, it's you," it seems to say. "You're back? Your mission's accomplished, I trust?" It had better be!

Aunt Renata was contrasting the portrait now to a postcard that she had taken from her purse, representing the Champaigne portrait of Richelieu in the British National Gallery.

"You see how static the London picture is. I am convinced that Champaigne must have painted it first. Richelieu is frozen on the spot, rather awkwardly holding a hat for which he has no apparent use. But now see what our artist does! He drops the hand with the hat, raises the other and lets the robes flow." She traced in the air the movement of the robes in the picture before us. "Richelieu may not be moving, but he just has been, and he will be again in a second. Champaigne was the poet of pause."

"I should say he was the poet of robes," I observed, taking in the multiple scarlet folds so richly painted.

"You know why, don't you? He was a Jansenist and wasn't permitted to paint the nude. He was limited to painting priests and nuns who were so covered up you couldn't even see their outlines. So what did he do? He made the robes organic! They fit the heads. In almost any other portrait, that marvelous robe of Richelieu's would dominate the wearer — dominate the whole canvas, in fact. But it doesn't because it's the body, and the body is dominated by the head. *That* head, anyway. Why, the whole picture centers in the command of those eyes. Look at them!"

"I *am* looking at them," I said. "It's impossible not to. They are the eyes of power. There is no threat in them. No anger. No praise. No approval, even. To him it's only a question of getting the job done. And to get it done he must use the individuals to hand. It may be necessary to reward this one by making him a duke. It may be necessary to punish another by cutting his head off. It doesn't really matter. The thing is that France must predominate. Oh, yes, I see it! Champaigne was not the poet of pause, or even of robes. He was the poet of power!"

I thought that my aunt looked at me rather curiously for a moment, but then we rose, and soon we were looking at the great Rigauds and pursuing the glorious effects of Richelieu's policy into the reign of his sovereign's son, Louis XIV. After that it was time to go back to the hotel and get ready for a performance of *Hernani* at the Comédie Française. Poor Aunt Ren! When she traveled with me, every breathing moment was given over to culture and history. Uncle Isidore would stay at the hotel or at a dealer's and wave us away. Chateaux, museums, art galleries, theaters — there was no end to it. She was always the best of sports. My enthusiasm seemed to sustain her in the inevitable moments when her own flagged.

One morning, at a dealer's, we sat before a picture that she was thinking of buying. It was a Greuze portrait of the young Napoleon. I objected that it did not seem a good likeness.

"Does it matter?" Aunt Renata returned. "All Nattier's princesses look alike, and they're all beautiful."

"But Greuze couldn't bear to reproduce hardness of character. He was too kind-hearted. Take his Robespierre. Who would dream the man was a monster? One would have said a clever, prosy, rather decent little lawyer from the provinces. And Napoleon! Would you ever see a despot, a world conqueror — would you ever see *power* — in that tense, sullen, romantic youth?"

"Let me tell you something, my dear." Aunt Renata turned away suddenly now from the portrait. "I've been thinking about your future career. Being an art historian may not be the right thing for you. Oh, now, don't look insulted. I don't mean that you couldn't be one. Of course, you could! But I'm beginning to wonder if your father isn't right. That perhaps you're meant for something ... well ... I don't know if bigger is the word. Perhaps more 'engaged.' "

"What on earth has happened in the past week to make you suddenly think that?"

"The fact that you're more interested in portraits than other pictures. Oh, much more interested. And portraits of statesmen. Politicians. Even sovereigns. People who govern. It seems to be power that fascinates you, rather than art."

"You think I want to be powerful?"

"Not necessarily. Though you might. What's wrong with that, if you want power for the right reason? But at the moment it seems to be the effect of power that concerns you. As seen in the holder's face. Perhaps you were meant for a career closer to public life."

"You mean politics?"

"I don't know. Maybe. Or law? Or journalism? It's hard to say, because you do things so well. You've got a brilliant mind and a lively imagination, but you're a doer, too."

"Auntie! You flatterer!"

"No, no, dear. I'm totally serious. I have to be, because I don't think you get all the help from your parents you need. Your ma ... well, you know how your ma is. She's a darling, but she lives in a world of her own. And your father is too ambitious for you. Maybe that's why you took up art history in the first place. In reaction to him."

"You mean to irritate him?"

"Well, yes, I suppose so. In part. All children like to irritate and disappoint their parents. It's a way of growing up, of sharpening their teeth. But even though it may be great fun to irritate Morris — I enjoy it myself at times — you mustn't give up the right career to do it."

I thought deeply about what Aunt Renata had said. I had been having doubts about a career in art, myself. At Yale I had become something of a radical. I should like to think that the wider knowledge of human suffering that came to me with my college reading was the true origin of my new concern for the welfare of my fellow beings. I had read all of *Das Kapital,* and *The Theory of the Leisure Class* had become my bible. But there are two types of reformers: those who wish to pull the world apart to remake it into something better, and those who simply wish to pull the world apart. The latter are apt to be motivated by hate, or at least animosity, toward the principal beneficiaries of the old world. I am afraid that I wanted to undermine the system that enabled my father and Uncle Jacob and even my beloved Aunt Renata's husband to live out their pompous philistine existences at the expense of the lower orders.

Once again, Mother may have had something to do with it. I saw her big hats and elaborate gowns, I saw the whole cluttered house on Riverside Drive with its profusion of bibelots and draperies, as the beads and feathers with which savage chiefs, according to Veblen, adorned their squaws to prove their prowess and virility. Did I even hark back to the Fauntleroy suit at school as further proof that Mother and I were simply part of the costly practice of "conspicuous consumption" for the greater glorification of the Leitners? It might seem that Mother was more responsible for all these items than Father, who was rarely at home and never cared what I wore, but what was this to my angry *id*? Father had made Mother his puppet and now sought to make me the same.

At the time, of course, there were no such underthoughts. I was convinced that I had been given my brains and health and youth to work for the benighted. The plight of the poor in crowded huddled cities, the misery of the blacks and poor whites in southern states, the helplessness of nonunionized workers, deeply affected me. And now it seemed to me that Aunt Renata had put her finger on the first sacrifice that I should have to make for the cause.

"You're right, Auntie," I told her the very next day. "I was not cut out to be an art historian. That ivory tower is simply evasion. But don't tell Father. Not yet, anyway."

"Because it would give him too much pleasure?"

I did not answer this. I did not even want to consider if it might be true. But whatever my reason, I did not tell Father, when I returned from Europe, that I was reconsidering my choice of career. I intended to do so, but I postponed it, and then all desire to do so vanished with my discovery that Father was still in the slum business. This I learned from Uncle Jacob when he came up to visit me in New Haven to be taken on a tour of Yale. Uncle Jacob was the driest, most factual kind of lawyer I have ever known. He was possessed of none of the romance in Aunt Renata or even, submerged though it might have been, in Father. He assessed the grounds and buildings of Yale as if it had been a future client.

"It's lucky for young dreamers like you that so many of our generous men of wealth have put their money into universities," he observed with a grunt. "You can look at pictures of naked women and write books about them amid green lawns and shady trees." His abrupt, sweeping gesture took in the Old Campus.

"Is that all you think I'm going to do, Uncle Jacob? What about pictures of naked men?"

"Don't be unnatural, Felix! No Leitner was ever a pervert."

Heyward and I, for my friend Heyward Satterlee had accompanied us on our tour, laughed in delight. "You speak of these men of wealth as generous, Uncle Jacob. Isn't it possible that they are simply expiating their guilt?"

"Guilt? For what?"

"For being what Teddy Roosevelt called malefactors of great wealth."

"That demagogue! I'm surprised you have the gall to quote him to me."

"But isn't it true of many men we know? Isn't it even true of *us?* Or at least, wasn't it, before Father got rid of his slums?"

"What do you mean by his slums? I wasn't aware he had any slums." But Uncle Jacob's conscience, exiguous though it may have been, was strong enough to cause him to pause here. "I suppose you mean those properties down on Hester Street."

"And on John Street. And on Lambert Road. It's all very well that we've sold them, but the guilt of having once owned them can't be washed away by a profitable sale!"

"I was not aware there had been a profitable sale," Uncle Jacob said drily.

"Well, a sale, then."

"I wasn't aware there had been a sale."

I tried to think afterward if Father had ever actually stated to me that he had disposed of these tenements and decided that he had not. But he had most certainly given me the impression that he had altered the essential character of his investments. It was bad enough to be the dependent son of a man who had made his fortune in this fashion. It was out of the question to remain the dependent son of a man who was still willfully so engaged!

I came home that weekend and confronted Father coldly at Saturday lunch with my discovery. He did not seem much perturbed.

"I had contracted to sell them, but the deal fell through. Now there's no market."

"I am afraid that I cannot accept any further money that comes from those wretched tenants!"

Father's dark complexion began to show a slowly deepening pink. "Do you want an accounting?" he asked in a harsher tone. "Shall I have Jack Fineberg prepare an allocation of my income between slums and other businesses? So that my morally fastidious son may have only pure dollars?"

"What are you two talking about?" Mother interposed. "Surely money is just money. Can one dollar be cleaner than another?"

"There speaks a woman," said Father with heavy irony. "They have no moral sense, do they, Felix? They don't understand the contamination of the source. Well, I guess I shall have to take a good look at my assets and reserve the wickedest pennies for my own poor needs. But what will your conscience accept? What about the dividends of Atlantic Steel? The company owns some buildings in Pittsburgh that make Hester Street look like the Waldorf. And how about the lease on the Armstrong warehouse? Two of the floors are rented by Georgia Phosphates. I am told the conditions in their mines are appalling."

"I guess I'd better renounce it all!" I exclaimed, flushing.

"That is at least logical. May I ask how you expect to complete your course at Yale? Not to speak of the degree you may need as an art historian?"

"I'll use what you've already given me to finish up. And then

I'll go to work to earn the money to pay you back. Every penny!"

Suddenly I had gone much further than I had planned. Suddenly there was something like hate in my heart. Why? This man had never really hurt me. He had failed to love me, but then he had never loved anyone. He was coarse and selfish, but no more so than half his world. I'm afraid that what I abominated was the idea that I could ever be like him, ever be part of him. I brushed him off me as if he had become an encasing mist.

Father suddenly seemed weary and deflated.

"Like all idealists you love the multitude, Felix," he said sadly. "But I fear you don't care much for the individual."

"What do you mean by that?"

"You don't care for me, that's for sure."

"Morris, how can you say such a foolish thing?"

"Is it not caring for you, Father, not to care for your money?"

"Yes! Because in despising it, you despise me!"

"*I* have the answer, Morris. If Felix won't take money from you, let him take it from me. Perhaps then it will have been sufficiently laundered."

Father's laugh was loud and unpleasant, but he did not even turn to Mother. He gave me a long, hard stare.

"Do you really mean what you say about the money, Felix? Think carefully before you answer."

"I mean every word of it. I shall not take another penny from you unless you assure me that you will clean up those slums. A sale will no longer be enough. No, no, they must be renovated!"

How prim, how smug I must have sounded! What is more irritating to older people than the high moral stands of the inexperienced young? I did not know that Father was already fatally ill with cancer of the lymphatic system. He had told nobody, and the symptoms were not yet detectable to the lay observer. It was he, not Mother, who needed my imaginary protection. The bitterness of my repudiation, on top of both my decision to go into art and his doctor's grim verdict, must have been black indeed.

"You may have brains," Father said more heavily now, "but I wonder if brains will get you far without judgment. And without a heart."

I was about to protest my continuing affection, but he cut me short with a rough gesture, and then he left the table. I returned to New Haven that afternoon. This was most unfortunate, for I never saw him again.

Three weeks later, without even telling Mother, he entered the hospital for surgery. He had been told there was some chance of success, but when the doctor cut into him he found the cancer too widely spread to be removed. Fortunately for Father, his heart gave out before he recovered from the anesthetic, and the first Mother and I heard of his illness was his death. It was like him never to bother anybody else with his troubles.

He had made a will dividing his property between me and Mother, but before entering the hospital he had added a codicil leaving everything to her. I felt that this was kind of him, for it helped to assuage my remorse. His real estate was in much worse condition than anyone, even Uncle Jacob, had guessed. It would have been difficult for him to renovate his tenements: rents were down, and he was heavily mortgaged. It was my satisfaction in the years that followed, despite the vigorous opposition from Uncle Jacob, to insist on maintaining Mother's scale of living as it had always been, even though this could be effected only by a steady erosion of her capital. After Uncle Jacob's death, only five years after Father's, I met no further resistance. Mother never inquired about money; she left everything in my hands.

I have said before that Mother had golden luck. She maintained this good fortune as long as she lived. During the Great Depression, when she was nearing the end of both her life and her capital, I was beginning to fear that the latter would expire before the former, leaving Mother on my financial hands, which I should have minded only because it might have humiliated her. I needn't have been concerned. Almost as the last assets were sold she died. There was nothing left of Father's fortune to embarrass me.

I did one other thing to prove to myself and to Father's shade that I bore him no immature resentment. When I made my decision to go to Harvard Law School I accepted the money for my tuition from Mother and refrained from asking myself too many searching questions about the fetid origin of my supporting cash. It was in this rather curious fashion that I saw fit to apologize to Father for my presumption and impertinence. It was not that I condoned his exploitation of slum areas. It was simply that I now realized that if I were to advance the moral standard of the Leitners in my own generation, it would be by my life and not by stagy gestures.

Letter to Roger Cutter from Heyward Satterlee, March 3, 1974

SIR:

You will have already observed, from the thickness of my envelope, that I have decided to comply — at least in part — with your request. Had I seen fit to decline — even had I given all of my excellent reasons for doing so — it would hardly have taken so many pages.

When I got your letter I was at first angry, then bitter, and finally resigned. How did *you*, who had been a witness, perhaps even an agent, of my humiliation in that summer of 1938, have the nerve to ask me to supply a chapter in the life of the man who had done me so cruel a wrong? But then I thought: no, if Felix Leitner merits a biography — and obviously he does — who is better qualified to write it than Roger Cutter? And if that be the case, is Cutter not bound to seek his facts wherever they are to be found? After this reflection came the bitterness. For *have* I any distinction in life greater than that of having been Felix's friend — except perhaps that of having ceased to be so? Is it not perhaps fitting that I should myself supply the sad little footnote that my sad long life has been? And so finally came the resignation. What difference does it all make now? Felix and I are old men. Wasn't it Talleyrand who said, "After eighty, there are no enemies, only survivors"?

You see, I can quote Talleyrand. I'm not quite the boob you Felix-worshipers think. That was Talleyrand's answer to the question of how he felt about Lafayette. I don't say I'm Lafayette or that Felix is Talleyrand, but certainly if you had to choose which most closely corresponded to which, that is the way it would come out. I suppose what I'm trying to show you — however disingenuously — is that where I was naive, Felix was crafty.

"What did Felix ever see in him?" That is what Felix's other friends always asked. Because I was a stockbroker, I had to be a philistine. You all forgot that at Yale I was an editor of the *Lit* before Felix was. And that he gave me credit in the foreword to his book on the crash of 1929 for my part in the chapter entitled "The Last Summer." And that we used to read Trollope together. *All* of Trollope. We would discuss the characters of the parliamentary novels on our fishing trips. It was a kind of shared hobby.

But I had better get to the point. I have said that I would comply in part with your request, and so I shall. I am going to describe for you the early days of my friendship with Felix. I am going to try to give you some sense of what he meant to me. But I have no intention of getting into the subject of how it all broke up. I do not believe, even now, that I am capable of the necessary objectivity. And anyway, you should know that chapter pretty well yourself. You were there, God knows. And if you played a role in it, may God forgive you. I couldn't. Even now.

I guess I've made it perfectly clear, Cutter, that what I am writing is for history's sake, not yours.

❊   ❊   ❊

Felix and I first met at the Driscoll School on Central Park West, which I attended in my seventeenth and eighteenth years. I suppose I should first explain what I — a Satterlee, a grandson of Bishop Potter, and the only son of Augustus Satterlee, senior partner of the old downtown law firm of Story, Satterlee & Strong — was doing at a school on the wrong side of Central Park, a good half of whose students were Jewish boys.

It was certainly with only the most reluctant consent of my "distinguished" father. Let me take a paragraph to describe him. His like does not exist today, although an odd parody of it occasionally appears in novels about "society" with characters called Wasps. Our chroniclers of fashion are apt to be a generation behind the times, or else they try to give the public what the public likes to think is truth. I noticed only last Monday, for example, on my weekly visit to my old office, that my partners had loaned one of our floors to a movie company that needed a set laid in a brokerage house. Some of our customers' men had volunteered to act as extras, but their services were politely declined. Why? Because they did not *look* like customers' men! Where were their white shirts and black knitted ties? Where were their gray flannel suits?

But to get back to Father. He looked like his portrait by Ellen Emmet Rand — grave, droopy-eyed, with a cream-colored vest, his gnarled fingers holding an open law reporter — provided the observer added the wrinkles, both on his face and in his clothes. For there *were* wrinkles there, just as there were prejudices in the mellifluous stream of his discourse and in the odd blind spots of his generally kindly vision. Father, by all accounts, was a fine lawyer and a powerful opponent in court; he was a strong trustee on charitable boards and had been a fearless opponent of city corruption during his term as president of the City Bar Association. He was also a devoted husband and father. But his rigid standards for inclusion in the narrow society in which he and Mother moved barred most of the New York world: Catholics, Jews, divorced persons, politicians, actors, retail business men . . . the list was endless. He also excluded financiers of doubtful integrity, even though he represented many such, and the too newly rich, unless they were plain and simple, something he called "nature's gentlemen."

Father never mixed business and pleasure, rarely asked a client to the house and never quite trusted a man who had earned all or none of his own money. But strangest of all was his sublime confidence that the world basically shared his values. When he returned to his habit of Newport summers, after a brief experiment with the Maine coast, he observed to me loftily: "Have you noticed how pleased the tradespeople are to have the Satterlees back?" I hadn't.

I have said enough to indicate that the selection of the Driscoll School did not come from him. You have undoubtedly deduced that our family must have contained a will even stronger than his. Mother was a shrewd, plain, vital, intense little woman who bustled about her house and the city, in sober black or brown, an irresistible force at home and in her church work. She rarely raised her voice or lost her temper, but she never released her grip once she had taken hold of something. She liked to quote the comic motto of her family: "God made the clay, but we are the Potters." She shared all of Father's prejudices, but she did not hesitate to make exceptions whenever it was convenient to do so. This fact alone made her the stronger of the two.

Being an only son of such a couple was not easy, and two younger sisters, pampered at least by Father, did not help. I realize now that Father loved me, but he rarely showed it, and I labored under a constant sense of disappointing him. I was always a poor student and never a leader, and my aptitude in athletics did not compensate in those days for other lacks, as it might have later. Father's total disinterest in sports, not uncommon to New York gentlemen of his generation, deprived me of my one chance to make good in his eyes. At Saint Paul's in New Hampshire, where I was sent at the age of fifteen, I did so badly in my classes that there was a question of dropping me to a lower form. Mother and Father came up from New York and successfully dissuaded the headmaster from this. They tried to be kind, but they were obviously both so concerned that I now became obsessed with marks in a desperate effort to justify their assurance to the headmaster that I could meet the standards of my contemporaries. This obsession destroyed the last remnants of my concentration; my grades dropped to the bottom; panic ensued. At the end of my second year, when I came home, Father announced to me gravely that I should not be going back.

Mother had made a survey of all the private day schools in Manhattan and had concluded that Driscoll was the one most likely to get me into Harvard. It combined a reputation for coping with backward students with one for academic excellence, so I should not have the stigma of attending a rehabilitation center for dunces. Mother made short shrift of Father's objections.

"Jewish boys?" she retorted. "Of course there are Jewish boys, and from some of their greatest families, too. Trust them to pick the best school! I always say: if you want a bargain, go where the Jews go."

This conversation had an effect on me that Mother could

never have anticipated. I was immensely relieved! For if I was being sent to a school that Father did not regard as fit for a gentleman's son, it could hardly so much matter what grades I received there. From the moment I entered Driscoll I had the exhilarating sense of being on my own. All was delightful to my liberated spirit: the boys seemed pleasant, the masters sympathetic, the courses interesting. My tensions were eased; my marks at last satisfactory. In short, I bloomed.

Felix Leitner, you will not be surprised to hear, stood number one in our class. We had adjoining desks in study hall, and he was very kind in advising a new student of the idiosyncrasies of the masters and the customs of the school. We soon became friends. I was never, of course, his intellectual equal, but that was not nearly so important among schoolboys as the fact that we both cared about soccer and girls. Felix, with his easy generosity, was willing to share his friends with me, and, thanks to him and to my new ease of mind, I felt more at home at Driscoll after two months than I had at Saint Paul's after two years.

Let me see if I can describe Felix as he looked then. He was considerably slighter than he later became. At first glance, and if one had not seen him sprinting down the soccer field, one might have inferred that he was delicate. Father thought he verged on the effeminate, but Father was biased. Mother considered him "beautiful," and both my kid sisters developed crushes on him. His skin was pale; his brow high, clear, poetic; his hair thick, blond and curly, with a tinge of red. His nose was more Roman than Jewish; his lips were thin and seemed tightly sealed when closed. His chin was square and more determined than seemed to fit with the pallor and delicacy that were one's general impression of him. But his eyes were his great asset. They were wide and of a pale gray-blue, flecked with green. Their expression was usually calm, quizzical, reflective, faintly amused. If there was a tendency to blandness, even lightness, in Felix's features as a whole, except for the chin, the eyes redeemed it. They would question you, smile at you, half reassure you . . . and then they would congeal into something more elusive, perhaps harder, certainly further away. You could never quite "catch" Felix.

When he asked me to his house I was impressed at the easy air of equality with which he treated his parents, so unlike my alternately too submissive or too resentful behavior to my own. I was dazzled by Mrs. Leitner, with her high-piled red hair and rustling taffetas, and found her house utterly exotic. But when I tried to describe her and her home to my parents they simply looked at each other and smiled. I soon realized that there was no point trying to make them admire my new friends. If Mother had ever admitted that Mrs. Leitner was even handsome, it would have been as if she had admitted that a particular horse was handsome.

Both my parents, however, behaved with perfect politeness to Felix when he came to our house. Father, after all, was a gentleman; he showed his prejudices only to those who shared them. Besides, like everyone else, he found Felix stimulating, even when they disagreed. I remember Felix facing him down, with perfect equanimity, over the issue of Theodore Roosevelt and the Panama Canal.

"It was an act of great statesmanship!" Father declared in his most emphatic, not-to-be-disagreed-with tone. "Roosevelt showed himself the equal of Jefferson. You will recall that at the time of the Louisiana Purchase nobody was sure that the Constitution permitted the president to add territory to the nation. But there was no time to wait for Congress or the courts. Napoleon might have changed his mind. Jefferson had to act, and he acted!"

"True, sir, but it was only a purchase. Jefferson had nothing to lose but what now seems an inconsiderable sum of money. Roosevelt's case, I submit, is altogether different. When he couldn't get the canal from Colombia, he sponsored the revolution that created the nation that *would* give it to him."

"Sponsored, you say? I believe the Panamanians were responsible for their own revolution."

"But Roosevelt prevented Colombia from suppressing it. I call that sponsoring it. Look what he said himself: 'I took the canal.'"

"Great Britain would have done the same!"

"Undoubtedly. But to me it is sad that we should be like our mother country already. We had such brave hopes when we were weaned!"

Father was completely stopped by this. He had not expected to be taught idealism by a Jewish boy. He was irritated, obviously, by my friend's cockiness, but he was also impressed. I noticed in the future that he was more cautious in his statements. Yet I think both he and Mother were always pleased when Felix came to the house. Certainly our meals were livelier.

Unfortunately for Felix's future relationship with my father, he was responsible for my choice of Yale over Harvard. He himself was going to Yale because he had been convinced by his favorite teacher at Driscoll that Yale had the best history department in the country, and he had no difficulty persuading me to go with him. Indeed, the idea of Harvard, branded as it was with the paternal preference, struck me as the nightmare of Saint Paul's all over again, and I resisted Father with a fierceness that at first astonished and finally disgusted him.

"I wouldn't expect your friend Leitner to understand distinctions that don't exist in his background. For example, that a Yale man is never quite a gentleman to the same degree a Harvard man is. It's a nuance, I admit, but still, it's there. What really upsets me is that you should prefer the advice of an inexperienced Jewish boy, smart though he may be, to that of your own father!"

Mother came to my aid again, and that settled the question. I am afraid that she was more influenced by the proximity of New Haven to New York than by the fact that Felix advocated Yale. She always liked to have her children nearby. But it was still a victory, and my first important one over Father. I never forgot that I owed it to Felix.

Yet Felix's own attitude toward a struggle so important to me was disappointing. He showed a rather chilling detachment and refused to condemn my father as I did.

"I don't know, Heyward, if I were you, that I shouldn't go along with him. He's so exquisite for his type. How many lawyers could you find on Wall Street who would refuse to acknowledge E. H. Harriman's nod? And maybe there's something in what he says, after all. Maybe a Harvard man *is* more of a gentleman."

"You can't think I care about *that?*"

"It's not what you and I care about. It's what *he* cares about. When you have a superb sample like that, don't you want to bottle it? Every chance you have to study your old man, you should grab, it seems to me. And you don't grab it by opposing him."

"You can't be serious!" I exclaimed, and broke off the discussion in an agony of apprehension as to what he might say next.

Felix wasn't altogether serious, of course, but he half was. He wanted to dissect Father, to anatomize him. Even *I* couldn't let him do that.

Felix also disappointed me by declining to room with me freshman year. He said that college was the opportunity to broaden our acquaintance and that roommates from the same preparatory school presented an "established intimacy" that might act as a repellant to a shy neighbor. He said that we should see as much of each other as ever, but I was not sure of this. I suspected that he thought I might be a drag on him when he cultivated the brilliant men of the class. Father, to my surprise, took just the opposite view.

"I must say that's very tactful of your friend," he said when I told him. "To be absolutely frank, I shouldn't have thought him capable of such delicacy of feeling. But I give him credit now. He sees that rooming with him might cut you out with some of the better elements of the class."

It had not occurred to me that my "social position," such as it was, would be much of an asset at Yale. At Saint Paul's most of the boys had had the same degree of it, and at Driscoll almost none, with the result that there had been very little talk of it in either school, at least to my awareness. Of course, my parents, particularly Father, were always conscious of it, but I had the feeling, developed no doubt from my own abysmal failure to excel in any of the things that they valued, that their social position was a thing that belonged to them personally and was not transmittable to me. I felt like a waif who had been adopted. I never associated myself with their rank in life.

At Yale, however, I began to find out that being a Satterlee and being handsome (for I *was* that — I can say it now) and being something of an athlete, opened plenty of doors to me. In my freshman year I made friends with most of the men who were to be the leaders of our class, and I was one of the first to be taken into the fraternity Psi U, which even my father conceded had almost the cachet of a Harvard club.

Felix, on the other hand, devoted himself exclusively to the class intellectuals and worked very hard at his courses. It seemed to me that he was always reading. We visited each other's rooms regularly and remained on much the same friendly terms as at Driscoll, but it was evident that our interests were increasingly disparate. I could not follow him as deeply into philosophy and government as he had gone, and he did not share my growing interest in sports and college activities. But we both enjoyed discussing how the world should be changed. Felix had become something of a radical, and I was always titillated at the prospect of the masses overturning Father's world.

You may imagine my surprise, therefore, in the middle of sophomore year, when Felix came to my room with a serious proposition. He wanted me to get him into Psi U! He came as close to looking embarrassed as he ever did, which was not very close. His eyes were fixed on me as if to show their determination not to glance aside.

"But I thought you didn't care for that sort of thing!"

"I don't, really. But I've come to see that it's part of the college experience. It seems to me now that it might be a mistake to miss it. The men in Psi U represent a class that is still immensely powerful in this country. I think it behooves me to know what they're like at first hand."

"You mean you want me to be a kind of Trojan horse? I can't do that, Felix. Those men are my friends!"

"And they shall be mine," Felix reassured me. "I didn't mean to sound so cold-blooded about it. I have no real ulterior purpose. I simply feel that I've been too narrowly intellectual. I want to broaden myself. I'd like to have different kinds of friends. I'd like to be more like *you*, Heyward."

Well, that did it! It had never occurred to me that I had anything that this remarkable friend could really want. In a single meeting he put all things right between us. You must remember that Felix was the first person who had ever treated me as having even normal brains and capabilities. I had been so cowed by my superior parents that I had come to consider myself a poor thing. Then Felix had picked me up and made me feel a man. It did not take him more than an afternoon to re-establish all his old ascendancy. I resolved to get him into my fraternity.

This turned out to be a considerable job. My friends at Psi U found Felix attractive, but they suspected him of being an intellectual snob. And, of course, there was the terrible hurdle of his Jewishness. At first it seemed insurmountable. I devoted myself to inquiries that I never thought I should make. I discovered that Felix's mother was not Jewish and that his father had abandoned the orthodox faith. I took the position with the fraternity leaders that Felix was not really a Jew at all. I pointed out tellingly that he did not look like one. My friends in Psi U did not know much about Jews; they were amateurs in prejudice. By putting every scrap of my own popularity on the counter I was able at last to secure Felix's rather grudging election.

I had hoped that he would be delighted. If he was, he did not show it. He was grateful, but not demonstratively so. Of course, he could not have known what my struggle had amounted to. Or could he have? He *did* give me a gold pin with the letters psi u in the center and our initials entwined on either side. When one of my prying sisters found this on my dresser at home and was mean enough to show it to Father, I had to endure the full explosion of his scorn.

"I never saw anything so vulgar, so innately Jewish in my life! I was right in the beginning about that young man. He's used you, Heyward, and he'll keep on using you until you take your blinders off!"

Felix came to the fraternity house often in the first months after his election and made himself thoroughly agreeable to everyone. I was even congratulated by some of his would-be blackballers on my perspicacity in proposing him. But after he had taken the full gauge of our members, he began to lose interest in the club. This was the beginning of his serious radical period, which was to culminate with his marriage to Frances Ward, who represented (except in the matter of birth) the opposite pole of all that Psi U had seemed to stand for. Felix was increasingly lost to his books and to what we at Psi U called "greasy grinds."

In the spring of junior year, when I was taken into Scroll and Key, Felix was not even "tapped" for a senior society. Even if one had wished to secure him, it could not have done so, for he declined to take his stand in the Old Campus with the rest of our class on Tap Day. I felt, still humbly, for all my own success, that he, at least, had put aside "childish things."

For the next half dozen years I saw little of Felix. He was a law student in Cambridge while I was a stockbroker in New York. Then he served as law clerk to Supreme Court Justice Miner in Washington. When he did move to New York, he and Frances lived in Greenwich Village, and his work for the U.S. Attorney along with the books and articles that he wrote were far removed from my little world of stocks and bonds. Besides, I was still living with my parents — as young bachelors of that day whose families had large, well-staffed houses still did — and Frances Leitner did not feel comfortable with a host like my father, who evidently regarded her, professional woman and outspoken reformer that she was, as a "traitor to her class." But Felix and I never allowed our friendship to drop. We corresponded; we occasionally lunched; and I came to some of his parties in the Village. We always had the bond of those years at Driscoll.

In 1917 I was twenty-seven and had just been commissioned a second lieutenant. I was about to be shipped overseas, and my only concern in life was to persuade Gladys Dunne, then only twenty, to marry me before I went. Gladys had been, at least to my enraptured eyes, the most fascinating debutante of the 1915 season. She was small, dark-eyed, bright, vivacious . . . but why make more of a fool of myself on paper than I did in fact such decades ago? I was simply crazy about her. And she? Well, she liked my looks and liked my dancing and even liked my jokes, but she did not consider me, in her engaging candor, sufficiently serious for what she liked to call *une grande passion*. No, I was just her "amiable teddy bear."

But now things were different. Now I was in uniform, with the glamorous prospect of early death in the trenches to wipe away smiles, obliterate condescension. Even my parents, who found Gladys too "giddy," and her own, who found her too young, were inclined to be benevolent about marriage among those whose future was so sadly in doubt. In the atmosphere of "seize the day" that now enveloped us, I saw that I was on the brink of sweeping Gladys off her feet. I decided that what I needed was the endorsement of someone totally dissociated with what she considered my "stuffy" background (not that hers was much better!), and whom better did I have to hand but Felix?

I took her to a party given by the Leitners in the Village. There were artists, poets, radicals, even pacifists there. Gladys was thrilled. She had never been exposed to anything quite like it before, and her opinion of me took a leap up. When Felix, whose biography of Theodore Roosevelt for the Bull Moose campaign she had read in preparation of the meeting (it being the shortest and easiest of his publications and already considered a minor classic), took her over to a corner to tell her what a fine guy I was, my wedding was as good as settled.

I had a different experience with Frances Leitner. I never knew quite what to make of her. She had been a surprising choice for Felix, being short and plain and on the verge of a word I hate and use hesitatingly . . . dumpy. Of course, she was a Ward and related to everyone in what Father called "old New York," but her branch of that family had always been poor, and her rather left-wing good works had discredited her in conservative circles for which she cared less than nothing. She was supposed to be brilliant, but what did Felix need with brilliance? I supposed that he was attracted by her obvious devotion to him. And then, too, I must admit, she had a winning amiability, an extremely good temper, even though I could not help reading in the steady gaze of her glinting blue eyes: "Now just what do *you* see in my friends, Heyward Satterlee? Admit you think they're all anarchists! Come, now, admit it!"

But what she said to me now was something quite different.

"Miss Dunne is utterly charming. I am so happy you brought her. Are you planning to be married soon?"

"If I have anything to do with it."

"Mightn't it be wiser to put it off till you come back?"

"But I may not come back!"

"Oh, yes, you will. Mark my words. This terrible war can't go on much longer. Flesh and blood won't stand it!"

"That's what they said in 1914."

"But even so, the time must come. Don't make decisions as if it were the end of the world."

I was suddenly shocked and angered by her gravely warning tone. How dared she talk to me in that way? She was younger than I! "You think I'll come back and she'll be tired of me!" I cried in anguish. I think there must have been sudden tears in my eyes.

Quickly Frances caught my hand in both of hers. "No, no, it's not that at all. I just think you may come back and find that you and she are different persons. Nice persons, of course, but not the same."

"Maybe better!"

Frances's smile was now perfectly without reservations. She nodded, as if to make up for her unseemly doubt, and squeezed my hand. "Maybe. I like to think that. I shall try to keep thinking that."

Gladys and I were married the following week. Felix was my best man. Father, who was becoming very old, became almost sentimental at my bachelor's dinner at the Racquet Club. After Felix's very funny speech and moving toast to the bride, he leaned over to me and whispered: "I have a confession to make, my boy. That man has been a better friend to you than I ever thought he would be. Bless you both!"

I thank whatever God there is that Father never knew what happened twenty years later. Isn't it odd? My strange, snobbish, violent old father, whose attitudes I so deplored all my days, proved the only human being in the end who ever really loved me.

First Chapter from the
Privately Printed Memoirs
of Frances Ward Leitner,
"My Life and Law"

WHEN I WAS TOLD in January of 1951 that my asthmatic
attacks were beginning to produce a dangerous strain
on my heart, I decided that, if I were ever going to, it was
time to write "that book" for my children and grandchildren.
While I was given no estimate of the time I might have left
("You may bury us all," Dr. Fitch told me in his jovial way),
I was left with the distinct impression that a "reasonable man,"
as we lawyers say, would arrange to put his affairs in order.
And so I decided to prepare these chapters for those of my
descendants, and the descendants of my parents, who may be
interested.

This one will tell the story of how I married Felix. So much
has been made in the family of our divorce that I am afraid
my offspring will think of our marriage as all unhappy. That
is very far from the truth. It was the greatest part of my life,

although I do not much care, as a staunch career woman, to have to admit it.

Later, I shall write a chapter on my legal career. And perhaps another on my ideas about legal aid and what the duty of the bar should be about it. And one, I think, if time permits, about my father. Maybe even one about my mother. Oh, ideas proliferate as one looks back to the past! I have evidently spent too much of my life living in the present.

No, I won't call this a book. I always said that I'd never write a book. Too many of my family already have. Wards have written about Wards; Chanlers about Chanlers; Livingstons about Livingstons. And *all* of them have written about the Astors, to whom, poor as my parents were, we were still kin. Even their titles were inclined to be proprietary, such as: *My Aunt, Julia Ward Howe,* or *My Cousin, Marion Crawford.* There was a kind of literary cannibalism in all these memoirs, into which I resolved I should never be tempted. And yet here I go. At least I have the excuse of a private circulation. I am not writing, let me remind my readers, for publication.

I have said that we were poor, and so we were by the standards of richer kin, but what did that mean in 1912, in our world, even on the fringes of it? It meant a shabby, comfortable brownstone house on East Twenty-third Street, tended by two loyal and devoted maids, and a summer shingle shack on the Hampton dunes. It meant economizing by spending a year in Fontainebleau, another in Dresden. It meant my going to Brooklyn Law School alone by trolley, without a chaperon. It meant my sisters and I wearing hand-me-downs. It meant darning our own socks.

Dad was the editor of the *Knickerbocker Monthly.* Its circulation was small but its literary reputation high. He had published stories by Crane and Dreiser. Mother wrote sentimental poetry on elevated topics for the evening papers. We were a cheerful and loving family who never envied our grander cousins. My three sisters and I used to compare ourselves to the March girls in *Little Women*.

But I must not make us seem too demure. Harriet, after all, became a surgeon, Lila a social worker in Harlem, and Sophie proclaimed her independence by living openly for twenty years with a married man. We were certainly emancipated by the standards of the era. I think poor Mommie and Dad were sometimes upset by our disregard of the proprieties, but there was never a time that any one of us felt the least failure in their love and support. Parents and daughters were always a unit.

What made us so liberal, or indeed so radical — as we were then considered? I think it may have been simply that we were intelligent and perhaps a bit more exposed than other girls of similar background to the appalling suffering that existed not far from our own front door. How could reasonable young women not surmise that there had to be something wrong with a society that permitted our Astor cousins to live in Renaissance splendor on Fifth Avenue while stinking slums existed a few blocks from our own brownstone?

But there was an important difference between our radicalism and the radicalism of many other young people. We never wanted anyone's blood. This is not a boast. Why should we have? We had never suffered poverty, filth, repression. Why should we have sought the heads of the rich? We were not frustrated social climbers. Mrs. Cornelius Vanderbilt asked Mommie and Dad to her balls. We were under no inner compulsion, in doing our paltry bit to improve the world, to ring tocsins or mount heads on pikes. We had inherited our father's basic reasonableness.

This, I feel sure, was one of the qualities that made us attractive to Felix when he first began to call. He always detested shouting, and he used to say in later years that bad manners alone had turned him from socialism. When he came out to see Dad in Westhampton in the summer of 1912, he felt immediately at home.

The Bull Moose campaign was in full swing, and Dad, a passionate admirer of Colonel Roosevelt, with whom he had some slight acquaintance, was busily editing and promoting party literature. Felix, who had just finished at Harvard Law and had been recommended to Dad by a friend in the law faculty as a volunteer, was engaged in writing the campaign biography of TR, a good copy of which is now a prime collector's item as its author's first published book. He spent far more time with the Wards than was warranted by what they had to contribute to the life of the candidate, and it soon became apparent that his interest had descended from the father to the daughters and from them to me.

Why me? I wasn't even pretty, though Mother used to say that my smile should catch me a husband. But Felix Leitner? I wasn't as charming as Sophie or as good as Lila or as bright as Harriet. I was a law student, it was true, as was Felix, but was that a thing to attract a man? You must remember, reader, that Felix was quite marvelous-looking at twenty-two (not that he ever wholly lost it), pale and shining, with a bit of red in the hair, a bit of green in the eyes, and a manner so cool and calm and assured! I could not help thinking of the sonnet of Elizabeth Barrett Browning's:

> *What hast thou to do*
> *With looking through the lattice lights at me,*
> *A poor tired wandering singer, singing through*
> *The dark, and leaning up a cypress tree?*

From the beginning he treated me the way the romantic Edwardian girl, only half-hidden behind the radical law student, wanted to be treated. He listened to my ideas with a grave attention that enchanted me, and he made only the gentlest fun of those with which he disagreed. He was strong without seeming aggressive, and he managed to imply an interest in my person without any of the gestures expected by girls today.

Here, for example, is how we discussed a woman's problem of combining a career with marriage:

"Of course, if she wanted children, she would have to take a few years off," I affirmed, "unless she could do her work at home. I suppose a lawyer could see clients that way."

"It would place her at a distinct competitive disadvantage. Think of it! Testators in the playroom. Why couldn't a nurse look after the children?"

"Would you want your children brought up by a nurse?"

"Why not? *I* was."

"But I think that's terrible!" I exclaimed with feeling. "A child needs a mother."

"She could be home in the evenings."

Of course, eventually this was very much how our two children *were* brought up, but at the time I was an idealist in everything. I wanted to have all my cakes and swallow them. Felix's ideas of family life struck me as very backward.

"Home in the evenings!" I exclaimed in disgust. "How can a mother give a child the attention and warmth it needs in an hour before bedtime?"

"I think *you* could, Fran," he said with a cryptic smile. "I think one shot of your electricity might keep that baby warm all night."

"And just what do you mean by that?"

"Simply that you're full of life and vitality. Don't look at me that way. It's a compliment!"

I suppose it was. Sensitive souls tend to admire qualities they lack themselves. Felix had plenty of vitality, but it was commonly said of him that he had a cool nature. Some people, like my sister Harriet, even found him cold. But I suspected that he was simply reserved, perhaps inhibited, and that he found in the friendly warmth of our family circle and in my own intense reactions a milieu that corresponded with something hidden behind his own polished, faintly formidable exterior. At least I hoped so, for I was already immensely attracted to him, although something like fear made me struggle with this attraction. Felix might be a man who would own a woman, and I had no intention of being owned.

Nothing, however, in his conversation betrayed the slightest inclination toward philistinism. He would discuss marriage with me as an institution, quite dispassionately, when we were still only friends.

"I should expect my wife to have any career she chose except the stage. And that is not in the least because I disapprove of the theater — my own mother was an actress — but simply because I should hate to have her away from home in the evenings. But there's no danger. I don't know any actresses."

"But your wife might become an actress after she married you!"

"True." Was he assessing, behind that calm, amused gaze, the possibility that Frances Ward might fling over her law books and tread the boards? An actress? What could I be but a comic? "One can only deal with likelihoods."

"You wouldn't repudiate her?"

"I should probably take to the grease paint myself. *That* should teach her a lesson."

Harriet did not like Felix. She thought him not only cold but calculating. She explained with pitiless ingenuity the seeming illogicality of his apparent preference for a plain, penniless girl like myself. As a dedicated socialist he could hardly saddle himself with a mere debutante. On the other hand, his innate snobbishness would cause him to turn up his nose at the girls he encountered in liberal circles. How many of these possessed my qualifications? How many "new women" with old backgrounds could he find?

I do not think that I realized how completely I had fallen in love with Felix until Harriet imparted this theory. I rejected it with a passion that gave me away.

"I'm sorry, Fran. I felt I had to say it."

"I guess that duty was more like a pleasure," I retorted with a sniff.

"Believe me, dear, this has been a very hard thing for me to do."

"Oh, stuff, Harriet!"

For what she told me was wormwood. It made a kind of ghastly sense. I felt like a butterfly — no, not even a butterfly, a poor brown moth — selected by an entomologist whose only passion was in classifications and impaled by the needle of my own sentiment to his crisp, clean chart. But in the whirlwind of my unhappiness I suddenly reached out and made a grab for hard earth. And I found it! Felix, already an intimate in our family circle, could hardly be seeking an illicit relationship with a daughter of Dad's. If his attentions pointed to anything, they had to point to marriage. And why on earth should he consider it worth his while, from any point of view, social or socialist, to marry *me*? Why would he not be better-off young and free? This idea afforded me a great relief. Felix might never ask me to marry him, but if he should — despite all that Harriet could say — it would have to be for love.

And then I learned something else. Dad, who was devoted to Felix, told me that a young Ward cousin, who had been at Yale with him, had related how Felix had turned his back on his old Jewish friends and had cultivated the socially elite of the class in order to get himself elected to an exclusive fraternity.

"I thought I'd tell you, Fran, because I see that you and Felix are becoming very good friends. You're old enough and independent enough not to be put off by that sort of talk, but it's also a good idea to know what's going around. Personally, I don't believe a word of it. People are always trying to put Jews in their place. If Johnny Ward wants to be elected to Psi U, it's because he wants a jolly place to eat and drink with his pals. But if Felix Leitner does, that's social climbing! I guess you and I are above that kind of spite."

Dad was, but I was not at all sure about myself. All the doubts aroused by Harriet flared up again. Felix was looking not only for a "society" girl; he was looking for a Gentile! Did he have a backbone at all behind that stiff back? Was he a man, a real man, like Dad?

Women have a reputation for subtlety, but it was not a characteristic of the female Wards. The very next time that Felix and I were alone together, I turned the conversation bluntly to Yale fraternities. It did not take him long to pick up the gist of my thoughts.

"You feel like my Uncle Jacob," he said. "He's always criticizing me for not having more Jewish friends. When I asked him once why he cared about my being Jewish or non-Jewish, he replied very candidly: 'Well, even if a man doesn't like his own club, he hates to see anyone else get out.'"

"What a cynical family you must have! I thought Jews were proud of being Jews."

"Many are. Some are not. And you've inherited more Christian prejudices than you're aware of, Fran."

"How can you say that? I respect everybody's religion! Or lack of religion."

"It's the last that I question. You accord liberty of religion to everyone but Jews. They have to be Jewish."

"That's not so. I believe in everyone's right to choose his own faith." I hesitated, but I was so tense now that I soon blurted it out. "Provided they don't choose it for social advantage!"

Felix now became as nearly angry as I had ever seen him. His cheeks became paler, and his eyes were hard and glinting. "I think you had better take a good look at yourself before you do any more preaching, Frances. You come of an old New York aristocracy whose rules and customs you take great pride in violating. You have chosen your own little world and your own little rules. Very well. That is fine by me. I shouldn't object if you became a converted Jew. But let me assure you, my friend, that I claim the same liberty for myself. I intend to select the association I want and join the clubs I want and live the life I want, regardless of what labels and motives small people may attach to my acts. If you wish to call that turning my back on my heritage for social advantage, you are quite at liberty to do so. But I don't intend to discuss this matter a second time. It's too demeaning."

After this I was more than just in love. I was pulverized. There is no better word for it. But that didn't mean I was convinced. Oh, no! I did not dare bring up the subject again, but I kept thinking of other questions that I longed to ask. Had he cultivated friends just to be elected? Did he go to see his Leitner cousins as much as he ought to? Did he prefer the Aunt Renata he was always talking about because she was the richest member of his family? I began to feel like Psyche, who was loved by the invisible Eros in the dark, or like Elsa who could not ask Lohengrin his name. I was in love with a stranger, perhaps not even a very nice one. I was helpless.

And then I would shake myself angrily. What sort of an ass was I to be dreaming of marriage to a man like Felix? Did that sort of thing happen to girls as drab as myself? No, I had long since made my plans: I was going to be a lawyer and represent the underprivileged. If I married at all, it would be to some good, plain, obscure, unromantic guy like the German professor who married Jo March in *Little Woman*. And that was going to be good enough for me, too. I hadn't been complaining!

I was more and more on my guard now with Felix. I was even occasionally antagonistic to him. When I went back to law school in the fall, Felix, who was still in New York writing for the campaign, used to take me out on weekends. Sometimes we went to the theater or a concert, but just as often we would stroll in Central Park and talk. I never had to be chaperoned, like my "uptown" cousins. But there were times when I almost envied them their lack of freedom. What was I going to do with mine?

Felix seemed in no hurry to "declare himself," as Grandmother Ward would have put it. Yet his conversation never seemed a curtain to disguise sexual timidity. I always had the sense that as soon as he wanted to change our relationship, he would change it. I was the only one in the throes of doubt. The nearest he came to wooing me was in an occasional, unexpected compliment.

"It's hard to believe that you and my mother can belong to the same sex," he told me once. "She hasn't entertained a serious thought since she had to decide between exposed legs and knickerbockers for Rosalind in *As You Like It*. And you, as a babe in arms, could have probably given her four good reasons why Sir Francis Bacon didn't write that play!"

Where the young Felix of this period most differed from his latter-day counterpart was in the quality of his political enthusiasm. He had a vibrant faith in a better world. He believed that progress was accelerating at such a rate that a violent upheaval might not be required to make the forces of greed give way to a benign and universal socialism. The world might find its own way, for the simple reason that that way would become so abundantly clear to all men. This was typical of the euphoria that invaded parts of Academe just before the Great War. I did not share it. I knew that the way would be long and hard, though I longed to believe otherwise.

He was immensely keen about Colonel Roosevelt, and this keenness was turned into something like worship after a day spent with the great man at Oyster Bay, which included a twelve-mile hike and a picnic of raw clams. When he told me about it, I made no comment.

"I'm beginning to recognize that gray questioning stare," he reproached me. "You don't agree with me about the colonel. Why not?"

"Well, there was that comment he made about his sons being soldiers and his daughters being mothers . . ."

"Don't take it out of context!" he interrupted. "He was talking about the importance of traditional challenges in developing character."

"Yes, but that emphasis on battles and babies, Felix! You can see what he really thinks of women. No wonder Mrs. Roosevelt insisted on her own sitting room at Sagamore. There had to be one place in that house where she would be spared the sight of horns and hoofs and claws!"

"I admit he may overdo the trophies. And, of course, there *is* the Rough Rider side of him. But how many presidents have we had — since the early days, anyway — who have read what he's read and done the things he's done? And whom have we had since Lincoln with a heart like that? The man's lovable, Frances. Think of it. A lovable president!"

"I'm not denying his lovability. You can love him all you want. What I question is his depth."

"You find him superficial?"

"On social issues, yes. I'm not impressed with what he's done about the trusts. He's like those keepers at the zoo who are so brave about going in and out of cages and sometimes even cuffing the big cats. But the moment any real snarling starts they're quick enough to get out of the way."

"You won't find that they take him so lightly on Wall Street!"

"Oh, but those people are always hollering before they're hurt. You know that, Felix. The American businessman gets hysterical at the very mention of the word *reform*. It proves his guilty conscience."

"I think you're going to find things different in nineteen thirteen. The colonel means every word he says!"

"We'll see. *If* he's elected."

＊　　＊　　＊

It was wonderful of my parents that neither found it in the least remarkable that I should have attracted such a prize as Felix. This was not, as my cousin Johnny Ward surmised, because they were Wards and he a Jew; snobbishness of that sort was unknown to them. It was simply that they thought no man in the world too good for their daughter. They were perfectly willing to welcome Felix into the family and to admire him — but not to be dazzled by him.

I had been nervous about meeting Mrs. Leitner, feeling sure that she, at least, would find me a frump. Like any woman, I was perfectly prepared to be cowed by and scornful of the exotic clothes and house I had heard of. But instead she won my heart. She seemed at once to separate herself from her Oriental trappings and to reach out cheerfully to meet me on my own ground. She applauded my decision to be a lawyer and cited her old acting days as proof of her basic feminism. There was such a quaint simplicity and honesty in those clear, gazing eyes (like Felix's) and in that high, childlike tone, that one dismissed her background as some kind of a crazy and irrelevant charade.

"You completely won Mother's heart," Felix told me afterward. "She whispered to me that if I let *you* slip between my fingers, I deserved to live and die a bachelor."

"Oh, she's just afraid you'll do worse." My nerves, at this suggestion of a proposal, made me petulant and scratchy. "She thinks you'll bring home a chorine."

He caught me by the hand. "Why do you fight me so, Frances?"

I jerked free. "Because I can't believe in you! What can you *see* in me?"

"Isn't that my affair?"

"No!"

"Very well, then." He stopped in the street and turned to contemplate me carefully, as though I had been a portrait. "To begin with, I like your spunk. Your spirit. I can't imagine you compromising on a moral issue."

What I said to this will show my reader how desperately I was at odds with myself. I had become two women: one bitterly critical; the other a lovesick fool.

"Meaning you're afraid you *might*?" I cried.

Felix flushed. At least he came as near flushing as I ever saw him. For one horrible moment I thought I might have alienated him forever. But then his tensity was suddenly relaxed. He even smiled. "Maybe," he said. "Maybe that's just it."

"You need me, then, like a calcium pill for a weak spine!"

"Frances!" It was almost a call of distress.

"Oh, I'm sorry, I'm being a beast!" And here, fortunately for both our sakes, I burst into tears. "Forgive me. I'm such an ass!"

When I told Mother about this scene, she quite agreed with my classification of myself. But she understood that I was overwrought, and she bathed me in maternal affection. She put her arms around the law student, the would-be judge, the savior of the poor and wretched, and crooned over me, telling me that I was as lovely as a princess and that Felix would be the luckiest man in the world if he were allowed to kiss my little finger.

"But you mustn't be *too* snippy, darling," she concluded. "That's a fine tactic for a time, but it can be very easily overdone."

This was just what I needed. I was now much calmer with Felix. How I remember the first night he kissed me! He always had his own way of doing things. There were no preliminaries, no timid request for permission, no gradual circling of my shoulder with an arm, no pressing closer. Very simply, at the bottom of our brownstone stoop, after I had bid him goodnight, he placed his hands firmly on my shoulders and kissed me on the lips. Then he gazed at me for a silent moment, with an air of mild gravity, nodded, and departed.

The next time we went out, no reference was made, on either side, to this kiss, but it was repeated. This time I seemed to make out, in that blue-green stare, a look of assured possession. Recalling it afterward in my bedroom, I felt a panic at least equal to my pleasure. What did he think of me? What did he expect of me?

After the third kiss I was ready for him. I did not turn to go up the stoop. "Why do you do that?" I asked him deliberately.

"Because it gives me great pleasure," he replied with equal deliberation. "I hope it gives you the same."

"I don't know what it gives me. What does it mean?"

"It means that I love you." When I simply stared, half in awe, he continued: "It means that I love you and want to marry you."

"Oh!"

"Is that something so terrible to hear?"

"I don't know," I said again, but this time desperately. "You'll have to give me time, Felix. You'll just have to give me time!"

And like a giddy fool of a girl, not at all like a law student or an emancipated woman, I turned and fled up the stoop.

*   *   *

The two things that helped me most to pull myself together were, first, Mother's unfailing encouragement and, second, my discovery that Felix had thrown away an inheritance because his father had refused to clean up his slums. He told me this one evening very simply, when we were discussing our careers. I was overjoyed. Until that moment I had been convinced that Felix was deeply attracted to the material pleasures of this world. His mother lived well, almost opulently. He, like her, loved fine clothes. He obviously envied his Aunt Renata her ability to purchase beautiful things. In theaters he always bought the best seats, and in restaurants he liked to show himself a gourmet. But now everything was different. He had turned his back on a fortune, or something like it, and for the most delicate of moral reasons. He said he loved me. God knows I loved him! How long could I keep on turning my back on a destiny that seemed obsessed with heaping my lap with gifts? The front of the picture was certainly handsome. I had turned it over and over and could find no spots on the back. I decided to accept Felix's offer of marriage.

As he had committed himself to a year in Washington as law clerk to Supreme Court Justice Miner, and as I had another year at Brooklyn Law, it was decided that we should not be married until the following spring. Mother, knowing that all my nervous doubts would be revived by separation from Felix, wisely urged me to go every other weekend to Washington, where I stayed with cousins until Justice and Mrs. Miner, very kindly, insisted on putting me up themselves. This worked out very well. Left to myself in New York, I should probably have broken our engagement three times over.

Felix had been disappointed not to have been chosen a secretary to Justice Holmes, but he never indulged his disappointments for long. He was always one to make the best of things, and soon he was taking the position that being secretary to so great a man as Holmes would be too overwhelming, that Holmes's amanuensis would have no chance to write opinions, whereas working for a less titanic individual, a man had a better chance to plumb the role of the judge in American political life.

Justice Miner was a type of conservative that I had not met before: the tory with no ax to grind, no visible advantage to be culled from an economic system of laissez-faire that he revered as if it had been incorporated in an eleventh commandment. He and Mrs. Miner had no personal wealth; they subsisted entirely on his judicial salary, out of which they had to support an invalid son with a wife and several children. Yet the judge, in his simple, plain, high-minded way, believed that if a state legislature were allowed to pass a law barring children from mines and sweatshops, or that if a federal court interfered with the political process in a southern state so as to enable a black man to cast a ballot, the Constitution had simply been torn to tatters. And yet this same man believed to his dying day that the Constitution, as he interpreted it and for which he would cheerfully have given up his life, was the greatest guarantee of human rights and human liberty in the history of the world!

He was still an enchanting old boy to know. He was kind and cozy and witty, a scholar in Greek and Latin, deeply versed in both common and constitutional law. He and his wife had taken Felix to their hearts, and they wanted to do the same with me. I was more reserved with Mrs. Miner, whose chatty desire for intimacy put my back up the slightest bit, but alone with the old judge, I had soon made him the depositary of all my secrets.

"You're afraid that Felix may love you for your brains and

political opinions? Is that it, my dear? But can't brains have sex appeal? Would you object if Felix loved you for your eyes or your lips or your hair? Not that he doesn't!"

"Yes, I think I would. I want to be loved for something that is me. Quintessentially me."

"And what is more that, pray, than the brain? Do you know that some of the ancients located the soul there?"

"Let me put it this way, sir. I'm not sure that Felix is really in love with me at all. I'm not sure he doesn't simply want a partner. Someone to work with him in his career."

"What are you describing but a beautiful marriage? And why should a man who seeks a beautiful marriage not be in love?"

Felix, like me, was fond of the old man, and he seemed to enjoy working for him. He was able to turn himself into the judge's mouthpiece more easily than I could have done, and he would actually chuckle to himself while drafting, in language superior to Miner's own, opinions with which he violently disagreed. And yet, in the long run, Felix was to show an objectivity with respect to his boss that I could not share and did not really envy.

One Saturday night as he dropped me back at the Miners' house after taking me to dinner, he handed me a typewritten manuscript.

"Be sure not to leave it around where the old man will see it," he warned me. "It's for your eyes alone — at least in this house."

"But, darling, what is it?"

"A study of the American judicial process — as manifested in the mental processes of Mr. Justice Miner."

I think the first time that I knew with absolute conviction that Felix was going to be a great writer was when I read that essay. It appeared years later, after Justice Miner's death, in somewhat altered form, as part of Felix's book on the due process clause. It was a little jewel of style and precision, a charming mixture of the personal and the historical, with its vivid contrast of the old man's sunny, saintlike disposition and his compulsion to interpret the Fourteenth Amendment in a way to transfer the rights of the manumitted slave to the great corporations. That so high-minded a man should dedicate himself to such a task was surely one of the ironies of American judicial history. Felix in writing of it seemed to combine the pens of Boswell and of Justice Holmes.

But there was still something that I didn't like about it. That Felix should sit month after month with this dear old fellow, discussing his cases, writing his opinions, having meals at his board, allowing himself to be treated as a kind of son, while all the while he was etching in acid his portrait for posterity, chilled me. I asked him if he planned to show his piece to the judge.

"Heavens, no!" he exclaimed with a laugh. "He's capable of getting a court order to keep me from publishing it."

"You mean you *would* publish it?"

"Well, not while I'm his clerk, of course not."

"But after?"

"Why, certainly, after."

"You wouldn't even wait till he died?"

"I might." Here he chuckled to lighten his words. "If he's not too long about it."

"But, Felix, is that loyal?"

He didn't seem in the least to resent this. "It's loyal to truth," he answered simply.

It was difficult for me to argue with this, but I was beginning to equate my cause with that of Justice Miner. I was also beginning to see that there was a side of Felix, perhaps even a whole of Felix, that was not going to be subject to the ordinary rules of human loyalty and human affection.

The real effect of Felix's Miner piece on me came when the old man urged Felix to spend a second year as his law clerk. I found that I was suddenly very determined that Felix should not do this. It seemed to me that the best way for him to counterbalance the cold, almost inhuman objectivity of his nature was to leap into the fray of courts and litigants, to get himself caught up with the tumultuous fracas of justice in a big city. Life in judicial chambers was austere, clerical, set apart. I dreaded the relentless eye that followed each turn and twist in the mental evolutions of the aging Miner.

But how was I to accomplish my goal without telling Felix of my fears and doubts? Very simply. All I had to do was tell him that I had morally committed myself to work for Legal Aid in New York after graduation and that I couldn't bear the idea of another year away from him. And indeed I couldn't! Felix seemed perfectly content to leave Washington. We agreed to marry in the spring, go abroad for a summer's honeymoon, and then settle in New York, where he had been offered a fine position in the U.S. Attorney's office.

The wedding took place in the parlor of my family's brownstone on Twenty-third Street. Mrs. Leitner looked very splendid in what I seem to remember as a green velvet eighteenth-century riding habit with a hat swathed in ostrich feathers. Mr. and Mrs. Justice Miner seemed a bit surprised at some of my sisters' friends but were reassured by the presence of the Ward cousins. The Leitner uncles and their families kept a bit truculently to themselves, but Aunt Renata was lovely to everybody. Felix spent too much time at our little reception talking to a *New York Times* editor about the possibilities of a major war in Europe. But that was always to be the way. I felt, on balance, that I had started well.

Manuscript of Felix Leitner's
"The Versailles Treaty and Me,"
Written in 1965 for Roger Cutter

L IKE MANY AMERICANS in the beginning of the First World
War, I tended to regard it as a conflict of imperialisms in
which the United States should take no active part. But as time
went on, and as it began to look as if the Allies might actually
lose, the majority became fiercely anti-German and interven-
tionist. The important thing that happened to me was my
discovery that I was not going to fall away from my initial
position, or at least that I was not going to fall away from it so
drastically. I always favored the British and French over the
Central Powers, but I never regarded the German militarists
as the persons solely responsible for Armageddon, and I never
thought that we should enter the conflict, except to supply the
Allies with arms and ships. I believed passionately that such
aid would give us a voice in the peace treaty and that that
voice would be the last hope of the civilized world.

I had to learn to be unpopular, but I have never found that
difficult. To tell the truth, I have always found it rather ex-

hilarating. When Frances decided to become an outspoken pacifist, I made no move to discourage her, although I have never believed, legally or morally, in the cause of the conscientious objector. We found ourselves increasingly isolated from old friends, but we supported each other stoutly and managed to continue to be happy.

I had become too absorbed in the course and origins of the war to continue working for the U.S. Attorney, so early in 1915 I resigned my office and accepted an income from Mother, who had always taken the position that half her money was morally mine. I then wrote the two little volumes that first made me known — if "notorious" be not a better word: *The Causes of the War* and *The Peace That Should Follow*, the first of which, as Frances's mother enthusiastically put it, caused more dyspepsia from undigested meals at angry dinner parties along the Eastern seaboard than any book since *Uncle Tom's Cabin*.

By the time America finally entered the war, I had become so convinced that the future of man would depend on the terms of the ultimate peace treaty that I considered it my duty, at any price, to find a way of working on them. I resolved that I must not waste my time or risk my life as a soldier. I know that this will strike my reader as either a piece of monstrous arrogance or a bald excuse for cowardice, if not both. All I can say, so far as my conscious thinking was concerned (one can never answer for the subconscious), is that I was at all times perfectly sincere. I truly believed that I had ideas that the world could not afford to lose and that a bullet through my brain would eliminate a feeble force for war, but a vital one for peace. I remember that Heyward Satterlee, who was afterward decorated for gallantry in combat, told me at the time:

"Gosh, Felix, I'd never have the guts to seek exemption from the draft on grounds like *that!*"

Well, seek it I did. I went down to Washington and saw Justice Miner. The dear old boy supported me enthusiastically and recommended me to Secretary Lansing. Thus it came about that I was commissioned an officer of the Department of State and put to work in a secret chamber where some half dozen men were laboring over maps and documents to prepare the background information that might some day be used to educate our peace commissioners. We were instructed to tell curious outsiders simply that we were in "intelligence."

Frances was pregnant with our daughter Felicia and running her Legal Aid office almost single-handedly; she could not come to Washington. I lived in a hotel room, worked almost every night and saw nobody but my fellow workers. Yet on the whole it was a happy period. It was impossible for me not to dream, as I struggled to make sense out of borders and populations, out of sea routes and land corridors, out of ethnic diversities and religious differences, that I was manipulating facts toward a solution of the insoluble, toward a bounteous period of peace and plenty that might even some day justify the distant daily slaughter — in those muddy, rat-filled trenches of northern France — of the finest youths of my generation.

With the coming of the Armistice and the appointment of the Peace Commission, I was an obvious staff candidate, and I had the good fortune to be selected as an aide by that benevolent and experienced old diplomat, Mr. Henry White. There was no idea of Frances going with me to Paris; our baby Felicia was an ailing child who hung between life and death a good part of the first two years of her life, a price that she may have paid for the robust health she has since enjoyed. I am afraid that I was too full of my sense of mission to give Frances the proper help and consolation at this time. She seemed, however, to take my preoccupation in good part, and our only real argument, in the days before I sailed, was over the prospects of a lasting peace treaty.

"The old imperialists will have it all their way," she warned me. "France and England will hoodwink Wilson. He's too new at the game."

"Everything can still work out if we can form a league of nations."

"What good will a league do you if it's run by the old guard? Will there be a single representative of the Russian government in Paris?"

"Of the Soviets? Of course not. Why should there be?"

Frances was one of the many American liberals who had great hopes for the Russian experiment. It was the first of what, alas, were to be our many basic differences. The Bolshevik slaughter of the upper and middle classes, including the brutal butchery of the imperial family, had given me a distaste for radical solutions that has lasted to this day. Frances tended to palliate these crimes as the regrettable but unavoidable excesses of a population too long repressed. She believed that bloodshed would disappear under a stable Communist government. I should add here in her defense that her faith did not survive the Soviet purges of the 1930s.

"Look at the make-up of your Peace Commission!" she exclaimed scornfully. "Who has Wilson chosen to go with himself and Lansing? Three old mossbacks: an Army general, a Texas millionaire and a social registrite ambassador. Do you think *they* are going to do over the world? Thank you very much, they like it the way it is!"

"Ah, but look who's going *with* them!" I replied with a smile that was meant to conceal a fatuity of which even I was then vaguely conscious.

I shall not describe the glowing ovation that greeted Wilson in Paris except to say that I was quite carried away by it. But at that time I still believed that the enthusiasm would be amply justified by the treaty that would follow. I shall also not bother to describe the work of the Peace Conference, which is now history. Suffice it to say that at a very early date I began to take cognizance of the massive roadblocks that lay in the path of a just and lasting peace — particularly in the nature of the agreements made by the other powers before we had even entered the war.

It was picky, frustrating work, with long hours of sessions, sometimes icily polite, sometimes merely time wasting, sometimes seething with rancor. My one relief and single recreation was in the companionship at meals and at an occasional quick visit to the Louvre, of a brilliant if opinionated French girl, an expert translator assigned to our staff, Mireille de Voe.

"I have read *The Causes of War*, Monsieur Leitner," she told me at our first meeting. "I found it brilliant. But, of course, I thought you were hard on my poor France. It is not our fault, surely, that *le bon Dieu* placed us to the south of the Hun!"

"I suppose the Hun may have felt the same way in the days of Napoleon. Not to speak of Louis XIV."

"Let us hope that those days have come again!"

Mireille took it upon herself to convert me to the French concept of *la gloire*. She was very well read and always good-tempered, but she could never understand that *la gloire* was not attractive to a non-Frenchman. After all, it could never really belong to him. She intrigued me because she seemed the very soul of *la vieille France,* convinced as she was that an ordered, clipped and formal Gallic civilization was the only true one on earth, and that the "lesser tribes without the law" should somehow concede this, even if they were the victims of dirty tricks by a Richelieu, a Bonaparte — or a Clemenceau.

"Your Monsieur Weelson is a very fine man," she would say. "But he cannot see that the Hun is never going to use a league of nations as anything but a device to disarm his neighbor while he secretly arms himself."

Mireille belonged to an old French family (*"noblesse de robe,"* she used to say with a deprecating smile) which, for the purposes of this narrative, I have called de Voe. She is no longer living, but no doubt she has relatives who are, and it is needless to hurt feelings. She was a pale, dark-haired, handsome woman, probably in her early thirties (I never determined her exact age) whose pleasant appearance and constant equanimity somehow detracted from what might otherwise have been a considerable sex appeal and may have explained her single state. She was one of those faithful and efficient civil servants who is a "treasure" in any foreign office, and she lived alone in a tiny jewel of an apartment, with some first-class eighteenth-century things, on the Place François I. She was a type of woman more commonly met in Europe than in America: one who had emancipated her own life from the restrictions of an upper-class background without in the least abandoning her faith in the family lares and penates. She was perfectly content to live as an acknowledged exception to an accepted system.

There was enough of the old maid about her to blind me, in the beginning of our friendship, to the idea that it would ever become anything else. My first suspicion should have been aroused when I saw how disconcerted she was at the discovery that I was half Jewish.

"I suppose it doesn't mean as much in America," she said.

"That's right," I replied, laughing. "We're a melting pot. You can never be quite sure who's black or white or red or yellow."

"It must be so odd," was her pensive reply to this.

"Yes, if we had a Dreyfus case, you might not know whom to cut."

"Ah, now you're laughing at me, Felix. I think you laugh at everything."

"I don't laugh at your Monsieur Clemenceau."

"I should hope not!"

If she minded my being Jewish, it was probably only because it pained her to imagine how her family would react to this. She had no prejudices herself except insofar as a respect for the prejudices of others might create one. She seemed to like and admire me as an individual utterly apart from her own background — as she might have regarded an attractive creature from outer space.

She was an expert on the Château de Versailles, where some of the conference took place, and we had frequent opportunities to explore the royal chambers.

"You are so set on your league," she told me once as we stood before the bed of Louis XIV, in the room toward which all of André Le Nôtre's vast network of alleys and waterways seems to converge. "But don't you see that Versailles, too, is a kind of universal concept? Everything here implies the ultimate world rule of order. The genius of man has subdued a whole countryside to this harmonious and symmetrical composition. It is only thus that true peace can come. By waves undulating outward from a center where government is seen as the ultimate art."

"A French government, you mean. Don't you see that everything in Versailles is sham? It is all curlicues and gilt and shields and medallions to hide from the observer that this *gloire*, as you call it, is nothing but a French military boot planted on the neck of a prostrate neighbor. Not to speak of a prostrate French peasant! That is why I abominate this palace as the site for our peace. It is the worst possible omen."

I think Mireille was a little bit thrilled, in spite of herself, when I spoke so forcefully. She was too intelligent, after all, to believe in all of what she professed. And I see now, in retrospect, that she may have already come to care enough for me to be a bit apprehensive about the effect of the disillusionment that she knew was in store for me. For she had enough Gallic realism to see that Clemenceau was certainly going to get the lion's share of the ugly peace for which he was so stubbornly striving.

For a long time I refused squarely to face the horrid probability that any treaty or league of nations that did emerge from the discussions at Versailles would be rejected by the United States Senate. Of course, it was always in the back of my mind. Poor old kind and wise Mr. White was haunted by the idea, and he was in constant correspondence with his friend Senator Lodge, in a vain effort to keep the latter from boiling over. Wilson had made a fatal error in putting only one Republican on the Peace Commission — and that one an elderly diplomat far removed from the fray of politics — and nobody was more aware of this than the humble but high-minded Harry White. He did his best, working day and night, to make the Republican leaders in Washington feel that they were abreast of what was going on, even that their opinions, as forwarded by himself, were receiving due consideration, but I sometimes wondered if the irritating reminder to Lodge — implied in this correspondence — of Wilson's arrogant assumption that he could deal with Republican opinion through a political nonentity, a dear old gentleman of affable manners and unimpeachable respectability, did not do more harm than good.

When White told me himself, on the eve of a trip to Washington, that he despaired of persuading "Cabot" of any concept of a league of nations, I at least recognized that everything I had done in the past two years had been in vain. I suppose that I must have been preparing myself subconsciously, because the picture of what was going to happen — and what of course did happen — sprang up suddenly in my mind in a sickening but vivid glare of blacks and whites. It was not the loss of my own work that bothered me; it was the loss of my whole faith in the future. It was the vision that the Versailles treaty was going to do more to produce another war than the war itself; that it might have been better for mankind had the conflict ended in a stalemate; that it might even have been better had the Germans won!

The extent of the blow to my psyche can only be understood if it is conceived in religious terms. I had never had any conventional religious faith. But I had believed passionately in man and in his ability to create a good life on this planet. My morals were the morals of a man seeking this good life. What contributed to a serene and contented society was good; what threatened its serenity and content was bad. I even believed that my capacities and labors toward this better world were such as to make me a contributor of more value than others. I hoped that I was not vain in that belief. Such talents as I had, had come to me as naturally and inevitably as the scent to the rose or the blue to the sky. I was a part of the world, that was all.

But a good world. That was the point. A potentially good world. And now I had awakened to a realm of horror, a dark sewer where black grubby pieces of insect life dug in and out of the mud and slime to eat each other. What a vision to have in Paris! But not all the beauty of the City of Light could veil it from me. I suppose what I suffered at this time was a kind of nervous breakdown.

I couldn't work. Oh, I appeared in the office at the Crillon; I shuffled papers; I attended conferences. I tried to look wise. Mr. White was away; nobody paid much attention to me. Paris was full of people, anyway, who only wanted to hear themselves talk. I spent more time with Mireille. She even took a week off to be free to take me on tours of Paris. Needless to say, she was an excellent guide.

It was now that she became my mistress. I use this essentially

European term advisedly. It seems truer to put it so than to say that we became lovers. Mireille was basically obliging me, as she did in all things. She sensed my desperation and wanted to help. Our affair might best be described as tranquil. Mireille was what many American husbands would consider the perfect mistress: discreet, cooperative, unpossessive. But although it is ungallant of me to say so, even in these antiseptic, quasi-historical pages, it may have been the very fact that she was the "dream girl" of timid, erring husbands that kept her from being a real woman. One can't have fire and passion without jealousy and anger.

In my strange, desperate state of mind I tried to intensify what should have been a pleasant interlude. I persuaded myself that I felt a Byronic love for Mireille, and I would accuse her bitterly of lack of feeling. I made believe that I was jealous and that she had another lover; I sought vainly to be introduced to her old parents who lived in Chartres; I told her that she was a snob and ashamed of me. I must have caused the poor woman endless pain, for actually I am afraid that she was in love with me. And finally, one evening at her apartment, when her maid was out and she was preparing dinner for us herself, I suggested that we marry. There was a clatter of a dish from the little kitchen. Mireille turned from the stove, removed her apron, brushed back her hair and came to the door.

"There!" she said. "I've spoiled the casserole. It's all your fault, *mon cher*. Now you'll have to take me out. A restaurant, in any event, is a better place for the little talk that you and I must have."

At Maxim's, sitting very straight beside me on the banquette after we had ordered, Mireille stared across the room.

"Have you contemplated the sort of life that you and I should lead after we have entered into this marriage that you so precipitately suggest?"

How I remember her use of that adverb! Mireille's English was almost too good. Nine out of ten Americans would have said "precipitously." But I plunged ahead with my self-indulgence. "Certainly I've thought of it. We'd live here. Well, in France anyway. Maybe in Chartres. I wouldn't dream of taking you to America. French women, like some wines, don't travel."

"*Merci du compliment!* But American men do? I can see you in Chartres, in what one of your compatriots so elegantly called our 'constipated' provincial society. A divorced man married to a renegade Catholic! We'd be very popular. My dear, you can't imagine how bored you'd be."

"You're quite wrong. I want to give up the world. I want to be a scholar. A kind of monk."

"A monk! That would be amusing for me."

"Well, not *that* much of a monk. Do you know something, Mireille? I think I could be content, for a year at least, just living near your incomparable cathedral. Perhaps I could write a book about it. A beautiful book, like Henry Adams's. Or like that man whose work you so admire . . . what's his name?"

"Huysmans. Well, I suppose it might last a year. No more. And a year is not enough, my friend. But let us put it on higher grounds. What about your wife? What about your little daughter?"

"Would they be happy with a man shackled to them who wanted to be free?"

"Oh, that is such an American argument. Of course, they'd be happy. As much as anyone is. But, Felix, let me come to the real point. Even if I felt that in the very bottom of your heart you wished to divorce Madame Leitner and marry me — which I don't — I could never contemplate it. No, my friend, I am not a home breaker. Marriage to us is a sacrament."

"But I was not married in your church!"

"I know there are Catholics who take that point of view. But

I am not one of them. I believe that God sanctioned your marriage, Felix, and that if I were to have any part in sundering you and your wife, my very soul would be in danger."

"Mireille, you can't be serious! What about what you and I have been doing in the past four weeks?"

"It has been a sin, *bien entendu*. But a sin that I intend to expiate by confession and penance. Oh, yes! When you have gone back to Madame Leitner and your child."

"You mean you really believe that what you and I have done is wicked?"

"I do, indeed. And I'll tell you something more, *mon cher*. I wouldn't want to live in a world where what you and I have done *wasn't* wrong!"

I had run into a French impasse, and I was to go no further. But the idea that Mireille regarded our love as sinful did not have the effect that it might have had on other men: to make it more exciting. On the contrary, it appalled me, and I abruptly ended our affair. It was time, anyway, for I came down with a late case of the terrible influenza and almost died. While I was delirious, I learned afterward, it was Mireille who, fearless of contagion, came to my hotel room and nursed me. It was she, too, who had the wisdom to send for my Aunt Renata, who was then in Madrid. What passed between the two women, I never knew, but my aunt took complete charge of my case, and when I became sensible again there was no Mireille to be seen. When I asked for her, Auntie soothed my brow and murmured:

"She's not here now, dear. She had to go to her father in Chartres. It appears that he, too, is ill. You are going to get well in my care, and when you're strong enough I'm going to take you to Spain, where it will be warm and lovely. After you've quite recovered, you can come back to Paris and thank Mademoiselle de Voe for the wonderful care she has taken of you.

She is a most charming person. You were very fortunate to have a friend like that in such a crisis."

So that was how it was. Of course, when I went home, through Paris, two months later, I did not see Mireille. I wrote her to give her my heartfelt thanks, and she answered, politely, charmingly, noncommitally. Two years later, when Frances and I were in Paris, Mireille gave a little dinner party for us. Everything went off very smoothly. I never knew if Frances suspected anything. If she did, she was smart enough to perceive that it was over.

*　　*　　*

Aunt Renata, now a widow and aging, wanted to crown her collection with an El Greco, and, as Toledo was the city for that, to Toledo we went. She was late for what she was after; Mrs. Havemeyer, a dozen years before, had carted away her *Grand Inquisitor* and her *View of Toledo*, and Maurice Barrès had refuted forever the silly theories that the great painter had been mad or astigmatic. But there were still a few of his saints and virgins to be had within my aunt's means, and she had taken a floor of a little palace on a narrow gray street, where we lived in quiet luxury, visiting churches and other palaces with our distinguished old guide — a count, no less — and going to bed soon after a sumptuous dinner with three wines.

I had recuperated to the point of taking a mild, passive interest in things around me. For the first time that I could remember I had no desire to read. I felt utterly removed from all my former life. Frances and the baby seemed creatures in a dream; Mireille had ceased to exist for me. I found this state of detachment vaguely intriguing.

Auntie was wonderful. She made no reference to the past or to my family. She was careful to cultivate only what was present to my fancy. When after two weeks of this placid existence, some of my natural curiosity began to revive, it attached itself, quite naturally, to her intense interest in El Greco.

"Do you really think he's the greatest painter of all?" I asked her.

"Oh, great, greater, greatest — what's the use of those terms? He excites me. That's all I care about. Next year someone else may excite me more. I hope so."

"What is it that excites you in him?"

"His vision. His sense of another world. All around us. With cloudier clouds and fierier fires and wonderful, elongated, emaciated saints."

"You make it sound like a nightmare."

"A glorious nightmare."

The next morning we returned to the Church of Santo Tomé for another long session before El Greco's masterpiece *The Burial of Count Orgáz.* I think that if Auntie could have had this painting for her collection at the price of a murder, some poor man's life might not have been safe. She sat before it in the wicker chair that our guide had produced, like an El Greco Virgin herself, her eyes raised as if to heaven. But when she spoke at last, she was intense, busy, factual, her usual self.

"You see, there are three levels of figures. First, there's the body being lowered into the grave by the two priests. Then there's the row of mourners. And finally, above, there's the dead man, naked now, being presented to the court of heaven. But note that the bottom and top levels are united by the same note of magnificence, the same awesome majesty. You see?"

"Of course. The priests' robes are magnificent."

"That's because they're not really priests. They're Saint Augustine and Saint Stephen. That was the miracle, you remember? They suddenly appeared at the funeral to inter the body with their own hands. So they are really part of the heavenly court. That is why their expressions, like those of the saints and angels above, are settled in serene reverence. They exist only to adore."

"How boring!"

Auntie ignored me. "And now look at the mourners. They are here. They are mortal. They are clay. They are presumably good Catholics, and they trust that their friend, for whose death they sincerely grieve, has gone to heaven, but it is all still a mystery. They know that they cannot take in the answer. Oh, yes, they have faith, but it's a muffled faith. They have a suspicion, but no real conception, of the splendor that surrounds them, right here, at that moment, in this church. But *we* see it! We see it because we share El Greco's vision."

"Auntie, you sound like a Catholic! Aren't you forgetting that we're in Toledo, which was filled with Jews, some of whom were burned alive, possibly by the very Catholics painted in this picture?"

"Well, of course, I know that. It was horrible, what they did to the Jews. I like to think it was our expulsion from the country that brought about the decadence of the empire. Served them right!"

"And don't you think El Greco himself may have approved of the burnings? After all, didn't he paint an inquisitor?"

"Ugh! I suppose so." Poor Auntie hugged herself as she always did in moments of emotional distress. "I try not to think of it. Maybe his god has forgiven him this because he was such a good painter."

"*His* god? But wouldn't his god have rubbed his hands in glee over the auto-da-fés? What would there have been to forgive?"

"I mean that if there *were* a god, he must have been a good god. So El Greco's god, whatever El Greco himself believed, would still have frowned on persecuting Jews. Or anyone else!"

"I've never asked you. Do *you* believe in God?"

Auntie became inscrutable. "I don't know. But I know this. I know that I like El Greco's feeling that what we see and hear is not all. That there's another world all around us and in us. You can divide the people in his pictures into those who sense this keenly and those who sense it only dimly. I can't think of any who don't sense it at all."

"But why do you *like* that?"

"Because it makes life more exciting! Anyway, it makes painting more exciting."

"And painting is your life."

"Oh, I have a few people in it, too," she said, reaching over to pat my hand. "A few people like yourself, my child."

I was well enough now to go back to Paris, and we traveled north by slow stages, stopping for a few days in Madrid. There a dealer brought to Auntie's suite at the Ritz a small painting that must have been an advance study for Mrs. Havemeyer's great portrait of the Cardinal de Guevara. It was overpriced, in Auntie's opinion, so she did not buy it, but we lived with it happily for a day. I was fascinated by the power in the hands grasping the arms of the chair and by the cold assessing stare of the eyes. It reminded me of the great Champaigne portrait of Richelieu that Auntie and I had looked at together in the Louvre so many years before.

"Where is the other world that *he* sees?" I asked her. "Isn't he an exception to your rule? He seems quite replete with the here and now."

"Perhaps," she conceded. "Perhaps that is what being an inquisitor did to him. No matter how good a Catholic he was when he started, the tortures and burnings may have removed the other world from his vision. But doesn't that prove what I was saying in the church in Toledo, that God, even *their* god, didn't approve? So the Grand Inquisitor begins to lose the mystic sense that the others have. He is of the earth — earthy!

He is trapped into one dimension of reality by the horrible things he thinks God wants him to do!"

I thought Auntie was being a bit too neat, but I did not demur. That afternoon we went to the Escorial to see El Greco's great *Dream of Philip II*. Here, as in the *Burial of Count Orgáz*, there is a heavenly court and a crowd below, but it is the Last Judgment; everyone in the canvas but the king himself is dead. It *is* the other world, as Philip II is allowed to envision it. All the figures are fully aware of it: with hope, in the case of the saved, and with horror, in the case of the damned. The king, in his mystic ecstasy, is almost translated to that higher sphere.

But not quite. That I noted carefully. He is still the king. He still has power below. What saved him from being as earthy as the Grand Inquisitor? A greater faith? A greater fanaticism?

And then I had an idea that filled me with sudden elation. It happened just like that! My depression, my illness, or the last shreds of it, simply exaporated. I knew now that I was going to be able to live in the world of 1919, bad as it might be. For if El Greco could find beauty in all the horror of Toledo in the Inquisition, so could I find it in a Europe that was preparing for a new war even before it had finished licking its wounds from the old one. If he could find relief in mysticism, I could find it in drama, which was very possibly the same thing.

The book that I planned that very night was *The Irreconcilables*, a study of the conflicting personalities of Woodrow Wilson and Henry Cabot Lodge. I would present their personalities dramatically; they would symbolize, respectively, the dream of world peace and the illusion of isolation. But behind the dream of peace would be the ruthless fanaticism of Philip II, as projected in Wilson, and behind the illusion of isolation would be the clever opportunism of the Grand Inquisitor, as seen in Lodge. Idealism marred by compromise would be pitted against selfishness tempered by high-mindedness. What could the poor world do but lose in such a tussle?

My aunt recognized at once that I was preoccupied and left me to myself. She made no inquiries, no fuss; she was tact itself. But she told me later that she had known I was "saved." By the time we reached Paris, I had prepared an outline for my book.

I found that I had been adequately replaced in Mr. White's office; in any event, our role was almost completed. No objection was made to my returning at once to New York and my family. For six months I worked night and day in the New York Public Library, and *The Irreconcilables* made its appearance in the full heat of the national debate over the treaty and the league. My first books had attracted considerable notice but nothing like what this one did. I enjoyed the experience of Lytton Strachey, who said, of the publication of *Eminent Victorians* in that same year, that he woke up to find himself famous.

It was through this book that I obtained my joint chair of government and constitutional law at New York University, which I held for ten years.

The Chapter on Marriage in the
Privately Printed Memoirs of
Frances Ward Leitner,
"My Life and Law."

M Y FAMILY and friends have always clung to the idea that
Gladys Satterlee single-handedly broke up what had
been, until her advent, a blissfully happy marriage. It seems to
me that if this little book has any functions, one should be to
correct such a misapprehension, and in this chapter I shall try
to describe how my relations with Felix had altered before her
"raid." I do not write it to excuse her, for Gladys was not a
woman to have let anything stand between herself and a goal.
If she had decided to smash my marriage, it little mattered to
her whether it was blissful or not. But I want to be fair to Felix.
I cannot leave my posterity under the illusion that I was a
model wife. I always loved him, yes. I never, as the saying goes,
so much as looked at another man. But a loving and faithful
wife can still be a pain in the neck. Oh, yes! That should be
the eleventh commandment: thou shalt not be a pain in the

neck. Or, as I am writing for a blunter generation, in any other part of the anatomy. It is going to be a painful chapter to write. I have been staring at my typewriter now for fifteen minutes. But here goes.

I had better start by admitting that during all of the year 1936 I was undergoing the tension of a difficult and somewhat premature menopause. It did not make me any easier to live with. It certainly did not improve my judgment or balance. I was inclined to make decisions emotionally just when I most needed calm and reflection.

It made matters worse, too, that I was not working. Felix had resigned his post in the Department of Justice to write a book, and I had decided to do the same. I had long wanted (or thought I had wanted) to write a monograph on legal aid, its problems and its future, and we agreed to take over my parents' summer house in Seal Cove and winterize it. Aunt Renata had died and left Felix a handsome legacy. The great fortune, of course, had been her husband's and "went back," as we used to say, to his nephews and nieces, but she had saved enough from her income to make us independent if we were sufficiently frugal. Felix, in the uncharacteristic role of Omar Khayyám, endeavored to persuade me that a winter on the lonely, beautiful Maine coast with just our books and ourselves, would be "paradise enow."

But everything seemed to go wrong from the very start. My book went badly; I had been too out of touch with legal aid during our Washington years. The ideas came slowly, and they struck me as banal and dated. Our daughter, Felicia, was away at boarding school and happy there, but our son, Frank, now thirteen, was beginning to show signs of the terrible depression and disorientation that were so to plague him later. He hated his new school and had to be taken out and tutored by Felix and myself. Felix was very good about this, but he obviously minded the loss of time from his book, so I eventually took over the whole job of teaching Frank and held it against his father. Oh, I was full of resentments! It was that time of my life.

But worst of all was my aching nostalgia for the immediate past of our wonderful three years in Washington. Felix had been only nominally in the Justice Department; his real role had been as a member of the president's famous "brain trust," dedicated to framing the legislation of the New Deal. I had taken a leave of absence from my New York office and worked as a volunteer drafter with Felix's group. We lived and breathed the New Deal. Even when we went to parties, and we went to a good many, it was principally to discuss how the statutes were working out and what new ones were needed.

I find it hard to convey the exhilaration of Washington in those days. Perhaps the best I can do is quote Wordsworth's great lines on the French Revolution:

> *Bliss was it in that dawn to be alive,*
> *But to be young was very heaven!*

Perhaps we weren't so young in years, but we were in spirit. I had a glorious sense of being part of the making of a new and better world. Felix was less exuberant — he never forgot his disillusionment at Versailles — but he was still intensely interested in what he was doing. Never had he and I been closer, never more of a team.

I think it was early in 1935 that I first became aware of a change in Felix's attitude. It struck me now as more that of a historian than of a reformer. He was more detached about his fellow workers and, at last, frankly critical of them. At dinner he would tell me stories about their ineptitudes, the folly of some of their visions. It simply amused him that I obviously hated this.

"You have the look of a grand inquisitor who scents apostasy in the air," he told me.

"Have you lost all faith in what we're doing?"

"Do we even know what we're doing? At the White House today I had the distinct impression that we were a bunch of kids building a fort with toy bricks. Who cares what tumbles down? It might even be part of the fun. Crash! Try Anything Once is Roosevelt's motto."

"I suppose you'd like us to go back to the bread lines! Until, as the great Mr. Hammond puts it, the 'natural bottom' of the market has been reached, and we can climb back up."

"Those bankers are not all crazy, you know. I talked to Ridley Hammond for two hours after his testimony before the Senate Finance Committee. He makes a lot of sense. And he's a good bit more open-minded than some of the men we work with."

"Oh, Felix, don't give me Ridley Hammond! Any other banking firm in the country, but not his. They're the very apostles of greed."

"There's no use talking to you about these things, Fran. You're too prejudiced."

"You've got to have some prejudices if you're not going to be totally wishy-washy. And I suggest that Ridley Hammond should be one of them."

It was here that I made my first big mistake. I should not have closed any door that gave me access to Felix's mind. It did not take much to make him avoid a topic altogether, and as a result of this initial outburst of mine — and, I fear, a few others — Felix began to tell me less and less of his growing doubts of the New Deal. Indeed, when he at last informed me of his decision to leave the government to write a book, it took me quite by surprise.

"A book? What sort of a book?"

"On what we've been doing down here."

And that was all he would say.

Seal Cove was a good enough place to write a book, if one had one to write. It was an intellectual summer community, full of camps and shingle houses, occupied largely by professors and artists, accessible to the excellent stores of nearby fashionable Butterfield Bay without any necessary involvement in the more hectic social life of that community. Felix was perfectly happy with his book and the long solitary walks by the ocean during which he would puzzle out his chapters, but when I began to find my material inadequate for the work that I had projected I became bored and restless. I found the cold, damp weather and the bleak, slaty sea oppressive. I yearned for the summer when the rest of the colony would return and when my parents, as agreed, would join us in the cottage. But the summer, when it came, brought another problem.

Felix's "great banker," Ridley Hammond, senior partner of Harris, Tweed & Sons, had an estate just south of Butterfield Bay in Jaffray Harbor. I mention the name of this village only because Mr. Hammond always insisted on it, loftily refusing to be identified either with the trivialities of Butterfield Bay or with what he called the "academic priggishness" of Seal Cove. To the big, rambling stone house that he had erected on a rocky peninsula jutting out to sea he invited economists, political philosophers, politicians and, of course, his own partners. His house parties were more like conferences. It almost seemed as if he used the summer vacation to educate the members of his firm to a higher concept of the role of banking in modern society. That, at any rate, was how Felix saw it.

Mr. Hammond was in the habit of borrowing a tycoon from Butterfield Bay or a brain from Seal Cove to add variety to his dinner parties. He made a great point of asking Felix, and of course I had to go, too. But I was determined that I would not be "summoned" by the great man.

"I am told you never go to anyone else's house in the summer," I said to my host after our second evening at his table. "But if we are to come again, you will have to dine with us first."

The answer startled me and all who overheard it. "But, my dear Mrs. Leitner, nothing would give me greater pleasure!"

I make immediate disclosure of my dislike of Mr. Hammond, so my readers may be on notice of possible prejudice in my description of him. But as a good lawyer I should be able to draw him as he was. He was certainly an attractive old man, lean and limber with a thick crop of wiry gray hair. His face was long and brown and wrinkled, his nose sharp, his chin pointed, but his small intent eyes were of a clear baby blue. He never showed temper. Perhaps he never felt it. It was as if he had long since decided that life was too short for him to be anything but rational.

He was, like so many financiers of his generation, the son of a New England Presbyterian minister, and he was inclined to be proud of his simple and austere background. It seemed to provide the needed contrast to the Tudor mansion on Seventieth Street in Manhattan, with its great library of Jacobean folios and quartos, and the huge, dark-paneled office that overlooked Trinity Church. Hammond loved to pose as the "intellectual" of Harris, Tweed & Sons. He had not only written a book on the King James version of the Bible; he had even been known to vote the Democratic ticket! You might have said it was one of his missions in life to keep people from taking him for granted.

Not only did he dine with us in Seal Cove; he actually drove over on occasion to talk with Felix and to take little strolls with him by the sea. When I asked Felix what they talked about on these excursions, he would simply say "everything under the sun." But I became jealously convinced that they were discussing Felix's book, and I noted one day that the old man left with a thick roll of typescript, which he handed to the driver of his big black car. Was he trying to influence Felix's book? Were they even collaborating? But when I put this to Felix, he roundly denied it.

"Why is he so interested then?"

"Because it's a passionately interesting book."

"What makes it so passionately interesting?"

"You'll see."

"Won't you even tell me what it's about?"

"I have told you. It's about the first two years of the New Deal. I am showing the origin and development of its political and economic concepts."

"You mean it's about the philosophy of the New Deal?"

"If you can call it a philosophy."

"Ah, there you are, Felix. I knew it. You're going to pan the whole thing!"

"It's precisely your using a term like 'pan' that makes me so reluctant to talk about it. I have a very difficult thesis to work out, and I need to be clear and objective."

"Yet you show it to Mr. Hammond."

"True. But I find him extremely helpful. He has an extraordinary grasp of economics."

"Robber baron economics! Piracy economics!"

"You see, Fran? You are incapable of objective judgment when it comes to politics. Your mind is too full of emotional preconceptions. Everything to you must have a direction. If the direction is left, it's good; if it's right, it's bad. The whole thing is just a game of cops and robbers."

I do not frequently lose my temper, but I lost it then. "I'm sorry I can't sit up there on Olympus with you and Mr. Hammond! I'm too concerned with poor people. Too little concerned with banks! My poor female mind is too full of sentiment."

"Don't bring sex into it."

"Why shouldn't I? You don't think any woman has a mind equal to yours, do you?"

"No woman that I've so far met. But that may be simply coincidence."

"Not even the great Mademoiselle de Voe?"

"Mireille does not really have a mind. She has a mental mirror that reflects a class system."

"Upper class, I assume, while mine is lower!"

Felix laughed quite cheerfully at this. "Well, I guess you'd like it to be!"

*   *   *

My father was what Felix used to call a "Century Club intellectual." By this I suppose he meant a benign old gentleman, with twinkling eyes, who thought he had become flamingly modern when he preferred Dreiser to Henry James, or Hemingway to William Dean Howells. Father was better than that, but there were certainly times, I must confess, when Felix's mild sarcasms seemed to fit the target, and one of these would be when Father discussed his favorite theory that Francis Bacon was the author of Shakespeare's plays. As girls, my sisters and I always knew that we had reached a dead end when this topic was introduced.

Old Lassiter Troy, the Shakespearean actor and our neighbor in Seal Cove, was a stout champion of what Daddy scornfully called "the school of the Stratford lout," and the two of them loved to engage in long, wordy, amiable arguments about the merits and demerits of their "candidates." Sometimes they would become noisily denunciatory, as when Daddy would insist that the man "Shaksper" was an illiterate, drunken poacher who could not even spell his own name, and Mr. Troy would retort that anyone who knew anything about theater could at once spot the author of *Hamlet* as an active member of a dramatic troupe. But it was always essentially a game between them.

When Mr. Hammond entered the discussion, it was as if a hawk had joined a couple of friendly chickadees at a bird feeder. It was not that his manners were not good. On the contrary, they were perfect. But he brought, for all his moderation of tone and for all his polite little smiles, an incisiveness and a drive that were at odds with the old spirit of the discussion. He was basically too serious.

"Of course, I could argue," he observed, "that there is no use attempting to rebut Mr. Ward's interesting theory until he has first established that the 'Stratford man' could *not* have written the plays. But I prefer to argue that anyone who is familiar with the whole of Elizabethan and Jacobean drama must acknowledge its basic homogeneity. Shakespeare was not essentially different in his subject material, his plots or his characterizations from his contemporaries. From Marston or Ford or Middleton. From Marlowe or Massinger or Tourneur. From Beaumont and Fletcher. He was simply a better poet, that is all. The age produced a particular type of drama, and that drama could be written by an aristocrat like Francis Beaumont or a bricklayer like Ben Jonson. Shakespeare did not *have* to be either a great aristocrat or a simple actor. If we knew nothing at all about him, he could have been either."

This was followed by a great clatter from Daddy, but Felix, who had followed Mr. Hammond's argument with particular attention, now abruptly changed the topic from Shakespeare to Shakespeare's era.

"Why do you suppose, Ridley, the age produced such great drama?"

"Because England had emerged from a century of civil war, and Europe had emerged from the Middle Ages. Man had discovered man. It was the Renaissance — a period of such hope as we find difficult to conceive in our time."

"Hope?" Felix retorted. "Do you find hope in Tourneur? Or in Webster? It's always seemed to me those tragedies flicker with the very flames of hell!"

"Ah, but that was after the disillusionment. That was in the reign of James. The golden promises were not fulfilled. The fine hope of the Elizabethans was lost in the corruption of the court, in the divine right of kings. Man was back in chains."

Felix's frown was sceptical. "And you think Cyril Tourneur and John Webster had those things in mind?"

"Not necessarily. They simply expressed the essence of their age. As great poets do. They saw the glory of man and his hopelessness."

Felix seemed suddenly very interested in this. "And mightn't that be true today? We had the hope of communism and then the horror of Soviet Russia. We had the hope of the New Deal..."

"And now the horror of Roosevelt!" Hammond finished with a chuckle.

"Oh, Mr. Hammond, for shame!" I protested.

"Yet there's something in it," my husband went on hastily, as if in fear of losing his thread by my interruption. "What started with a burst of hope in the future of man and his superiority to the old cycle of prosperity and depression is already being crushed under a mountain of law and regulation. But where is our drama to celebrate the hope and its failure?"

"Perhaps we don't go in so much for plays today," Hammond responded. "Perhaps it's the age of a different kind of literature. Why shouldn't *you* be our Webster or Tourneur, Felix?"

"Why not our Shakespeare?" asked dear old Mr. Troy.

"Why not our Bacon?" amended my father.

Well, all this may sound harmless enough, but it didn't, at the time, to me. It made me ill to think that this old pirate — for so Hammond was, lurking under his urbane exterior — should be taking over Felix's beautiful mind. But Felix still insisted that no such thing was occurring.

"I don't know what's got into you this summer," he told me later that same evening. "You seem to have entirely lost your perspective. Why should everyone have to agree with you about your sacred New Deal? Can't you imagine that a rational man might see it as the unwarrantable abridgment of ancient liberties?"

"A rational man, perhaps. But old Hammond isn't controlled by his thoughts. He's controlled by his feeling — his feeling for his money bags!"

But the real crisis came at a dinner party at Hammond's, where I was given the seat of honor on my host's right. The old man turned to me with what struck me as a leer.

"I have a bribe to offer you, Frances."

"You're very frank. Shouldn't you call it a gift?"

"Oh, I wouldn't equivocate with *you*. I'm not such an ass. Nor would I be such a fool as to offer you riches or power or position, though these might be the natural consequents of my bribe. I wouldn't even offer you a place among the saints or a seat on the right hand of God, for you would certainly smell an appeal to your ego."

"You begin to intrigue me. What is this bribe that brings riches as consequents?"

"Your husband's happiness."

Something clutched at my heart as I stared into those glinting eyes. I realized that he took in the full depth of my dislike of him and did not in the least care. "What makes you think he's unhappy now?"

"I don't say he's unhappy. I merely suggest that he might

find a greater happiness in making the fullest possible use of what I do not scruple to call his genius."

"And that, I suppose, would be in your banking firm?"

"Precisely. As a full partner, with his capital contributed by an easy loan. I thought you'd guess it."

I knew there was no point arguing with this man. But by sparring with him I might hope to pick up an argument to use in the coming struggle with Felix. "I don't know that my husband's talent is for finance," I said guardedly, "although I'm sure he has a mind that could be turned to anything he chose. But is there really such a future in your line of work? Isn't it all going to be regulated by Uncle Sam?"

"No doubt the bureaucrats, like the poor, will be always with us. But don't believe, my dear, that the age of the capitalist is over yet. Or should I say, don't let that little red wish be father to so black a thought!" Here he placed an avuncular hand on mine. I jerked it away.

"I'm sorry. It makes me nervous to be touched."

"I suppose that depends on who does it," he retorted with a chuckle. "But to the point. Some people insist that communism is getting more capitalistic and capitalism more communistic and that one day the twain shall meet, in a benign bath of socialism. I say that's twaddle. Communism has not changed its spots because a few Soviet bureaucrats drive around in limousines. And capitalism isn't going to collapse because Franklin Roosevelt likes to play games. No, the only doomed system is socialism. It's too weak, too flabby, to prevail."

"That hasn't been proved."

"You will live to see it proved. The world will be ultimately divided between the Communist and the 'managerial' states. The latter will be run by cooperating teams of statesmen, business managers, and engineers."

"Isn't that fascism?"

Hammond shrugged. "Labels merely express emotion. Let me put it this way. The great corporations will not be at liberty to wreck the economy. Neither will the labor unions. Neither will the politicians."

"Not even the people?" He shook his head. "You don't believe in democracy?"

"My dear lady, I should like nothing better than to believe in it. But can we afford it? That's the question."

"I think we can," I responded firmly. "Perhaps we'd better get back to the subject of Felix. What will his role be in your managerial state?"

"That will be up to him. But I should like to see him working with the forces that must ultimately carry this nation to its economic salvation."

"And that's your bank? That's where the archangels are? And I suppose, as an incident to his march to glory, Felix will make a fortune?"

"I have no doubt of it."

"And even help add to yours?"

"Ah, my dear, surely you don't accuse a man of my years and means of being mercenary?"

"No." I looked at him now with frank dislike. "No, I'll grant that you have no personal ax to grind. It's worse than that. You really believe in the whole rotten business!"

Seated at my other side was Grant Stowe, the solid, portly senior partner of the law firm that acted as general counsel to Harris, Tweed. It was to him I now abruptly turned. I had already concluded that he was just the kind of factotum that a man like Hammond would choose: loyal, efficient, and quite incapable of providing the smallest competition to the boss-client's theatricalism.

"I have just insulted our host," I told him flatly.

"Did it make you feel better?"

"Much!"

"Then he'd be the first to say you did the right thing."

"He doesn't bear grudges?"

"He has no time for them." Stowe seemed perfectly serious. "Like myself, he was born poor. A young man who wants to get ahead must learn to hide his grudges. If he still has them when he gets to the top of the ladder, that's a sign he's picked the wrong ladder."

"And you lost your grudges?"

The thick round shoulders were elevated in a slight shrug. "Oh, yes. There was one old curmudgeon of a partner in my firm whom, as a clerk, I always thought I wanted to get back at. But when I became a partner myself . . . well, he was a sad, sick old man, that was all. I even kept the others from forcing him to retire."

"Then you don't think Mr. Hammond will push me into an oubliette after dinner? Or even get you to do it for him?"

"I suppose at Legal Aid you learned to regard Wall Street lawyers as the slaves of their clients. But I assure you, Mrs. Leitner, I don't do anything I don't want to do."

His small eyes struck me as the eyes of a bear, friendly for the moment but dangerous. "But maybe you *want* to push me into an oubliette."

Stowe merely grunted in response to this. "What did Ridley Hammond do to deserve his insult?"

"He has designs on my husband. Machiavellian designs."

"Ah, well, insults will get you nowhere, then. Hammond usually gets what he wants."

When Felix drove me home that night, he was angry, with a cold, hard anger. Hammond, of course, had told him of our little interchange.

"I think you might have the courtesy — if such a term has any place in your conception of the marriage relationship —

to consult me in advance, or at least to warn me, before you kick a man in the teeth who is offering me a fortune."

"But he's a fascist, Felix!"

"I reserve the right to make up my own mind about accepting or declining fortunes, even from fascists. Which, incidentally, I don't for a minute concede that he is."

"You didn't hear what he told me!"

"No, but I can imagine it. Hammond is very free with his speculations about the future. Why should he not be? He happens to believe that our constitutional system is going to undergo certain drastic changes. He does not advocate these changes. He does not work to bring them about. He is an old man and does not even expect to live to see them. He simply likes to peer into what he deems his crystal ball. You call him a pessimist, if you wish, but you have no business calling him a fascist."

"A pessimist?" I grabbed wildly at this note of hope. "Then *you* do not advocate the managerial state?"

"Not in the least. For what do you take me?"

"Do you think it will come about?"

"Not if we keep our wits about us."

"And you won't become a partner in Harris, Tweed?"

"I had already declined the offer. That was why Ridley turned to you. He wanted you to intervene."

"Oh, Felix! I'm so happy!"

"But I'm not." How I remember his tone as he said that! He was very rough with me that night. "You have chosen to muddy my friendship with a wise old man whose understanding of economics — despite an occasional wild deduction — is second to nobody's in this country. I am sick and tired of your intrusiveness. If I have occasion in the future to alter my political views or even to change my profession, I shall make my decisions alone."

"Please, Felix! Don't punish me any more!"

"I'm sorry, Frances, but you have hurt me tonight. Deeply. Very deeply. I cannot forget it."

We drove the rest of the way home in silence. I tried to keep my mind on the fact, the wonderful fact, that Felix was not going to be a Wall Street banker, that he had not sold out to the forces of reaction, that he was the same bright, brave altruist I had married. But deep in my heart was a small, growing fear that even if he were all of that, I might still, by my folly, have lost him.

＊　　＊　　＊

Felix and my father took young Frank off on a fishing trip to a camp in the northern part of the state a few weeks later. Felix had been contributing a weekly column to Mark Truro's New York paper, *The New Dealer,* and he told me to be sure to read the one that would appear on the Friday after he left. When I begged him to tell me why, he simply smiled as if it were a tremendous joke, and in that spirit I tried to accept his secrecy.

It turned out to be a very bad joke. I thought then, and I think now, that it was about as mean a trick as a husband could play on a wife. For the column that met my astounded eyes that Friday simply announced that Felix Leitner, the noted liberal, Felix Leitner, the drafter of some of the New Deal's most important legislation, Felix Leitner, the seeker after world peace, the advocate of the "good life," was going to vote for Alfred Landon!

Oh, yes, he had his reasons: the growth of bureaucracy, the threat of too much government, the excessive deficits, the loss of "freedom." Felix was concerned for his right to walk through the jungle and be consumed by lions!

Was it possible that he could have come to such an inane conclusion if he had not been influenced by that old devil, Ridley Hammond? And would he have been subject to such an influence if he had not hoped to gain something from it? Was he not polishing up Wall Street, so to speak, giving it a spring cleaning, before becoming a part of it himself?

My worst fears were confirmed when I received a letter from Felix from his camp, carried out by a guide and mailed from the nearest box. It told me of his new plans.

> I am writing you this, my dear, because my mind has been made up and my decision taken, and argument would only distress us both. Grant Stowe has offered me a partnership in his law firm in New York, and I have accepted it. My specialty will be constitutional law, and I expect that I shall very much enjoy myself. It will provide us with an income four times as large as we have ever enjoyed. The time has come to turn an eye to the children's economic security. You will be able to return to your legal aid work in the city. I think everything will work out."

My head spun. How could I have so misconceived my enemy? It was the lawyer, not the client, that I should have feared! And now, was I going to have to sit by and watch Felix attack in court the very statutes that he had helped to draw? For what else had so astute a reactionary as Grant Stowe hired him? For what else, but to join the latter's fine stable of Trojan horses? Did Felix think that *I* would continue to be at his side? Surely, it had become my simple duty to separate myself from the apostate, at least until he had seen the error of his ways.

My mother had gone to visit one of my sisters. I had no one to consult but Felix's mother, who had just arrived for the weekend.

*   *   *

When Felix and I were first married, I had tended to dread his mother's visits. It had seemed to me that I could never provide the proper elegance for her. But I soon learned that all her little rules and habits in clothes and household arrangements were designed solely for herself. She expected nothing at all of others. So long as her hair was properly set and dyed, so long as her satins were smoothly pressed and her facial make-up just right, she did not care if the rest of the world was arrayed in potato sacks. Consequently she was the easiest visitor in the world, even the easiest house guest. She would busily convert her bedroom into her own little fragrant bower and then emerge to be serenely at home in the rest of the house.

At Seal Cove she would sit contentedly, if rather regally, on the porch in an old wicker armchair with a peacock-tail back and gaze placidly over the water. She always declined to go out to parties with us but was perfectly content to have her meals alone on these occasions. When, on the second afternoon of her present visit, I at last told her of Felix's letter and my sense of outrage, she remained absolutely motionless for several moments. Then, like a stork, she turned the small, pretty head on the long, pale neck to face me with a cool glare of what I would have thought was hostility had I not known her better. I knew now that it was the defensive posture behind which she hid her bewilderment at the strangeness of others.

"You ask what you should *do*, my child? Why, in heaven's name, should you do anything? I always know that people are going to get into worse trouble when they talk of having to do things."

"How can I go on living with a man whose political views I abominate!"

"But you say he's changed them. Why not wait and see if he won't change them back? Felix has always been mercurial."

"You mean he has no principles?"

"I rather think he may have too many."

"Isn't that the same thing?"

"Not at all. Listen to me, my dear. Felix is a very good husband. You're not going to get a better one."

"But I don't want another husband! That's not the point at all. I *love* Felix. You know that, Mrs. Leitner. I simply wonder what further use I can be to him, if he rejects my advice and makes his major commitments without consulting me."

"That was the way it was with his uncle Isidore and aunt Renata," Mrs. Leitner pointed out with sudden eagerness, as if she had just discovered an analogy that would solve all my problems. "Isidore really never cared much for paintings, except academic things where naked slave girls were being sold at Arab auctions. He liked bronzes and golden bowls and porcelains — things he could touch. But Renata went right ahead and bought what she wanted. Isidore took it very well; he always paid up. So things worked out. Between them they put together a most distinguished collection."

"Except for the slave girls."

"Well, I think even they went to the Metropolitan. They're probably in the cellar now."

"Where I suppose I should be," I said gloomily. But I felt already that there might be a funny kind of therapy in my mother-in-law's attitude. That she should equate my concern for my fellow man with Uncle Isidore's prurient canvases was a sobering thought. Was it possible that I was taking the whole thing in general, and myself in particular, too seriously?

"The one thing I will say about myself as a mother," Mrs. Leitner continued, "is that I recognized early that I was never going to have the slightest effect on Felix's decisions. It has made our relationship much pleasanter that I haven't tried. Let me suggest that you borrow a leaf, my dear, from your old mother-in-law's notebook."

"Oh, Mrs. Leitner, I don't know what to do!"

"Then don't do anything." Now she gazed at me silently

until my eyes met hers. It seemed to me that I could make out something like feeling in them. Certainly I found it in her words. "We are not demonstrative folk, Felix and I. I cannot ever be sure what he feels or does not feel. But I can say this. I love you, my child. And I should be very sad indeed if anything were to happen between you and Felix. I simply cannot believe that a national election or a job in Wall Street can be as important as your joint happiness."

Well, there we were. She was a wonderful woman, my mother-in-law. I had never until that moment properly appreciated her. Arguments about my duty as a wife or in defense of Felix's political acrobatics would have merely aroused my ire. She had the wisdom to rest her case on a simple plea for our joint happiness. I had been in the habit of assuming that there did not exist two women more different than myself and Florine Leitner. Now, suddenly, we were united in love. For I found that I *did* love that straight, powdered figure with the dyed hair and the bright clear smile.

I threw my arms around her and wept. Could I make up to her for my long undervaluation? No. I saw at once in her gentle embarrassment that I had gone as far toward intimacy as I ever should go. So I dried my eyes. When Mrs. Leitner had said that she was not demonstrative, she meant it. I comprehended at last why she had been so slight a loss to the stage.

And so it was that I tried to accept her — and to accept her son — for what they were, or at least for what they appeared to be. I resolved to say no more about the national election, and I was good to my resolution. I did not even indulge in crowing when Felix's candidate carried only two states in November. And I learned to behave myself as the wife of a partner of Dinwiddie, Stowe & Whelan.

Nobody, least of all Felix, ever gave me proper credit for my change. Of course, it is almost impossible for families to recognize any fundamental change in a member, though they are quick to spot a superficial one. I had established a reputation for constantly proselytizing for my political views, and I suppose I shall die with it. As my friends and relatives can easily figure out what side I am on in any major public issue, they are quick to assume that I am canvassing for it. Perhaps in a way they are right. The unspoken word can be thunderous.

Memorandum of Grant Stowe Concerning the Partnership of Felix Leitner, Prepared in 1959 in Connection with His History of Dinwiddie, Stowe & Whelan

A T THE TIME of this writing the big downtown law firms of Manhattan have reached so great a size that most of them have senior partners, or committees of senior partners, who devote at least as much of their time to office administration as to the practice of law. They have learned that if overhead is not constantly watched, it will eat up the very fattest profits, and that if they fail to keep abreast of the latest business machines, they will soon find their competitive position impaired. And what they *all* now recognize must receive their first attention is the esprit de corps of the associate lawyers. If these are not made to feel that they have a future in the firm, if, on the contrary, they come to see themselves as mere hacks to be driven as hard as possible and rewarded only when they have jacked themselves into a position to run off with an important client, then the firm will become a joyless factory whose vital professional spirit will soon sputter out.

I pride myself that I was a pioneer in these matters. I saw as early as 1923, when I became a member of the venerable Wall Street firm of Walker & Whelan, that the essential problem was somehow not to lose the old-fashioned individualistic practitioner in the disciplined corps of highly specialized attorneys needed to service the great corporations. The key to the happy partner would be the happy clerk. I made it a rule of our firm to choose partners only from the body of our associates and to obtain good jobs for those who were "passed over." As we took only law review men from the best law schools, a Walker & Whelan "graduate" was assured a high resale value. After only a few years of implementing this policy we had the most dedicated and hard-working clerks in Manhattan. Of course, I was called a "slave driver" and a "little Napoleon" by my rivals, but they all copied me.

I have never pretended to be wholly consistent. I knew that exceptions had to be made, and I did not hesitate to make them. The most important deviation occurred when I persuaded the membership to invite George Dinwiddie to come in as senior partner and to change our firm name to Dinwiddie, Stowe & Whelan. I intended this to reflect our final emergence from the nineteenth century and our resolution to be the first corporation law firm of the nation.

George Dinwiddie in 1925 was sixty years old and the most renowned appellant pleader of the federal courts. He had been governor of his native state, Virginia, a United States senator, and, briefly, Secretary of State. Tall, silver-haired, with a strong, resonant voice and an inimitable charm of manner, he seemed the essence of all that was finest in the Southern tradition. He was a Democrat, but a Jeffersonian one, quite acceptable to even our darkest Republican clients. During the depression, disgusted with the New Deal, he ceased even to vote for his party. As senior partner he devoted himself to his own great cases and left the management of the firm to me. It was an excellent arrangement. He was admired by the junior partners and clerks, and his benign disposition cast a glowing curtain over some of the inevitable rough spots of my just but realistic administration.

Dinwiddie gave the firm immense prestige. Perhaps I should have been content with his contribution and made no further exceptions to my rule of choosing partners from within. But I was greedy. I wanted the moon. I wanted the firm to be attractive not only to the business world but to the intellectuals. I wanted to appeal to the young people, and it occurred to me that we might attract the brightest third-year law students away from rival employers if we could somehow appear less stuffy than they. Suppose we had as a leading partner a man with a reputation as a writer, a teacher, a social philosopher? Suppose we had such a star as Felix Leitner?

There was method in my madness. His notoriety as a New Dealer had been canceled by his much excoriated (by the left) vote for Alfred Landon. I figured that some of our corporate clients might regard him as a brand plucked from the burning — or perhaps as a redeemed prodigal to be feasted. They might even come to see him as a kind of Trojan horse in which they could invade the capitol. I estimated — correctly, as it turned out — that his advice would be extremely valuable in dealing with the administrative agencies that were springing up everywhere. But what was there in it for Leitner? A large income, of course. I had reason to believe that the heavy psychiatric expenses of his son would make this attractive. Felix, indeed, accepted my offer with alacrity. He became a member of the firm on January 1, 1937.

What I did *not* anticipate was that he should become, in the first six months of his partnership, the right hand man of George Dinwiddie. Our leader was engaged in a series of great constitutional cases challenging the legislation of Franklin Roosevelt's first term, and he proceeded quietly, but with his usual firmness, to preempt all of Felix's time as a brief-writer. This was not precisely the function that I had visualized for our new recruit, but it was certainly a part of it, and I decided to make no comment but to watch the situation and read all drafts of the Dinwiddie briefs.

One of these was a succession of short, connected arguments, each following the other with a formidable logic and moving to a seemingly inevitable conclusion. The concise, crushing paragraphs were arranged like stanzas on the pages, separated by large blank spaces. I called in one of Dinwiddie's litigation assistants and asked him why they were so printed.

"Oh, that's Mr. Leitner's method," he explained. "He writes the argument and then gives it to us to fill in the cases."

"You mean he writes the brief *before* reading the law?"

"Oh, yes, sir, quite on purpose. He says a good lawyer should be able to find a precedent for anything."

At a partners' lunch later that day I sat by Felix and quizzed him about his method. He was perfectly frank about it.

"But doesn't that imply a certain contempt for precedent?" I asked.

"It implies a total contempt for precedent."

"Is that an example of 'advanced thinking'?"

"It's an example of everybody's thinking. Few, perhaps, acknowledge it quite so frankly as I. But the true basis of most judges' thinking on any constitutional point is, Where do I want to come out? Once he's decided that, he arranges the precedents and his interpretation of them accordingly."

"I did not realize you were such a cynic."

"My dear Grant, it's not a question of cynicism. It's a question of fact. The Constitution can be made to yield to any interpretation. It has in the past, and it will in the future. As one British friend of mine put it, What is the point of a document that requires your bar to play word games every time an important change in national policy is required?"

"I trust you don't air these views outside the firm."

I put this a bit in my managing partner's tone, with a toothy smile and a hint of gruffness, but it struck me there and then that this was not going to work with Felix. After all, I had not had the indoctrinating of him. He gave me a rather odd stare as I turned from him to address the table on a matter of firm business, and I made a mental note to postpone the matter of his constitutional views for a later day.

We did not discuss them again until June, on a barge trip down the Canal du Midi in France. Since the death of Mrs. Dinwiddie three years before, Matilda and I had accompanied the old man on his annual summer trip to Europe. It had been Matilda's idea to charter this luxurious passenger barge, with a crew of five, at Toulouse, and she had not been much pleased when Dinwiddie had suggested that the Leitners be included in our little party. However, we could hardly refuse, and I was secretly pleased at the opportunity of a more intimate acquaintance, not only with Felix but with his interesting wife. I hoped it might be my chance to weave them both more intimately into the firm family.

The trip itself was a delight. We reclined in deck chairs as the big, slow craft nosed its way down the placid narrow waterway, past hot, still fields and misty hills, which succeeded each other like Cézanne landscapes in an exhibition, and through small, sleepy, whitewashed villages. A motor car followed and met us at the docks to take us on excursions to castles and churches, to Roman ruins and caverns. I enjoyed strolling ahead on the old towpath while our barge waited its turn in the little locks; sometimes I would lend a hand at the crank or with the lines. It was a life of indolence against a background of seeming indolence, the perfect relief from our Wall Street frenzy.

We three men got on very well. By tacit agreement we left the law behind and immersed ourselves in the history and culture of southern France. Felix, who seemed to know everything, was casually instructive, charmingly so. Dinwiddie listened to him with the graceful deference that truly great men are apt to manifest in fields not their own, and immersed himself in the evenings in the books that Felix had brought for the trip. One would have thought, to talk to Dinwiddie, that he had no interest in the world but the early crusades and the persecution of the Albigensians. Frances Leitner, small and quiet, with her wise little smile, seemed not to miss a trick, historical, geographical or contemporary. She was curious but hard to impress, tolerant but hard to persuade. Like me, like Felix, even like old Dinwiddie, she seemed always on an even keel. We were a good traveling group.

It will be noted that I have defined the group as good travelers before coming to the fifth member. I yield to nobody in admiration of my late wife, Matilda, whom I loved and largely obeyed throughout the forty years of our very happy marriage. She was at all times a devoted and exemplary wife and mother, but I trust that I do not denigrate her memory in admitting that she had a temper. Few who felt it have forgotten it. When it was over, it was over — Matilda was not a grudge bearer — but while it lasted, well . . . enough said.

Matilda had one great virtue: she was always expansively benign and agreeable when she had her own way. Now this may sound sarcastic, but it is not intended to be. Many American women of her class and generation were perennial malcontents; they grumbled as much on their good days as on their bad. But Matilda was usually beaming, for the simple reason that people, starting with myself, usually gave in to her. I set the example, not, I insist, because I was weak, but because from the beginning I perceived that what Matilda desired above all things was my own good. There was no selfishness in her, unless one accepts the theory that a wife who identifies herself with her husband is disguising her own egotism under his. That is not a theory to which I have ever subscribed.

Matilda made almost a fetish of Dinwiddie, Stowe. She always referred to the firm in this abbreviated fashion, but our children used to say that, had my name occupied the first position, she would have abbreviated it still further. Children today have little reverence. Matilda believed that in a divinely ordained system of free enterprise, the corporation lawyers were the high priests of the Deity. It was to the great downtown firms such as mine that He had entrusted the moral rules of competition for the business community. If Matilda envisioned tycoons such as Harrison Williams or Thomas J. Watson as playing the roles of Henry II or Louis XIII, she saw George Dinwiddie and myself in the nobler ones of Thomas à Becket or Richelieu. However much she respected birth and wealth — and she did so, freely and frankly, without being in the least a toady — she reserved her highest esteem for those whose function it was to interpret laws that were to her as holy and as absolute as any that Moses received on the mountain top.

It followed, of course, that Matilda took with the utmost seriousness her duties as wife of the managing partner. She was constantly arranging social events for the partners, for the clients, for the associates, sometimes with their wives, sometimes without, either in our big, white, constantly redecorated house in Bronxville or in clubs or restaurants in the city. No problem was too small for her, no younger clerk's newly wedded wife too humble. She was always kind and helpful, and always free with advice as to doctors, merchants, real estate brokers and summer rentals. She was even ready, if necessary, to advance funds. But there was undeniably a note of imperium in her assistance. She was perfectly democratic — so long as her rank was perfectly understood.

I had hoped that our cruise would be the occasion of enlightening Felix's wife, whom I knew to be a most intelligent woman, as to the essentially harmless nature of Matilda's expectations. It was really so easy to make Matilda happy! But I was wrong. Frances Leitner, for all her quiet and inoffensive reserve, managed somehow to stick out noticeably as not belonging to Matilda's domain. Perhaps it was not conceivable to Frances that anyone could see the world quite as Matilda saw it.

For example, when Matilda, at one of our meals, was describing, in her high comic style of mock gravity, how a poor clerk at an office Christmas party had got drunk and accused Mr. Dinwiddie to his face of being the "apostle of greed and the prophet of grab," Frances, not comprehending that such heresy was being treated lightly only because the audience was a "safe" one, laughed with an amusement obviously sympathetic to the culprit and offered this comment:

"I wonder if the opportunity for that kind of catharsis shouldn't be considered one of the advantages of an office party. Perhaps the invitations should read: 'each guest shall have an "indulgence" to insult one partner. Senior associates may insult two.'"

Matilda's obvious dismay was made worse by George Dinwiddie's merriment.

"Would the indulgences be exchangeable?" he asked. "How many would a clerk have to collect before he could let fly at the managing partner? Eh, Grant?"

I took this in good part, for I knew that my senior sometimes chafed at the tightness of my management. Matilda, however, was convinced that Frances was introducing a serious note of dissension into our legal family. Later that day, as she and I strolled on the towpath, she placed the matter squarely between me and the Gallic scenery.

"I begin to wonder if Frances Leitner is ever going to be a true member of Dinwiddie, Stowe. I had my doubts about her last May when she failed to show up at my tea for the wives. When I suggested to her that she must have got her dates mixed, she said, no, she hadn't forgotten at all; she simply couldn't abide 'hen parties.' She said this as if it were something that I should naturally understand. As if I had been giving a garden party and she had hay fever!"

"I suppose she's never had to be on a team before."

"But she might at least have the imagination to know what it is. She's supposed to be so brilliant. Well, in my opinion she's either very stupid, or she's playing some funny game."

I could not explain to Matilda that there were people — intelligent, rational people — who thought that the kind of organization that I had labored so long and so hard to build up was not only inhumane but actually antisocial. Matilda believed in absolutes, and she was much too useful to me to be allowed to be shaken in these beliefs. I decided to take the tack that Frances was a kind of harmless freak who had to be accepted and perhaps gently isolated.

"If you let her be, you'll find she's little enough trouble," I suggested. "She's very quiet, after all. Rather a little mouse. Nobody's going to notice her much."

"Don't underestimate that woman, Grant!" my good spouse insisted hotly. "She may look like a mouse, but she has a pile of will power. Don't forget she's a lawyer and has acted for all kinds of desperate criminals in her legal aid work. And then, she's a radical, too. Did you know that she believes in a hundred percent inheritance tax?"

"Did she volunteer that or did you get it out of her?"

Matilda paused to reflect. She was always a truthful woman. "I don't recall. It came out in one of our talks. She thinks each generation should have to make its own way."

"I've heard you say something rather like that yourself. Anyway, Frances Leitner is not a congresswoman, so she can't initiate money bills. We needn't care what she thinks."

"That's all very well, Grant, but consider where she's getting it from. Do you know that your partner Felix is writing a book? About constitutional law? Hadn't you better ask him about it?"

"I suppose his book is his own business."

"*Is* it? I'm warning you, Grant. Don't ever say I didn't."

"Never fear, darling. I shan't."

But the very next morning, pacing the walls of Carcassonne with George Dinwiddie and Felix, I was reminded of Matilda's forebodings. George was enraptured by the vision of battlements and towers that stretched below us. He said that it reminded him of a castle in the background of a painting in a book of hours. It was not so much the Middle Ages as the legend of the Middle Ages, a faery keep, the palace of some mighty wizard or hideous giant in a tale of enchantment.

"Legend, indeed!" Felix agreed with a chuckle. "But it's the legend of Viollet-le-Duc. I confess I'm not partial to reconstructions. I prefer the grimmest, most shapeless pile of old stones to the fanciest restoration."

"Why, in God's name?" George asked in astonishment.

"Because it's true!"

"But even if it isn't just like *the* old castle," I protested, "isn't it like *a* castle? I agree with George. To me Carcassonne is a kind of hymn to the Middle Ages."

"Well, it may be my loss that I don't have that kind of imagination," Felix said, with at least assumed humility. "I can never forgive Richelieu for destroying the great fortresses. What a sightseer's paradise this country might have been!"

"He had to do it," George said, in his placid tone. "He had to break the power of the nobles. He had to forge France into a strong unit."

"Why, in God's name?" Felix demanded, echoing George's emphasis.

"You know that as well as I do, Felix. Would you have preserved a few old castles at the price of general looting and bloodshed? Of course, you wouldn't."

"I'm not at all sure. If beautiful things are to be preserved, maybe government shouldn't be too strong. Isn't that your thesis at home, Mr. D.? Aren't you considered the archenemy of the welfare state?"

"Of the welfare state, sir. Not of the strong state."

"Well, I guess I'm one of those anachronisms that still believe the best government is the least government."

"Does that make you what is now being called a 'strict constructionist'?" Dinwiddie asked.

"Of the Constitution? Perhaps not. I have more faith in legislation than I do in constitutions. More faith in legislation, to tell the truth, than I do in courts."

"You would not, I trust, challenge the power of the courts to declare an act of the legislature unconstitutional?"

"Would I not, Mr. D?" But Felix, seeing that his interlocutor was more than half serious, smiled. "Not before *you*, anyway!"

This conversation made me considerably more curious about the nature of Felix's book. I mentioned it to Matilda before our lunch at the hotel in the castle that day, and she told me later that this was what caused her to send a cable to Jim Allerton, a junior partner in the firm who was my particular assistant in administration and who was Matilda's favorite "young man." But I suspect that what really caused her to take so drastic a step was the exasperation that Frances caused her at that very lunch.

Matilda was telling one of her "grand client" stories. She

loved, in "safe" company, to hold forth on the humorous aspects of the manners of such clients as Mrs. Jay Baldwin, an octogenarian millionairess, whose comic air of self-importance was a source of many legends in New York. I suspected that the reason Mrs. Baldwin saw so much of her lawyers and doctors and financial advisers was that only in the company of those whom she paid could she command the deference that her naive but essentially good-natured ego required. Matilda now related the story of our visit to Mrs. Baldwin over the previous Labor Day weekend. We had been surprised to find that we were expected to leave Sunday night and had reminded the butler of what the morrow was. "Mrs. Baldwin does not recognize Labor Day," he gravely explained to us.

Frances smiled with the perfunctoriness of one who has heard that story many times before.

"I'm not surprised that Cousin Daisy should hate Labor Day," she observed. "After all, her father came close to being murdered in Pittsburgh in the nineties. But she's still a perfect darling when it's a question of an individual worker and not a union. I went to her once about an old valet of Cousin Jay's, who I heard was in financial trouble, and she at once pensioned the poor fellow."

The effect of this on Matilda was nothing less than massive. I watched with restrained amusement as her round, pale, almost lineless face took on the faint pink of incipient battle. Matilda came from Omaha; she had never mastered the labyrinthine relationships of old New York. France's background was a total enigma to her. By Matilda's standards, Frances, being married to a Jew, should not be related to people like Mrs. Baldwin. Even though I had told her of Frances's Knickerbocker genealogy, she could not really believe that any woman without looks, fortune or clothes, and destitute, moreover, of the least air of distinction, could really have any social pretensions.

"You call Mrs. Baldwin 'Cousin Daisy'?" my wife was now startled enough to ask.

"Does it sound absurdly old-fashioned? I always preferred 'Mr.' or 'Mrs.' to the eternal 'Cousin This' and 'Cousin That.' But I was brought up to it, and it's a hard habit to break."

"Then she *is* your cousin?"

"Oh, not her. Good Lord, no, not with that fortune. None of my poor branch of the Ward family ever had two nickels to rub together. But Cousin Jay, her husband, was a first cousin of *both* my parents. Does that sound incestuous? It isn't really. You see his mother was a Ward and Daddy's aunt, and his father was a nephew of my grandmother Livingston. It's all ridiculously complicated, but I was made to learn these things as a child, and, for the life of me, I can't forget them."

What I think was most galling to Matilda was the evident sincerity of Frances's manner, which disclaimed any grandeur in such connections. She was like an archduchess who has shed her rank to join the commoners. She had her memories, and she would correct you on facts, if necessary. But only if necessary.

"Then Harry and Arthur Baldwin are your . . . second cousins?"

"Double second, to be exact. Which makes them the same blood kin as first. And I'll tell you a funny story in that connection. We used to have to pass the hat at Christmas for a poor Irving cousin who lived up the Hudson in what was almost a shack. Mother had the bright idea of asking Cousin Daisy to help, hoping, of course, that she would take over the whole thing, but Father pointed out that this particular Irving was no relation of Cousin Jay's. Well, we all pooh-poohed this and said it was impossible, and we got out the family tree to prove it, but, alas! Every branch we traced had either the poor Irving or Cousin Jay, but never both. Father was quite right. They were not related."

"Couldn't you have asked the Baldwins, anyway?" George asked with a wink. "They'd *never* have known."

"Oh, of course, they wouldn't have!" Frances agreed. "And Cousin Daisy, who used to refer to her iron ore millions as 'the lovely fortune that enables me to help so many people,' would have written any check we asked. But there were rules. Poor relatives had to be supported, but they had to be *related*. Oh, we were very strict indeed — about some things. Yes, New Yorkers of that ilk, for all their provincialism, had a few standards. More, anyway, than Cousin Daisy's robber baron progenitors. If that's saying anything!'

George and Felix chuckled. I smiled, but Matilda did not. I knew that she was inwardly seething. That so dim a little creature as Frances Leitner should pre-empt the great Mrs. Baldwin was bad enough. That she should toss her away was far worse. My wife now changed the subject firmly, but I knew that I had not heard the end of it.

Matilda left the barge in Béziers for "a morning's shopping," during which she actually telephoned Jim Allerton in New York. When she returned she led me to our little stateroom and closed the door.

"It may interest you to know that your loyal partner, Mr. Leitner, is entitling his forthcoming book *The Great American Myth*. And do you know what the great American myth is? The Constitution! Leitner maintains ... now let me get this straight." Here Matilda busily consulted the notes of her telephone parley. "Leitner maintains that except for the Bill of Rights, the Constitution was designed simply to set up the machinery of government. And that even the Bill of Rights applies only to people ... am I correct? Yes, to people, that is, to human beings. Not to businesses and corporations. Jim said you'd be interested in *that!*"

I was. I listened grimly now until she had finished and then went up to the foyer. I found Felix reading galleys and remembered that he had received a large package in our Béziers mail delivery.

"Is that by any chance *The Great American Myth?*"

He looked up, surprised, but by no means perturbed. "How did you know? Would you care to look at it? I have two sets."

"Very much."

That afternoon I remained on board while the others visited a medieval abbey, and read Felix's little book from start to finish. Of course, it was brilliant. In half a dozen essays he traced, with devastating wit and accuracy, the tortured word games that our judiciary has had to play — ever since John Marshall's assumption of the power to outlaw unconstitutional laws — in order to prove to the world that we always had and always should obey the sacred document of 1787. It was a beautiful book. It was perhaps a work of art. But what had I to do with beautiful books and works of art?

That evening I took Felix for a stroll on the towpath and asked him if he had ever thought of using a pen name.

"I could, of course," he replied. "But I wouldn't. Why should I?"

"Does it not occur to you, my friend, that your thesis might embarrass the firm? To say nothing of embarrassing George Dinwiddie?"

"You astound me, Grant. Why should anyone be embarrassed? Except possibly myself, when the law school professors start to pull me apart."

"Because we are representing clients whose very existence may depend upon the present interpretation of the commerce and due process clauses. How do we look, arguing the sanctity of those clauses in the highest court of the land, when one of our partners — indeed the one who may have written the very brief before the bench — advertises to the world that he regards the Constitution as a rag?"

"Surely there is a difference between an attorney's arguments and his private convictions?"

"You sound like a raw law student! Do you think that when corporations as vast as Magnum Steel and the Bank of Commerce retain general counsel, they don't expect them to be generally consistent in *all* their public utterances?"

"I don't think I care what they think. So long as I write the best briefs that can be written for them, that's all they're entitled to expect. Surely I have a right to my own opinions."

"A right? Who's talking about rights? When you're in the business of representing a company like Magnum, you do it twenty-four hours a day — or decline the retainer. That's what being a corporation lawyer is all about. If you want to be a criminal attorney and represent a murderer one day and his victim the next, like the old-time repertory ham who played Hamlet one night and Figaro another, that's your affair. We have a different philosophy at 65 Wall."

"So I see." When I knew Felix better, I learned to recognize the opaque look that I now saw in his eyes. It was the mark of his limit. He could be charming, persuasive, wonderfully amiable, up to a certain point. And then, suddenly, he would stop. And when he stopped, nothing — bribes, arguments, love, sentiment, torture, death — would move him. The ego was solid, closed, complete. "I guess I'm an old repertory ham."

"I don't suppose one philosophy is necessarily better than the other," I decided to concede. "A lawyer who changes his opinion with each client is called a mouthpiece. And one, like myself, who adheres to a few corporations, is said to be 'kept.' But the choice must still be made."

"And I've made it. The book will be published as planned, under my own name. Do you want me to resign from the firm?"

We faced each other, quite without anger. I was not angry because I had trained myself never to be angry in crises. Felix was not angry because he was above it all. He actually smiled.

"I'll speak to George," I said. And then I returned to the barge.

Felix tactfully took Frances out to dinner in Béziers, and George and I and Matilda dined on the barge. But the conversation did not go at all as I had expected. George was not like his usual serene self. He drank more wine than was his wont and became very grumpy.

"I can see where you're leading, Grant, and I tell you right now, I won't have it! I don't mind saying I've grown quite dependent on Felix in the last six months. I like the way his mind works. I like his arguments. We've become a team. I'm not prepared to lose Felix Leitner because of your exaggerated theeories of what we owe our clients."

"It seems to me, George, that a company that employs twenty thousand men and supplies the nation with a commodity essential to its business and necessary to its defense may feel entitled to counsel who at least profess lip service to the legal and economic theories that support its continuance."

"I know, I know. It's a question of how far you carry it. You forget, Grant, that I started life as a small-town practitioner in Wythe County where I was happy to take any brief that came my way. I remember defending a man who was charged with robbing a bank of which my uncle was a director."

"I'm very well aware of your early days, George. I hope one day to write a chapter about them for our firm history. But what was right in Wythe County may not be right in Wall Street."

"Felix may cost you some of your clients, George!" Matilda warned him.

"My dear Matilda, I must ask you to leave this matter to the professionals, where it unhappily belongs." George here made my wife a stiff little bow and gave her a severe little smile, and I knew that even Matilda would not open her mouth on the subject again. "I think that even if what you say is generally true, Grant, a firm the size of ours can afford an exception, and I should be pleased if you would make one of Felix."

"Well, of course, George, there's nothing I wouldn't do for you. But I still want to point out that you are the one who is going to suffer from any inconsistency between Leitner books and Leitner briefs."

"I may even profit from it!" George exclaimed. "I wonder if I haven't become too much of a stereotype. And you've had a hand in it, my friend."

"Me?"

"Yes, you. Grant Stowe, the P. T. Barnum of law firms. Don't think I don't know what you've been up to, in the past ten years. You've been shaping me into a public image. The silver-haired, silver-tongued prophet of laissez faire! A kind of now stern, now twinkling Uncle Sam, first pointing a bony finger as in a war poster and then patting a small child's tousled head."

This was too much for Matilda. "How can you say a thing like that, George? Don't you know that my husband worships the very ground you walk on? *You* should be married to him!"

"In a way I am, Matilda," George said more gently now. "At least we walk on that same ground. But seriously, do you know what that fellow Frankfurter says of me? That I'm like Tennyson. Mellifluous, sonorous, high sounding — with no thought content."

"Well, who *cares* what a smart-alecky Jewish law professor thinks?" Matilda cried angrily.

"*I* care!" George retorted. "And maybe, my dear, you have some of that same prejudice about our own Felix. What I maintain is that he is keeping me younger and making my image sharper. And that I like it. And that I like him! What do you say to that, Grant?"

"Simply that what goes with you, George, goes with me. I withdraw my objections to Felix Leitner and to his books. To this book, anyway."

George chuckled, his usual serenity restored with victory. "I thought you'd qualify your general statement. You remind me of an old colored butler we had in Richmond. His name was Jesse. Once when Mrs. Dinwiddie and Jesse's wife, who was her maid, were particularly pleased at the prospect of fine weather and a country fair, I said to him: 'Jesse, our women folk seem in a good mood today.' He looked at his watch and replied, 'Say they's in a good mood at this minute, twelve-sixteen.'"

Later that night when I was alone topside, smoking a cigar and watching the lights in the little village square by which we were moored, Frances Leitner came up and took a seat beside me.

"May I talk with you?" she asked. "I mean, of course, frankly and personally."

"That's as it should be between partner and partner's wife."

"I gather there's been a sort of crisis, but that it's passed. For the time being, anyway."

"That is correct."

"And that you were about to ask Felix to resign from the firm, but that Mr. Dinwiddie was against you and prevailed."

"No, that is not quite the case. I felt that the publication of Felix's new book might be harmful to the firm and that this was a matter that should be discussed. George did not wish even to discuss it. I bowed to his wishes. That is all."

"But it *could* have resulted in Felix's leaving the firm?"

"Conceivably. Anyway, it didn't."

"So now it's all over? Just like that? And the five of us will continue the trip happily together?"

"So far as I'm concerned. There was nothing personal or acrimonious involved. It was simply a matter of opinion. Perhaps of philosophy. Hasn't Felix told you about it?"

"He has. What I marvel at is the calm way in which you take it."

"Why should I not take it calmly?"

"Because you've presumably lost what you consider an important administrative battle."

"Perhaps. But a good administrator should be accustomed to losing battles. Even important ones."

"You're an interesting man, Grant. And a formidable opponent. You see all around a question, and you don't lose your temper."

"Oh, I've been known to!"

"Probably only because you figured you could gain something by losing it. I'm afraid that if I were pitted against you, I should become more interested in the battle than in what we were fighting about. You make the fighting so interesting."

"Is that a compliment?"

"I don't honestly know. Of course, you and I *are* pitted against each other. We believe in different worlds."

"You mean because you stand somewhere to the left of where I do?"

"Oh, come now, Grant, you know all about me! You had to look me up carefully before you took Felix into the firm. You wanted to be sure I wasn't a Communist. And you're perfectly well aware that Matilda and I dislike each other. And that I don't share your ecstatic admiration for Mr. Dinwiddie, although I am very fond of the old boy. The only person you haven't made out is Felix. Why were you so sure that you could control him?"

"I wasn't. I took a chance."

"Didn't you figure that respectability would get him in the end? That Wall Street and the Social Register would prevail?"

It was impossible to be irritated with this friendly, smiling, persistent and perceptive little woman. "Maybe they still will," I suggested.

"Maybe. But I think you'll find that Felix can be led just so far and no further."

"He has no basic loyalty?"

"Only to truth."

"You don't think he may sometimes identify truth with Felix Leitner?"

Frances looked at me curiously. "Now why do you put it that way? Why don't you ask me if he doesn't identify truth with what is good for Felix Leitner?"

"I asked what I meant to ask."

"That truth *is* Felix Leitner!" She shook her head almost sorrowfully. "You accuse him of extraordinary egotism."

"I accuse him of nothing."

"You suggest it, then."

"Don't you suggest it of *me*?"

"I suppose I do." She actually reached over to give me a little peck of a pat on the shoulder. "But I respect you. I even like you. So we'll continue our merry cruise. It should be fun for the watchers, anyway."

"What will you watch for?"

"To see if you can recoup the ground you've lost with Mr. Dinwiddie. It should be like watching the hare and the tortoise. Felix can bound ahead brilliantly. After all, he snatched away the senior partner from under your very nose. But we all know who won the race."

Perhaps it was just as well that our cruise was almost over. In two more days we moored under the walls of Aigues-Mortes, the beautiful, miraculously preserved little medieval seaport from which Saint Louis embarked on his crusade. Matilda's temper had become very short, and I had been under some apprehension of an explosion. As it was, we parted company with the Leitners very politely, and the Dinwiddies and the Stowes proceeded north to Paris by rail.

I had been perfectly serious in speaking to Frances of her husband's ego. I was not in the least impressed by his vaunted search for truth. I had come to the conclusion that my choice of him for a partner had been an error. The man was an egotist, pure and simple. He was incapable of conforming to any pattern, noble or ignoble. Sooner or later he was bound to separate himself from the team, whatever team it might be, and redefine himself in relation to it in less than complimentary terms. The reason that he was so dangerous was that the pleasure that he derived in separating himself from the team was greater than any material or even moral advantage that he might possibly derive from staying with it.

I had allowed Frances Leitner to believe that I never lost my temper and perhaps to deduce from this that I never hated anybody. I did not want her to know that I was beginning to dislike her husband. The man was a kind of monster of self, and nothing in his subsequent career has served to mitigate this harsh but considered judgment.

❖   ❖   ❖

Some months later I sat in the United States Supreme Court building, not at counsel's bench, where Felix Leitner and others of my firm were sitting, but with the public, in back, and listened to George Dinwiddie argue the rights of East Coast Inland Coal and certain of its employees against two labor unions in a case arising under the National Labor Relations Act. I had not even told George that I should be there; I preferred the anonymity of my public seat.

Never had I heard George Dinwiddie more eloquent or more persuasive. The old man's voice rose to near passion as he described the plight of the non-union man, hounded by pickets, bombarded by threatening letters, his family living in fear, his future dark. The great employer company was exalted to the role of a defender of his liberty, perhaps of his very life; the unions were shown as captious, cranky, despotic. If we were to preserve the old-line, independent artisan, the Yankee individualist, if we were to resist a new world of gray uniformity and egalitarianism, we had to brandish the due process clause before the very fangs of the enemy. George came closer to a tirade than I had ever heard him. He veered and soared and yet, like a kite, he was always attached to the ground by a firm cord. I recognized that cord as the anchor cable of Felix Leitner's logic. It was an astonishing performance, a union of fire and steel.

But the first question from the bench was from Roosevelt's first appointee, Hugo Black. He had a volume in his hand, and I had little difficulty in recognizing the color of the dust jacket.

"Let me read you a sentence, Mr. Dinwiddie, from a recent publication by Felix Leitner, whose name is associated with yours in the brief before us today. He writes: 'To deny Congress the power to regulate the relations between business and labor in our time would have been like denying the Venetian Republic the power to regulate its canals or telling an American frontier state that it had no jurisdiction over horse trades. A great nation must be able to solve its mercantile problems, whatever were the fixed ideas of a handful of southern planters a century and a half ago.' Would you like to comment on that, Mr. Dinwiddie, in the light of the argument you have just made?"

"Who was it who said: 'Oh, that mine enemy would write a

book!'" George replied with his most winning smile. "Well, *I* say: 'Oh, that my partners would not!'"

But Justice Black would not let him off so easily. "I believe it was Sir Francis Bacon who wrote: 'Books will speak plain when counsellors blanch.'"

"Very good, your honor! But did he not also say: 'Some books are to be read only in part — and not curiously'?"

Obviously, George had been prepared for the attack. But the decision went against us five to four. I was too familiar with the line-up of opinion on the Court at that time to believe that any of the judges had been influenced by the inconsistency between Leitner the advocate and Leitner the author, but there was no question about its influence on the subsequent decision of Magnum Steel to transfer its next big constitutional case to Sullivan & Cromwell. I received the following epistle from Magnum's president:

"It hurts me to do this, but I have no option, in the opinion of our directors. Of course, you will continue as our general counsel, but let me tell you frankly that we do not intend to be represented by your firm in the federal courts so long as Mr. Leitner is associated with your litigation department."

I did not show this letter to George Dinwiddie at the time. I thought it would be better to let him draw his own deductions from the action of Magnum. In time he did, and less than a year later he told me that, following a long weekend's discussion with Felix, the latter had decided to withdraw from the firm.

Roger Cutter (3)

I HAD KNOWN Felix Leitner since my childhood, but it was at Seal Cove, Maine, in my twenty-second year that we first became friends. Seal Cove contained a small but rather intensely intellectual summer community of which my parents and the Leitners were charter members and of which the Lassiter Troys were the undisputed leaders. Lassiter Troy, who in 1938 was in his early eighties, was the splendid, white-haired veteran of American repertory, a relic of the school of Henry Irving, who had performed across the nation in *Cyrano, Richelieu* and *The Green Goddess*, and was to many school children of the generation preceding mine the physical embodiment of King Lear and Macbeth. I had seen his farewell performance as Falstaff and had admired the powerful, resonant voice and the gravely mocking, sharply staring eyes, even though to my more modern way of thinking his interpretation smacked more of Santa Claus than of Shakespeare's dissipated old reprobate.

Mrs. Troy, a fine, plain, faintly grim New England crone, had never been on the boards and had never, I suspected, quite approved of the world of paint and pasteboard, but her conjugal loyalty (unlike his) had been absolute, and in a marriage that had lasted more than five decades she had kept his homes in trim order, brought up his children with a discipline rare in theatrical circles and invested his earnings so as to turn them into a small fortune. The Troys, like most of our Seal Cove community, lived in a camp, but their principal log cabin boasted an immense two-story living room with a balcony that ran around three of the walls, a huge stone fireplace and an alarming collection of heads and fangs and spread antlers. This room was the social center of Seal.

My parents' cabin was the next down the cove, not nearly so large but commodious, in the easy style of pre-World War I arrangements. Daddy, a professor of philosophy at Columbia, moderately famous in that day, could never bear to be separated from his books, and he had built shelves to the ceiling in our living room. But although he was inclined to read at night in the city during Columbia's term, he loved the social life at Seal, and his great bearlike figure and shaggy, shaking gray head could be seen at any party at the Troys, where he loved to take active part in the most complicated charades, leading his obedient team in or out of the hall like a drill sergeant after preparing, or performing, his scenes. Mother was quite different. She never participated in the games, but made up a serene audience of one, engaged in the needlepoint that she always brought with her, her broad clear forehead and unwaved gray hair creating for her inner privacy a barrier that was pliant yet unyielding, a kind of willow fence, a sash of some pale Indian material that protected without unduly decorating.

The summer of 1938 was a dark one for me, for it followed the spring in which I had suffered a near-fatal attack of diabetes. One of the complications of this terrible disease was the development of sexual impotence, at first believed by the doctors to be temporary, but which, alas, has not proven so. As I was still virgin to woman, a situation more common in a man of twenty-two in that day than now, my deprivation was only prospective, but its effect on my psyche was nonetheless shattering. I developed none of the physical characteristics of a eunuch, but I felt that I had been turned into something unclean, a kind of leper. It seemed to me now that sexuality was essential to a man's success in any field, even the arts, and that I was condemned to be at most a dilettante. But worst of all was Daddy's attitude, or more strictly speaking, what I deemed to be Daddy's attitude.

I had felt from infancy that he was disappointed in me. It had not made things easier that he had tried so hard to conceal it. He had too much imagination not to feel the load that his great personality and reputation placed on the shoulders of an uninspired and uninspiring only child, but his attempted playfulness was a bit like that of a bulldog with a kitten. And then he had never really loved me. He never really loved anyone, even Mother. He had too much ego. He might, like other egotists, have been capable of a great romantic passion — he was supposed to have had a tempestuous love affair with the actress Bella Simes, long before his marriage at the age of forty-five — but passions have little place in the family circle. Daddy perhaps could light a bonfire in his heart but not a candle. He may have suffered for me in my deprivation, but only as he suffered for all the ailing. I had no business, in his mind, to be a freak. I was his blood, was I not? He endured me; he was scrupulously kind, heavily gentle. But I felt his shame.

Mother's lack of response to my trouble was almost worse. She had remained an old maid in marriage, a darling old maid, to be sure — sweet, unruffled and affectionate — but she was always disappointing in the way she failed to respond to the deeper love that she evoked in me. It was not that she actually rejected me; she was always happy to run a hand gently through my hair or lightly touch her cheek to mine. But she never understood that people needed more of such responses than she did herself. She did not really comprehend that the pleasures of sex could be much of a loss.

When I first learned from Felix Leitner that my father had confided my condition in him, I felt a moment of wild resentment, but Felix quickly made me understand that I was wrong.

"Only a man of your father's imagination could accept the fact that you obviously need a younger parent. Believe me, Roger, he wants me to tell you things that neither he nor your mother can tell you. You see, he *knows* he's failed you. It's hard for a proud man to admit that."

"But why should *you* do his job?"

"Because I care."

Did he? Felix Leitner? And yet there was that about him that stopped denial in my throat. If he, who knew everything, said that he cared about a plain, sexless young man, undistinguished in mind or spirit, who was I to deny it? Did not gods care?

Mountain climbing, as we called it, though none of the hills along the coast were over three thousand feet, was a popular diversion in Seal Cove, and Felix took me up the steep trail of Blaine's Peak on a beautiful afternoon when we could see over a sapphire sea as far as Bald Rock, twenty miles out in the Atlantic. Climbing, to one as self-conscious as myself, was the perfect way to communicate. I was always ahead of or behind my companion and only had to look him in the face in the moments when we paused to rest.

On the first level area above the tree tops, where we stopped to gaze down at the shore line, Felix announced that he wished to discuss my "condition." He folded his arms and eyed me with the famous stare, half quizzical, half defiant, with just a hint of amusement that he adopted when addressing chiefs of state on some topic known to be distasteful to them. It worked immediately to dispel the last shred of my resentment. If *he* was going to honor me thus, what could I do but humbly acknowledge the honor?

"Very well," I said meekly.

He turned to walk on ahead of me. "We are all dealt different hands to play. If we are to be judged, it must be on how we play them. Surely it is no great thing to make a grand slam if you hold all the high honors. Now you have probably been thinking that your hand is too poor even to bid on. But you're wrong. There have been times in my life when I have wondered if the mating urge was not more of a liability than an asset."

This was a bit too much, even for me. "I suppose one could always remedy that. Eunuchs in the East were made, not born."

"Eunuchs in China occupied great positions," Felix said seriously. "Had I belonged to the court of the dowager empress I might have considered an operation. But that was not what I was thinking of. I was thinking of the tranquility one might gain. You have always been interested in writing. Is it not possible that you may secure a detachment that will ultimately serve you?"

"But shouldn't a literary artist, a novelist, a poet, say, be subject to the great passions he writes about?"

"But you have felt them, my dear boy! I am sure you must have. Passion is at its keenest in the early teens. How old was Juliet? Or Romeo? Everything that follows is simply variation on an early theme. You have your eyes and ears to watch the rest of us. You have your memory. Didn't Wordsworth define poetry as emotion recollected in tranquility?'

"But have I accumulated a sufficient capital?"

"You have your childhood. What else did Proust spend his

life recapturing? Do you think for a moment he didn't have more joy in writing "Un Amour de Swann" than in all of his clandestine affairs with chauffeurs and waiters? Of course, he did! There is no ecstasy like that of creation." Felix paused to turn back to me as he warmed to this theme. "There are idiotic professors who will tell you that Shakespeare must have been in a depressed and misanthropic mood when he wrote *Hamlet* and *Lear*. I'll wager those were the happiest moments in his life! I'll bet he joined Ben Jonson at the Mermaid after finishing the scene on the heath and ordered a tankard of ale and sang a bawdy song. God, he must have been hilarious!"

"*If* he knew how good he was."

"They always know! Even if it spoils things a bit for them to think they might have been better."

"Well, perhaps. But I've always envied *you*." I wanted to get away from Shakespeare. How could I relate to Shakespeare? "And you strike me as being . . . so complete. You're strong and handsome. You play wonderful tennis. You're a happy husband and father. All that in addition to the finest brain of our time."

It was always easy to compliment Felix, because he took no notice of it. There were no smirks, no false denials. He knew very well how good his brain was.

"Shall I tell you something?" he asked. "Something I've never told anyone else?"

His back was to me, but I was so surprised that I stopped. "Why should you tell *me*?"

He paused, but did not turn. "Because I want to help you. Now listen to me, Roger. I am going to tell you an important truth. Of course, it's confidential. I trust you entirely."

"Oh, Felix, you know I'd never . . ."

"Very well," he interrupted quickly. "Enough of that. Here it is. I love my wife. I love my children. I enjoy my health. I like to exercise. But if I had to choose between the use of my intellect as I now use it, and everything else: health, love, vigor, family, friends . . . well, it would be an easy choice. I'd take my intellect."

A sad little yellow thought flickered for a second in my brain. Was it the strength of his passion for thought or the weakness of his passion for the rest? But almost at once, I rejected the idea. I even frowned at myself! Felix's love of his family was quite as strong as anyone else's. It was simply that his love of his genius was stronger than anything. And that was just as it should be.

"Well, if I had your talent," I pointed out, "I shouldn't so much mind being impotent. Perhaps I shouldn't mind anything. But I haven't your talent."

"How do you know you haven't?"

"Oh, Felix."

He turned now to slap me hard on the shoulder. "God, man, you have to have faith! You have to try! There are two kinds of intellectual life. There is mine, where the whole aim is to see life steadily and see it whole. And there is yours, to turn away from life and create a better one. The critic and the artist. Their joys are equal."

"Ah, but what makes you think I *am* an artist?"

"You can try, man. You can try."

It should not be difficult for my reader to understand that after this conversation I loved Felix Leitner more than anyone in the whole world. Before I had simply admired him; now I worshiped him. I even ceased to be frightened by the idea that I should surely disappoint him as a writer; it might be enough of a function for me in one lifetime that I had excited his compassion and elicited his deepest confidence. As I looked back and considered the things that I had been privileged to observe, there was nothing to approach this.

Encouraged by Felix, I began to take more interest in things around me. I had graduated from Columbia, and I had no particular plans for a career, other than vague notions of writing, but I decided that I could now at least widen my circumference of observation, and I began to accept invitations. By this I do not mean the social gatherings at Seal Cove, where because of my parents I was always welcome, but to the grander affairs of Butterfield Bay.

Butterfield Bay, ten miles south of Seal Cove, was generally considered its diametric opposite. Butterfield, to Seal Covites, was Philistia, a place that one visited only under boring obligation, but a source of temptation to the young and giddy, a community that served to remind one, if reminder were necessary, that money and fashion do not have to offer charm or wit or even food or drink in any unusual profusion to corrupt.

Butterfield Bay had been founded, as a summer community, by the same sort of people who had later gone to Seal Cove — professors, writers and artists — but it had been taken over by the worldly, who are always quick to recognize that the academics have a sharp nose for the loveliest country spots. The original settlers had been driven north by these richer invaders who had made the prices of everything, from beaches to turnips, impossible, and now, where cabins and primitive boat houses had once existed, the coast was lined with Tudor mansions and French chateaux and dark piles of Romanesque shingle. The center of this community was the swimming club, with its huge pool by the ocean, where the salt sea water was warmed by the sun and then pumped up, under green lawns and tennis courts, and delivered, filtered and crystal blue, to a shining rectangular basin surrounded by a flagged terrace with umbrella tables where elderly ladies in large hats sipped cocktails and watched the young swim and listened to the red-coated Hungarian orchestra, which played Victor Herbert from the porch of the clubhouse. It was all quite unreal. As Frances

Leitner once observed, one could not even read a newspaper in Butterfield Bay.

Felix, as might have been expected, was as much in demand in Butterfield as in Seal, and he liked to go there. As he once put it to me: "Who would not occasionally prefer a well-served dinner party, where beautiful ladies with diamonds hang on one's words, to a picnic with pine needles in the salad and mosquitoes in one's ear?" Frances, on the other hand, had a total contempt for Butterfield, which she took little enough pains to conceal, and after some heated disputes on the subject, they had agreed on a compromise: Felix was allowed one dinner party a week in Butterfield, and Frances was exempted from going there altogether. This seemed to please all parties for a while. The Butterfield hostesses were enchanted to have Felix without his critical, dowdy wife, and Frances was perfectly content to have an evening alone with her books. This lasted until the advent of Gladys Satterlee.

An additional inducement, and even an excuse for Felix's visits to Butterfield, was the presence there of Mark Truro in The Mount — the great, craggy stone mansion, huddled on top of the hill overlooking the village, that he had inherited from his railroad pioneer grandfather. Mark had founded the liberal New York paper *The New Dealer,* to which Felix had been a frequent, and was still an occasional, contributor. Mark was between marriages in 1938, and as he hated to be alone, he kept his house filled with people. He was a strikingly handsome and well-proportioned man of fifty, with thick long gray hair, a firm Roman nose, and large, hazy, sexy, smiling blue eyes. Felix used to say that even stripped of his vast wealth and fine figure, those eyes alone would have accounted for Truro's prodigious success with women. I suppose that Truro liked Felix as much as he liked anyone, but I wondered how much that was. He was convinced, I believe, that everyone was after his money, and he had accepted this, but only at the price of disdaining mankind. Mark Truro seemed almost to feel that his money cheapened not only the regard of others for himself but in some curious way his own native good qualities. If people looked past his charm, his quick wit and his vivid imagination to the gold that lay behind, was it not because the gold was worth more?

Felix brought me to one of the Truro parties, where any friend of his was welcome, and because I was lucky enough to amuse my rather languid host with what I fear was a rather unkind description of Seal Cove (I was quick to toss my cradle on the fiery altar of social success), I was invited to come again on my own.

"Any time you hear of anyone coming here to a 'do' at The Mount, don't hesitate to join them. We can always add a place for an amusing young man."

I took to going to The Mount a good deal — far more, certainly, than my parents approved. Daddy was inclined to inveigh against my new friend as a political dilettante, a parlor pink, a jaded epicure who, tired of wine and women, now played with politics. Mother, of course, deplored what she assumed to be the moral looseness of the Truro atmosphere. When I pointed out to them that Felix went there, they retorted that Felix had to go everywhere, that he was a kind of roving reporter, but Mother always added that he did wrong to dine out without his wife.

"But she lets him!"

"That's just as wrong of her."

It was at The Mount that I became friendly with Mrs. Heyward Satterlee, who, if not the "leading hostess" of Butterfield Bay, as the village social rag would have put it, was certainly the liveliest and by far the most enchanting of them. She was in her early forties at this time, thin, mannered, much made up, husky voiced, with a rather violent laugh and a habit of twitching her shoulders and jangling heavy gold bracelets. She was perhaps what the French call *une belle laide.* Her face was oval and very pale, her chin round, her lips a small thick crimson blurb, her nose small and turned up, her eyes a luminous, speculating black. She affected long sashes and very high heels, and she smoked Turkish cigarettes in a long ebony holder. Yet at the same time she seemed sensible and down to earth. She had a keen sense of humor, which she used devastatingly against the very society that she dominated. I was captivated.

"Felix tells me we're fellow Switzers," she observed to me at Sunday lunch. "That we're neutrals in the hundred years' war between Seal and Butterfield."

"You astound me. I thought I had the honor of sitting next to the commander-in-chief of the enemy."

"Oh, no. I'm more of a fifth column."

"You mean you bore from within? How is that neutral?"

"I hope I don't bore. But I do observe." She included the table in her quick gesture. "I watch the world. Like Felix. What do you do?"

"Oh, I watch Felix."

"Isn't he the most wonderful man in the world?"

"Well, *I* think that. But do you? Really?"

"I cross my heart." Which she did, with two long strokes and much rattling of jewelry.

I did not know what to make of her. But as we talked I credited her with a virtue that I had found as rare in Butterfield Bay as in Seal Cove. She gave me her total, undivided attention. There was nobody, it seemed, in the room but myself, and she spoke with a frankness that gave me the oddest feeling that we were alone. Later I discovered that she was this way with everybody — but that only made this virtue the more remarkable. It was certainly the secret of her charm. When she talked about herself she seemed to be talking about *you*. And, in a way, she was.

Heyward Satterlee had been a Yale classmate of Felix's and, oddly enough — for they could not have been more different men — an early friend and admirer. It was one of those youthful intimacies that had survived every vicissitude. The two, perhaps sensibly, did not try to bridge the gap in their lives: they met in New York only to lunch and in Maine only to fish. Their wives hardly knew each other. Heyward had the kind of square, florid good looks that cause you, in a man nearing fifty, to say: "How handsome he must have been!" His well-brushed thinning hair was a light brown; his features were a bit too small for his countenance. He was brisk and tweedy and addicted to loud, emphatic throat clearings. So far as I could make out, he had very little imagination; he seemed to be trying to take in everything that was said, urging people to refute or explain before he gave vent to his cheerful but humorless laugh. In New York he was a stockbroker, a partner in a small, odd-lots firm. He and Gladys were reputed to live over their income, but she had expectancies from a rich old mother. Their house in Maine was not large — a conventional shingle "cottage" — but Gladys made up in entertaining for what she saved in décor, and maintained similarly modest establishments in New York, Long Island and Florida. She seemed, indeed, to be economizing when she was actually at her most extravagant.

They had one child, a daughter, Fiona, a rather somber girl of eighteen who had a withered leg supported in a steel brace as a result of infantile paralysis. When I was invited to the Satterlees', it occurred to me that Gladys might have heard of my misfortune and thought me an appropriate companion for her child. But, of course, there was no allusion to this.

"Do look at Fiona's water colors," Gladys urged me, in the presence of her sullenly frowning daughter. "I'm sure you'll think them as good as I do. But, of course, a mother's opinion goes for *nothing*. A mother's simply dirt. I know. I understand. I'm just that way with my own."

"Mummie, please. Mr. Cutter is quite capable of making up his own mind."

"I didn't say he wasn't! But how is he even to know you paint if I don't tell him? I'll leave you now, and you can both chew me up. What else is a parent for but to sharpen a child's teeth? Don't take me too seriously, Roger. Fiona and I are really quite devoted to each other — in our own peculiar way."

Gladys was right about one thing. Fiona's water colors were startlingly good. She would draw tiny houses or villages with a meticulous skill and then subordinate them to painted atmospheres of Turneresque violence. Her pictures conveyed a sense of the microscopic neatness of man pitifully, yet perhaps not uncourageously, out of tune with a swirling, pointless universe. But Gladys was not right in her assumption that Fiona was critical of her. Fiona, it was true, watched her parents and their mild domestic bickering with a steady eye, but it was not so much critical as judicial. She liked to discuss them, but as if with an objective of discovering some important truth. Heyward and Gladys seemed to constitute the total theater of her practical experience.

"People are inclined to feel sorry for Pa," she told me seriously, "because Mummie lives in too many places and spends too much money. But what they don't see is that he basically adores parties and has a much better social position with Mummie than he could possibly have without her. Mummie would object to my speaking of 'social position.' She would find the term vulgar. I find it precise. Pa could perfectly well control her extravagance if he really wanted to. On the other hand, people give Mummie much too much sympathy for being married to a man so much less intellectual than she is. She may put up a better show at dinner — indeed, a considerably better show — but fundamentally she's not much smarter than he is. I'm sure he'd get the better grade in a general intelligence test. But, of course, she'd never be so dumb as to take one."

Gladys Satterlee professed a great interest in the social life of Seal Cove, which she described as "forbidden fruit" to her. Her husband went there to fish with Felix, but he and she had never been invited to the Leitners' or to the Troys'. Felix, she said, had warned her, only half humorously, that she might be fatal to the northern community.

"He says that women like me operate as a chemical. That the whole place would be dipped in Gladys Satterlee and dyed a different color. I don't think that's very polite, do you? What does he mean by 'women like me'? There aren't any women like me, are there?"

"Of course not. But I see what he means. Your charm might be fatal. Would you care to come over and lunch with my parents? They're expendable. We could use them as guinea pigs. If they survive the experiment, we could try you on the Troys."

"I'd love it!" She clapped her hands. "Heyward has to go to New York next week. Suppose we say Tuesday? And could we climb one of your mountains first? Felix tells me that's the only proper indoctrination for Seal Cove."

Mother had asked the Aleck Nickersons, old Troy's daughter and son-in-law, for lunch that Tuesday, but she was perfectly willing to have Mrs. Satterlee as well. For all her Boston austerity, she had her share of female curiosity and was perhaps a bit proud that her son should have so famous a hostess as a friend. Daddy never cared much whom I asked, but he rumbled a bit about Mrs. Satterlee's "condescension" in coming to our "humble board." However, I was accustomed to that.

I selected the smallest of our "mountains" for the climb, Beehive, which was hardly six hundred feet, but Gladys arrived in boots and a corduroy suit that might have been designed for the Matterhorn. She wore a red hat, a red scarf and red socks, and I assumed she was thinking more of her appearance at lunch than in the woods. But she seemed genuinely excited by what she termed her "adventure" and was disposed to be confidential.

"You can't imagine what fun this is for me, Roger. Oh, I know, you probably suppose that I live for pleasure, and in a way I suppose I do, but that doesn't mean I get it. Far from it. Pleasure is the most elusive thing in the world. One has to work and work for it. To be up here on — what do you call it? Beehive? how rather disingenuous — but anyway, to be up here, without anyone in the world knowing where I am, for I've told nobody — I never tell anyone — makes me feel, well, that just for a minute I own my soul again."

Now, a remark like this, made to a young man by a middle-aged married woman in the dark Maine woods, might have seemed a come-on. But Gladys was so obviously sure of herself and of her own attractions that she would not have used the slightest subterfuge had she had designs (however futile) on my own poor self. I was not alarmed. Only when she turned the conversation to her daughter did I feel that we were talking about me.

"Everyone is so sympathetic about Fiona," she said with a shrug, "and, of course, the poor darling had much to suffer about and is a perfect angel. But there are assets in her condition. Whatever she manages to accomplish in life, being against such great odds, will be more worthwhile. She won't have the bitterness that so many of us have, of seeing what a mess she's made of her natural advantages."

"You don't mean that *you* have? Of yours?"

"Why not?"

"But you're such a success, Gladys!"

"Don't make me laugh. All my life I've thrown things to the winds. My landscape is knee deep in litter."

"What have you ever thrown away?"

But Gladys was not going to be tied down. She hurried on ahead of me now, ascending more rapidly, as if to give emphasis to her feeling "It's a crime, the way we leave everything to the young! Oh, we warn them, yes. We tell them they're impatient, inexperienced, reckless, naive, green. But when you come right down to it, we let them make all the basic decisions they're not qualified to make — what life to lead, what career to choose, what person to marry. Yes, we let the poor creatures make their beds, and then we sternly tell them to lie in them!"

"But surely your marriage is happy, Gladys. And didn't you choose for yourself?"

"Did I?" She turned back to mark the pitch of her impending confidence. I saw that she was determined to be indiscreet. But why? I had half an inclination to warn her, but she plunged ahead. "I fell head over heels for the handsomest man in his class at Yale. I was nineteen. Heyward was perfect. He had no vices; he was an athlete; he came of a good family. And he was going off to war. He was probably going to be killed! When he proposed to me after an opera matinee in Bryant Park, I rushed home to tell my parents. They raised their hands simultaneously and cried, 'We couldn't be more pleased!' God! I think a little voice must have tried to warn me at that moment. But I brushed it aside. 'We couldn't be more pleased!' Death knell!"

"You mean you wish you hadn't married him?"

"I mean that my whole life shouldn't have been decided then and there for the simple reason that I wanted to sleep with Heyward Satterlee. There. Have I shocked you?"

"I suppose you have. I thought you and Heyward were so happy together."

"We are. As happy as most people, anyway. I'm only saying that we make very important choices on very slim grounds. I think what first attracted me to Heyward was the peculiar glow in his eyes. It was moisture, probably. His eyes are quite dry now."

"That's what lawyers call a failure of consideration. The contract falls."

"But mine stands up!"

"Would you go back to arranged marriages?"

"What good would that have done me?" She raised her arms in a picture of mock despair. "My parents would have chosen Heyward!" She strode on rapidly now. We had almost reached the top of Beehive where there was no view, as it was covered with trees. "Why do I tell you these things? What is it about you, Roger, that makes me gas on so?"

What indeed?

When we arrived at my home we found Daddy and Mother on the terrace with Aleck and Lila Nickerson. Aleck Nickerson, rotund, bald, bright eyed, was an editor of *The New York Times* and was considered, after Felix and my father, the leading brain of Seal Cove. His manners were very gentle, and he voiced his carefully thought out opinions in a most moderate tone. He smoked constantly and watched people carefully with his small, fixed eyes. He seemed always to be waiting for the world to turn itself into news. Lila, his wife, was one of those persons who just miss the top in every quality. Her nose was too large and her chin too pointed for beauty; her manners were too good not to seem insincere; her wit was too sharp for profundity and her laugh too quick not to hurt. She wanted the world and found it wanting. In Butterfield Bay, where Aleck, like Felix, was in constant demand, she missed the intellectual play of Seal Cove, but in the latter community she found the women frumpy and even her revered parents faintly ridiculous.

As Felix said of her once, she was an unhappy woman who wanted everyone else to be unhappy.

As I now read this over, I see that I have made her somewhat less attractive than she was. It must be remembered that I am looking back with considerable hindsight. Lila was generally considered good company. She liked to own people, it was true, but it was not altogether unpleasant to be owned by Lila. She thought she owned Felix; she even thought that as small a catch as myself, being Felix's disciple, was part of her property. She regarded the intrusion of Gladys Satterlee into Seal Cove as an act of simple trespass. As Gladys now drew the entire attention of Daddy and Aleck, Lila moved over to the bar table where I was mixing drinks.

"Are you Paris, Roger, abducting *la belle* Hélène to Troy?"

"Is that how you see it?"

"Or are you a spy, with a crafty Greek in a Trojan horse? I think the latter. I think you have her here to deliver us into her power."

"Do you think she needs the likes of *me*? Why, Gladys has but to appear on the border, and our troops would flock to her standard!"

Lila did her best to suppress the instant irritation in her tone. "Ah, but she needs a subtler victory. She wants to deliver us to the enemy in such a way that we shall not even know what has happened."

"Why should she be so merciful?"

"Because she was a problem. She is married to a dunce. If the borders are to be opened, she must be sure that he will be well received. Heyward Satterlee has never been to any house in Seal Cove. He has been too afraid. Now that she wants us, she must ensure his good reception."

"But I thought Heyward did exactly as he was told."

"Far from it. He can be very difficult. Dunces always are.

Besides, she has Felix to cope with. Felix would not want Heyward to be unhappy."

"Are they really such friends?"

"It seems strange, doesn't it? But not when you put it together. You must picture them in New Haven in 1910. Each had what the other lacked. Heyward had the glorious looks, the athletic reputation, the social position. Felix had his genius and charm, but it was not an Anglo-Saxon genius or an Anglo-Saxon charm. And he was an intellectual, a Jew. It was a symbiotic relationship. Felix, of course, soon left poor Heyward a million miles behind, but he has always been generous, and he remembers early favors: weekends with the Satterlees in Newport and so forth. Oh, yes, Felix is loyal. And Heyward . . . well, to have been the friend of Felix Leitner is simply the one great event of his humdrum life."

"But the Satterlees and the Leitners have been coming to Maine for years! Why, all of a sudden, should it be so important for Gladys to conquer Seal Cove?"

"Why, indeed?" Lila glanced over at the object of our discussion sitting between Daddy and Aleck. "Why should she be acting the Lorelei with your gallant father? And pulverizing my dear husband! Poor Aleck, he has no defenses against a woman with an atom of sophistication. His farm background betrays itself! But look who approaches. Don't try to tell *me*, Roger Cutter, that a certain pundit didn't have wind of your lady's proposed visit!"

And, sure enough, I looked up to behold Felix Leitner approaching our dock in his scull. It was so clear a day that he had been able to row down the stream from his camp and right across the cove. As he got out of his boat and leaned down to raise it up and place it on the dock, I suddenly felt that he was showing off his strength. I looked up at Lila, and I did not like her smile.

Mother, of course, asked Felix to stay for lunch, and the seven of us were soon gathered about the long log table on our porch. Daddy poured wine and talked about Hitler. He was inclined to think that the Nazis were bluffing and that a firm resistance would make them back down. Felix was less sure. He suspected a paralysis of will in the democracies, the hangover of a guilt complex at having won the last war and lost the peace.

"What do *you* think?" he asked, turning suddenly to Gladys.

"Oh, we poor women. What can we do when you gods thunder?"

"But you have the most important function of all."

"And what is that?"

"To ask the right questions."

Gladys smiled as she gazed over the water. "Very well. Let me try one. You pointed out in your article in the *Atlantic* last month that the Nazis face a dilemma. They depend absolutely on leadership — they must have a great Führer. Yet their system of education — or obfuscation, as you called it — is designed to produce only followers, and servile ones at that. Suppose we wait until they're led by an idiot?"

"Very good. If they'll give us the time."

"Oh, we can always stall, can't we? And in the meantime we could be arming. What I can't see is why, if we are so inclined to lose peaces, we think we can afford to win wars?"

Lila, who could no longer contain her jealousy, interrupted sharply. "It's one thing to lose a peace. It's quite another, I'm afraid you'll find, Mrs. Satterlee, to lose a war."

"Germany did. So did Russia. Yet everyone trembles before them now."

"Germany would dictate a monstrous peace," Felix suggested.

"Isn't that what you said we did in 1919?"

"There may be degrees in monstrosity."

"Perhaps in Butterfield Bay, the Nazis seem less monstrous," Lila surmised with a sneer. "They might prefer Hitler to Roosevelt. What is it they say of Mussolini? That he made the trains run on time?"

But Gladys seemed merely amused. "Do they say that?"

"Well, don't they?"

Gladys shrugged, as she smiled again at Felix. "I'm afraid that's not the right question."

Roger Cutter (4)

THE LASSITER TROYS gave their larger dinner parties on Saturdays, and nobody in Seal Cove presumed to entertain on that night without first checking to see if it were clear. There was always a strong nucleus of the principal Troy friends at Troy parties, but the addition of weekend house guests, sometimes very important persons, gave the needed variety. Dinner in the big room with all the antlers and fangs was served from a buffet, and the guests seated themselves as they chose, at three long tables. After dinner we always played parlor games, such as charades or twenty questions.

I enjoyed the long cocktail hour and the animated talk at dinner, usually dominated by my father and Felix, with an occasional roar from our venerable host, but I dreaded the games. Nobody was exempted, except my modest and retiring mother, and participation was noisy and hilarious. There was always the danger that Mrs. Troy, a devilishly resourceful old woman, would come up with some new and more embarrassing one. One of my regular Seal Cove nightmares was that I was made to strip bare and parade down one of the long tables before the gaping guests.

Mrs. Troy was inclined to be superior about Butterfield Bay

and to accuse its visitors to the social precincts of Seal Cove of "slumming," but she always had one or two carefully selected Butterfield couples at her Saturday nights. The first time that Heyward and Gladys Satterlee appeared at one of these, I found myself chosen by the former to be his guide and interpreter. Heyward seemed enchanted by everything: the cabin, the game heads, the distinguished hosts, the bright, alert assembly. Even Mrs. Troy could not have detected condescension behind his smiling naiveté.

"Of course, I know we're only asked because of Gladys," he confided in me with cheerful humility. "Nobody here would want a duffer like me. Even Felix never asks me to his parties. No, I mean it! Why should he? I come over once a week, and we go fishing. That's good enough for old Heyward. Truly. That way I have the great man all to myself. And sometimes he dines with us, because he likes a smart party. He picks up bits of news, you know. Why not? That's his stock in trade, and I'm tickled pink if I can help him. Every time Gladys and I catch something in our net, we ask, Will he do for Felix? But these people tonight — they beat everything! I thought they'd be discussing the Rhineland or the Saar Territory, but do you know what old man Troy's been talking about? Shakespeare! God, I haven't read any Shakespeare since I took Billy Phelps's course at Yale. But I remember Troy in *Macbeth*. He used a beam of light for the dagger, and it jumped all about the stage to lead him to Duncan. We thought it very clever."

When I turned to hear the discussion, I found that it was indeed about Shakespeare. Lassiter Troy was holding forth, in his deep, mellifluous tones, on the final comedies.

"It is pleasant to contemplate that, after the dark, melancholy years that produced the sublime tragedies of *Lear* and *Hamlet*, our bard should have found peace in the semi-retirement of Stratford. The bitter rivalries, the savage strivings of

London, were past. In his rose garden at New House, he was able to conceive the enchanted fairyland of *The Tempest,* the sweet rusticity of *The Winter's Tale,* the glorious dirge in *Cymbeline.* He was concerned now with flowers, with songs, with magic, with reconciliation. Oh, I know why Lord Tennyson directed that his copy of *Cymbeline* should be buried with him! I have told Prudence that I want *The Tempest* placed in my lifeless hands."

Daddy now jumped noisily into the fray, like an antichorus. A stranger to Seal Cove ways might have thought the evening had been rehearsed.

"With all due respect, Lassiter, I am compelled to call that tommyrot." Some of the new guests, including Heyward, audibly gasped, but Troy waved his arms benignly and nodded his head to urge his old friend to continue. "One must have a very strong preconception in favor of a tranquil fairyland to close one's eyes to the monsters in these last comedies. Why, they outdo Goneril and Iago! How benign is the queen in *Cymbeline* who tests her poisons on the servants? Or Posthumous, who orders the murder of his wife on evidence of infidelity that wouldn't have fooled even Othello? Or Leontes, who exposes his newborn babe to the wilderness because its mother happened to smile at his oldest friend? No, no, Lassiter, you shan't persuade me that our poet had achieved any lasting peace. On the contrary, I suspect that he came back to Stratford to find a middle-aged, nagging wife who made him pine for London and the Globe!"

"It occurs to me that you may both be right," Felix now intervened, in his slow, level voice, which seemed almost to chew the words and which commanded the instant attention of all. "Or perhaps, by the same token, that you may both be wrong. I hazard a different theory. I follow Lytton Strachey. I suggest that Shakespeare had moved beyond plots and beyond characters in this final phase. There is no consistency between the sudden passion and sudden repentance of Leontes. There is none between the wickedness and patriotism of Cymbeline's queen. Or between the philosophical calm and crabbed petulance of Prospero. The librettos leap over time and space. They spurn logic and sequence. Knotty problems are solved by magic; the long lost are found again, and ancient wrongs are dramatically righted. What is Shakespeare up to? What has happened to the subtle psychologist who created Macbeth and Cleopatra?"

A pause was followed by Gladys's sudden, clear "What?"

"The words ran away with him!" Felix exclaimed, turning at once to her, his voice rising to a pitch of enthusiasm unusual to him. "The words that had always been his love, his passion, suddenly ceased to be his tools. He gave himself up to them; he became their slave, not their master. So character went by the board, plot went by the board, nothing was left but a peerless poetry caught in a void. Look at *Timon.* Its plot is absurd and its hero a bore, but his tirades are greater than Lear's. Shakespeare's final victory was a Pyrrhic one. The words destroyed his plays. It was a love-death, a warning to all of us here!"

Mrs. Troy now interrupted to herd us to the buffet. I filled my plate and took the empty seat between Gladys and Lila, who talked, or rather sparred, across me. Gladys made a bit of an ass of herself. She was a very clever woman, but there were certain things she never learned. When literary people talk about literature, they may be sentimental, like Lassiter Troy; or violent, like Daddy; or intent upon novel concepts, like Felix — but they are always involved. They do not talk merely for effect, as Gladys now did, unaware that she was enunciating one of the most banal theories in Shakespearean criticism.

"I've always thought that when Prospero broke his wand, it was Shakespeare saying farewell to the stage," she remarked in a high, faintly melancholy tone, intended, no doubt, to show the depth of her feeling. "When he says: 'Our revels now are ended,' isn't he thinking of the wonderful years at the Globe, now ending, and all those golden comedies and tragedies? Leaving 'not a rack behind'? If he had only known!"

I should have blushed for Gladys had not the yellow stare in Lila's eyes made me feel sorry for her instead.

"Did you hear that, Felix?" Lila called down the table. "Mrs. Satterlee has a novel theory about *The Tempest*. That Prospero is really Shakespeare and his magic, the playwright's art. So, when he breaks his wand, we know it must be the last play. Isn't it wonderful that such an interesting idea should come to us from Butterfield Bay? We thought they only cared for parties there!"

Felix's tone betrayed nothing. "I think it *is* an interesting idea. And very likely true."

Gladys might have made a mistake, but it did not take her more than a minute to change her tactics, recover lost ground and carry the campaign deep into enemy territory. "Oh, of course, we're hopelessly fashionable in Butterfield Bay, Mrs. Nickerson. I plead guilty to that. We are poor butterflies. But what else do you leave us? You ladies at Seal have all the lore and the learning. Oh, you are formidable! But do you know something? If Shakespeare were alive in Maine today, I wonder if he wouldn't spend more of his time in Butterfield than in Seal. What do *you* think of that, Professor Cutter? Aren't great artists and writers notoriously drawn to gilded courts and lovely women?"

I marveled at her skill. Not only had she managed to put Lila, who prided herself on moving with equal ease in both communities, in the position of a dowdy bluestocking who

would be hopelessly out of place in any smart
had somehow divined that my father would take h
could not possibly have known that she had touched
of his favorite subjects: the vulnerability of the creative a
to the lure of society.

"Quite so, dear lady," he boomed. "When Dr. Johnson was
asked if he would rather meet a duke or a great writer, he said
a duke, of course. For, once he had known the duke, he could
meet all the writers in the world!"

"I wonder if that would hold today," Lila protested, obviously irked. "Not that I suggest we have yet achieved the
classless society. But we have come a long way from Dr. Johnson. Certainly dukes aren't what they were."

"Nor are literary men," said Leo Troy unexpectedly. He was
our host's only son, a small, tense bachelor engineer of fifty
who was reputed to be a near genius. "I believe that only two
classes of people will survive the coming revolution; the only
two that no society, capitalist or communist, can get on without. These are the technicians and the beautiful women. Well,
I'm a technician, and I've chosen Mrs. Satterlee!"

A round of surprised laughter from the whole table greeted
this.

"What will you do with Heyward?" Felix demanded with a
chuckle.

"Oh, I'll send him to Siberia with the rest of you!"

At this, the general conversation broke up, and after dinner,
as usual, we played charades. Felix and Mrs. Troy were cap-
tains of the rival teams, and I noted that Felix chose Gladys
as his first recruit. But not till near the end of the evening did
they act out a word together. It was "cloak" from the quotation
"Not alone my inky cloak, good mother," and it took them
only a moment to do it, but that moment became fixed in my
memory and in the memory of all who were then present.

ıy. The little scene was simple and
ce of cardboard around her neck to
understood was a ruff collar, walked
n easy, loping stride and then paused
truction in her path. Felix hurried for-
coat and flung it across her path. Smiling,
ıd we all roared "cloak." It was easy, of
ınd Felix remained for a small fraction of
time, s maybe, after the guess was made, still
forming their tableau, she looking down at him, charmingly
smiling, he crouching, his hand still holding the coat, gazing
up at her, his eyes aglow. There was an immediate communication to the whole room of a new relationship.

Then, to everybody's embarrassment, somebody clapped. It
was Heyward.

"Bravo!" he absurdly cried, absurdly meaning it.

The next day, I had a talk with Frances Leitner at the Seal
Cove Sailing Club. She, herself, did not sail, but her fifteen-
year-old son, Frank, did, and she drove him there almost every
day. I had just come in from an afternoon cruise when I saw
her with her knitting on the terrace. She waved to me and
asked me to have a drink.

"You've been spending a lot of time in Butterfield this summer," she commented when I sat down. "We hardly see you
at all any more."

"An extra man is much in demand there. They make it
pleasant for one."

I must endeavor to be fair in my description of Frances
Leitner, for her subsequent strong dislike of me could well
bring down on my head the suspicion of resentment. I think
I have none, but a chronicler must always be on his guard
against it. Frances at the time was forty-seven, exactly her
husband's age. Unfortunately, where he was a splendidly fit
example for his years, she seemed older than hers. She was a

small gray woman, with a tendency to roundness; nothing about her figure or presence did justice to her admirable brain or elevated character. She was reputed to be a kind of saint; she hardly ever lost her temper, or even her calm. She would sit at a party at Seal Cove, absolutely still except for her busy hands, her mild, lined, pleasant countenance turned to the speaker, her lips fixed in that half smile that preceded her invariably intelligent qualification to every uttered generality. Frances's concern for humanity had almost obliterated her interest in the things that so many women (at least in her day) cared about: clothes, parties, jewels, houses, all the paraphernalia of social life. She was too bright and had too keen a sense of humor to let herself become a bore about this, but I always felt the drop in her interest whenever the topic changed from the broad to the particular, or whenever it even bordered on "gossip," as she was prone to label any discussion, however friendly, of the personalities of our acquaintances. I sometimes wondered if "people" had not replaced individuals in Frances's heart and if this perhaps was not the rather unlovable characteristic of saints, but if so, she made a notable exception for Felix. There was never any question that he occupied the central position in her life.

"I've never seen Felix more brilliant than he was last night," I began, a bit mischievously, for I knew that she thought his brilliance was wasted at parties.

"You mean at that silly game?"

"He was much applauded."

"That kind of applause doesn't do Felix any good."

"It doesn't?"

"He likes it too much. Felix has quite enough appetite for social life as it is. He doesn't need any encouragement."

"Oh, come, Frances, you're being too severe. If ever a man deserved a little relaxation, it's Felix."

"Relaxation, yes. But Butterfield Bay is not relaxation."

"I had thought we were in Seal Cove last night."

"Don't play games with me, Roger. We had a delegation from Butterfield Bay, as you well know. They changed the character of the whole evening. A party to us may be simply a diversion. To them it is simply the whole of life."

"You take them too seriously."

"Because I see them so clearly. They corrupt people." Frances's smile and soft tone did not in the least mitigate the rigor of her sentence.

"Why should they want to do that?"

"It may be a form of self-defense. Perhaps an instinct. Society people arrange the outward appearance of their lives so as to make the observer think they are not only attractive but virtuous. If the observer has been inclined to consider them a public nuisance, and the system that fosters them an economic anachronism, he may now be persuaded to moderate his views. It's the old business of Ramsay MacDonald being tamed by the Tories who put him in court breeches."

"You can't think Felix would change his opinions because of a few dinner parties in Butterfield Bay?"

"Can't I? Felix in the last four years has been moving steadily to the right."

"But that's been the maturing of his vision!"

"Well, I don't think it desirable that such maturing, if that's what it is, should be accelerated by society people. Did you hear what he said about Shakespeare falling victim in the end to his own words?"

"Yes. And I thought it beautifully put."

Frances sniffed. "He was describing his own danger. Felix has always been fascinated by words. I believe there are times when he would like to substitute them for actions."

"But words are his life!"

"Words can never be life. Not in themselves. Words are aids

to action. The most beautiful thought in the world is not worth a fig if it isn't made to help people."

"But it isn't Felix's job to implement his own ideas! There have to be people whose only role is to comment and guide."

"I won't positively deny that, though there's a good deal I could say against it. Let's leave it aside for the moment. What I affirm is that Felix's role should be more than commenting. When I first met him, he wanted to change the world. Now I sometimes fear he wants simply to entertain it."

"But with the highest form of entertainment! As Shakespeare entertains us with *Hamlet*."

"That's art, Roger. Don't get things mixed up. Felix is concerned with politics and government. There's no borderline in the fight for a good society between doing and thinking. They must fuse."

"They needn't!"

Frances saw that she was not going to convince me. Her slightly broadened smile was her way of indicating that she now gave it up. "Well, if you want to put him in an ivory tower, let's see that it *is* ivory. Let's see that it's tall and clean, with a fine view of the world below. And not a shingle monstrosity in Butterfield Bay."

"You just don't like Gladys Satterlee."

"I certainly don't!" Frances's whole tone changed now, and I had that uneasy sense of lost security that comes to us when an adult who has always treated us, however kindly and politely, as a child, suddenly admits us to the company of grownups. It can be flattering, even exhilarating, but there is a corresponding loss of exemption. "I certainly do *not* like Gladys Satterlee. The woman is rotten to the core. She sees that Felix has a quality beyond anything that exists in her tawdry world, and she wants to stamp it out. Oh, she doesn't *think* that she wants to stamp it out. No, she believes she wants to wear it around her neck, like a glittering diamond. But once it's around that neck, it will lose its glitter. Count on it, Roger."

"Of course I have to believe you're exaggerating. Probably on purpose."

"Of course you do. Here come our drinks. Let's talk of something else."

The next morning, early, Felix called me for a walk up Blaine's Peak. I had never seen him in a mood of such strenuous cheer. I had almost to run up the mountain after him. At the top he stared out over the ocean, like stout Cortez, or as Keats should have put it, like Balboa.

"Would you believe, Roger, that the same summer could mark the happiest time in a man's whole life *and* the most miserable? That ineffable joy and atrocious agony can be simultaneous?"

I had only to read my answer in the burning pink of his eyes.

Gladys Leitner's Account of the Summer of 1938, Written for Roger Cutter in 1974

W̲E̲ ̲A̲L̲L̲ ̲T̲E̲N̲D̲ to think that our parents lived under fixed and inhibiting rules and that we know much more of life than they ever could have. Yet I am sure that my daughter, Fiona, thinks there is little to choose between her grandmother's life and mine. Distinctions blur as we look back more than one generation. How much do I distinguish between the moral codes of my great-grandmothers and my great-greats'?

Still, looking back on my youth, my mother seems to me an innocent, even if she was an innocent wrapped in whalebone. I was born in the eighteen-nineties; she in the seventies. Romantic ideas may have permeated her generation; they may have considered themselves flamboyant and passionate compared to their own, more composed and placid progenitors (illusions perhaps of the daguerreotype). Some of them had affairs; a few even divorced. But my contemporaries were of the First World War; they drank too much and smoked too much and married too much. I insist that the "generation gap" was at its widest in 1919.

Mother's conservatism, I must admit, seemed quite voluntary. It appeared to emanate not so much from a repression exercised upon her by people or doctrines as from her own simple enchantment with life exactly as it was. It did not matter to her that Ephraim Dunne, my father, was a gentle, unimaginative, methodical gentleman who had obviously married her because she was the daughter of the president of the Bank of Commerce. She seemed just as pleased with the kind of mild, exclusive devotion that he offered her as she was with the garden parties and card games and card droppings and dinner parties (oh, the length of them!) that made up so much of her very routinized existence. Mother did not see why anyone should want anything more than she had. America was the greatest of nations and had the greatest future; business was constantly improving the lot of the human race, and science would eventually find a solution to all the horrid diseases that threatened even a woman as robustly healthy as Isabel Dunne.

I grew up in New York and Butterfield Bay, like all the other children of my parents' friends. When we were in our teens we talked boldly of the possibility of "platonic" friendships with men, and by the time we were debutantes we believed that every woman's life should contain at least one "great passion." Only so, we proclaimed, could a woman be "fulfilled." We did not consider that our mothers had ever been fulfilled. Their entire generation (think of it!) had been spiritually wasted, with the possible exceptions of Cousin Maud Tilson, who had run off with her son's violin teacher, and Father's college roommate, who was supposed to have had an affair with the diva Olive Fremstad.

As I grew older, I grew a bit bolder. I took dancing lessons and acting lessons and even once played a maid's part in a parlor comedy on Broadway. I smoked and drank in circles where it was still considered daring to do so and went a good deal further with men than other girls did. But not too far. I was basically a fake. I was basically my mother's daughter. When I made my war marriage to Heyward Satterlee I was still a virgin. And when he returned from France in 1919 — my soldier, my hero, my lover — when I went with bursting heart to meet his troop ship at the pier, I knew at the first sight of his shining face on the gangplank that I had made the mistake of my life!

What will seem scarcely credible to young people in 1974 is that I remained faithful to Heyward for almost two decades. But fidelity was not so unfashionable in those days as it is now, and Heyward was an amiable and adoring husband who let me do anything I wanted and bought far more things for me than either of us could afford. I lived through the roaring twenties and went to a thousand parties. I think I even made him happy.

But, oh, dear me, I tried to give him some bad times! If I was going to live vicariously, it would be with a vengeance. I turned life into a book, written by myself, of which I, of course, was the heroine. I would write letters that I didn't send, sometimes to people I didn't know or who didn't even exist, and would leave them about, as if to invite a reading. I kept a diary with no other purpose, that I could make out, than that of entering my near indiscretions. My carelessly (or carefully?) scattered documents kept Heyward only too painfully abreast, not of what was going on, but of what I wanted to have go on, and there would be noisy scenes, which I would then write up in full detail in my diary. Was he made wretched? Or did the whole business simply titillate him? I was never sure.

I always cherished the idea that one day I would go in for the real thing. So many of my friends did. There *had* to be something more in life than what I enjoyed! But Heyward was always so good, and then, also, he was very connubial. For years I compromised; I kept men dangling in attendance. There were epicene young men who did not in the least object to my limitations, and beefier types who did. But all the while, I was looking, waiting, hoping for that . . . all right, that *prince* who would never come!

In the spring of 1938, desperate and forty-two, I made a crucial decision. I was going to find my great passion before the year was out. I was not going to wait any longer; I was going to give romance and nature a deliberate shove, and the man who seemed to be directly in my chosen path was Mark Truro.

He had always intrigued me. He had been given so much: a huge fortune; fine, aristocratic, graying good looks; sleepy, sexy, laughing eyes; grace of bearing; a sharp wit and a liberal philosophy. What more could a godchild of luck demand? Of course, many of my crowd detested him for what they called his radicalism. Some even said he was a Red. "He's so bloody rich," they would sneer, "that he doesn't give a tinker's damn what that madman in the White House is up to." We had emerged from the worst of the depression, but none of us had anything like what he had had in 1929. I was spending capital in a way that my mother thought damnable. Heyward disapproved, but he made it a rule not to interfere with what I did with my own money. I suppose I figured — if I thought about it at all — that he or Mother would have enough to keep me off the streets if I spent it all. I was becoming a great one for seizing the day.

Mark Truro had been three times divorced, and he liked to make it known that he would never marry again. The children of his various unions lived mostly with their mothers, but they were apt to spend their summers with him at The Mount, that ugly old castle of his long-deceased grandfather's in Butterfield Bay, now so oddly hung with Mark's collection of modern paintings. The children adored him; the servants adored him; the sycophant house guests, employees of the liberal periodicals and institutions that he supported, pretended to adore him. Butterfield Bay, dazzled and disapproving, watched him warily. But everything — adoration, distrust, even outright hostility — amused Mark. He seemed as incapable of anger as he was of reverence.

My contemporaries liked to accuse the younger generation of silly romantic illusions, but in fact my daughter, Fiona, and her friends were hard boiled compared to me and mine. I conceived the crazy idea that Mark Truro, an aging Byronic corsair, hardened by disillusionment, immune to flattery, despairing of love, walled up in his rugged tower of cynicism, was now ripe for the one great passion of his lifetime. I even pictured him as a Lord Nelson, weary of victories and adulation, and myself as a Lady Hamilton, seeking something deeper than the frivolous flirtations of the Neapolitan court. We had always been good, if casual, friends, had always laughed lightheartedly at the same things, but Mark, whose sensitivity to women was uncanny, picked up my intensification of feeling almost the very day it occurred. He promptly reacted.

Heyward and I were now invited to every event at The Mount; we went out on the great sailing yacht; we played in the desperately serious croquet matches on Mark's lawn, every square inch of which had been tested by a leveler. When Heyward went down to New York — as he did (quite unnecessarily, I thought) every other week to preside conscientiously over market operations, which his subordinates could have done as well or better than he — Mark would place me at the end of his table as his hostess. He did so as calmly as a feudal seigneur helping himself to the services of an underlord. Did not the latter's very wife and children belong to him?

I waited with carefully suppressed excitement for Mark to

make the first serious move. We had talked intimately of ourselves and of our lives but never of our feelings toward each other. I shall not relate that I had said nothing to Mark that I could not have said to Heyward, because I had said a great many harsh things to Mark about my poor husband and how he bored me, but I had said nothing to him about my own heart that Heyward could not have heard. Mark told me about his children's troubles and his own dissatisfaction with his role in political life. He wanted something more, something larger, something more challenging. I thought I knew what form this something would take.

I knew that Mark would not fumble, that when he was ready, he would move with absolute assurance. I imagined his fixing those blue eyes on me gravely, taking my hand gently in his and saying: "Now, Gladys, don't you think the time has come when you and I can express what we really feel?" But when our relationship at last developed to its crisis, it did so in a very different way.

On an afternoon's sail as far north as Mount Desert Island, Mark and I were sitting on the divan on the fantail, contemplating the gray and green shoreline. The children and other guests were up forward; it was already their discreet habit to leave us alone when the occasion seemed to invite personal communication. Mark had just left the tiller to his skipper; he had on his commodore's cap and was smoking a pipe.

"Let me tell you something, Gladys," he began, with what struck me as a look of constraint, rare indeed for him. "Something that is not easy to say."

"Then I must assume it is not romantic, for you have always found *those* things very easy to say. Poor Gladys! She shouldn't have got her hopes up."

"It is not romantic, and yet it is."

"A conundrum? Take it to Seal Cove. I'm told Mrs. Troy adores them."

"A plague on Mrs. Troy! Listen to me, Gladys. You and I understand each other only too well. We are two tired world-lings. There isn't really much that we could give each other."

"You mean you've been trifling with me? Trifling with an innocent girl's affections?"

"We could perhaps amuse each other for a season. We could even fancy that we were hurt, bereft . . ."

"You won't marry me! Say it! You wouldn't have dared to treat me so had my old father lived! But I see it all. We are only the playthings of you men."

"Gladys, if you will only be serious . . ."

"Don't flatter yourself that nothing can make up for your withdrawn love. A diamond necklace might make all the difference."

"What would Heyward say?"

"I'd tell him it was paste. Haven't you read *any* French novels?"

"I insist on saying what I sat down here to say. Despite your wall of brittle persiflage. I know perfectly well what you're up to, Gladys Satterlee. You're bored. You have a sense of waste, of futility. You and I together would simply compound each other's faults. But there *is* a man, in my opinion one of the most remarkable men of our time, who admires you deeply. He is someone who could do as much for you as you for him."

I stared, too astonished to be indignant. "Are you by any chance speaking of Felix Leitner?"

"I am."

"Has he told you this?"

"We have not spoken of you. Except as a charming friend."

"Thanks!"

"Now don't go middle class on me, Gladys. Be large of spirit. I know Felix very well. I can imagine what you represent to him."

"What? Society? Parties? Champagne?"

"No. Charm in living. Beauty in living. Life as an art. Life as something to wonder at. Felix has toiled and struggled, surrounded by people of high thinking and high ideals. He has existed in a kind of intellectual monastery. Look at that drab little wife of his. All she can think of is her poor and needy. Felix must rescue the downtrodden multitudes! The poor guy's almost forgotten that a man has to love as well as think."

I found myself rapidly, almost frenetically, reviewing the recent evenings when I had sat next to Felix. They had given me, certainly, considerable pleasure, but the pleasure had been qualified by the fear of making a fool of myself. What could I say to a man with a brain like that? Yet I had also to admit he had been cheerful, attentive, seemingly appreciative. Had he not been the great Felix Leitner, I might have preferred him to Mark. Had he not been the great Felix Leitner, I might have noticed that he was interested!

"So," I replied, in the same bantering tone, "I am to fill the emotional gap in the great man's life? You have it all worked out. But what is he to do for *me*? Or doesn't that matter? I suppose I should consider myself lucky if he even deigns to notice me."

"Of course I have it all worked out. One has no business interfering in other peoples' lives unless one has it all worked out. What Felix can give you is something you've been pining for: the life of the mind. You've spent all of your existence with your intellectual inferiors: your mother, Heyward, this whole vapid crowd up here. Fiona, I suspect, may be as bright as they come, but you can't make a life out of a daughter. You need Felix. He needs you. It's a union made in heaven."

"In heaven! I should rather have thought it was the other place. What about Heyward? What about poor Mrs. Leitner?"

"Frankly, I don't give a damn about Heyward. Or about Frances Leitner. I'm not saying that you and Felix should run off together. I'm not even suggesting you should have an affair, though I can't imagine that any friendship between two such electric personalities would end any other way. If so, your spouses should try to be understanding."

"Mark Truro, I think you must be the most immoral man I've ever known."

"Amoral, call it. I've never believed that marriage passes title to another human being. Felix has outgrown Frances. You started off too tall for Heyward. They should allow you both a degree of latitude. If not . . . *tant pis*. I have no patience with possessive spouses. Live and let live, I say."

A steward now came up with a tray, and I was very glad indeed to have a drink. My mind was a tumult, but what kept bobbing to the surface, like a piece of Ivory soap in a frothy bath, was the fine, fresh white, clean, brand new idea that I might be seriously attractive to such a man as Felix Leitner. Was he "gone" on me, as we used to say? Had he confessed as much to Mark? Certainly he had spent more time in Butterfield Bay that summer than ever before. Everyone had noticed it.

"Admit the idea intrigues you, Gladys."

Mark should not have said this. It threw too hard in my face the crude fact that in ten minutes' time I had switched an errant fancy from him to Felix. Who the hell did Mark Truro think he was to play God with the rest of us?

"And what does our Mark need?" I demanded, in a sweet sarcastic tone. "He knows what *we* need, but what of him? Or is he above needs? No, not quite. He has a little secret. He has grown tired of people who want things from him. First they wanted his money. Then they wanted his parties and good times. Then they wanted his beautiful body. And finally they grew greedier yet. They wanted his love! Poor Mark! Even in his great castle he is not safe. Even in his white yacht breasting the billows. So now he dreams of a little girl who will give him all and ask for nothing."

"And where will he find her?" Mark's rather quivering smile showed that I had hit a sore spot. I hastened to drive the point home.

"Not in Butterfield Bay. Or even in Seal Cove. No, she will come from what my mother calls simpler folk. She may be a stenographer in your estate office, or the daughter of a caretaker, or merely a street urchin glimpsed by your highness from the window of your Hispano Suiza. But her love will be total. It will make up for her other lacks: birth, position, education — all. It will be the climax of the tempestuous Truro career. King Cophetua will marry his beggar maid!" Here I paused for several moments, and then deliberately smashed the silence with a shrill ending: "Next chapter? She *takes* the doting old boy. Right down to his last red cent!"

Mark flushed, which was as near as he ever came to showing anger. Then he rose without comment to go back to the tiller. I had certainly not made myself agreeable, but I had predicted, as it turned out, very much what actually happened when he married the little Murphy girl. Of course, she didn't get his last red cent, but a "usually reliable source" has since informed me that he paid three million to be rid of her.

＊　＊　＊

When I lunched the following week at The Mount (Mark never harbored resentment) I was hardly surprised to find myself seated by Felix. We were both in the highest spirits. I wondered if Mark had had a similar talk with him, and if he, like myself, was covering his embarrassment with exhilaration. Never had he seemed better looking to me. The long, thin, bony face under the high wide brow was extraordinarily rejuvenated by the large, blue-green eyes; and the curly, reddish blond hair was almost boyish. What was particularly attractive to me was the way he seemed to vary between an almost delicate, romantic, poetic figure of the deepest sensitivity, and one rather cruder. If his eyes were soulful, his chuckle was certainly earthy. Beside him, even Mark seemed almost haggard.

I was too wise to ask him about the absent Frances, but when he brought her into the conversation, I tried to be frank.

"I'm surprised she lets you loose among the beauties of Butterfield Bay. Is it really quite complimentary to a husband to trust him so?"

"I could ask the same thing about Heyward and you."

"But that's altogether different. Heyward can hardly expect me to sit home while he makes perfectly unnecessary trips to New York."

"Why do you call them unnecessary?"

"Because they are. Heyward's like my father. He thinks he's doing something in his office just by being there. Men are different from women that way."

"Is that your idea of Wall Street? That it's only a formality?"

"Only half of Wall Street. The half made up of people trying to look like tycoons. Of course, there's another half: that of the real tycoon. But Heyward doesn't know the difference."

"Aren't you being a bit hard on him?"

I turned to face him squarely at this. "I know that a woman's considered a fool to run down her husband to another man. But I'm not going to treat you as another man. You're supposed to be a paragon. Very well. Heyward's an ass. You know that as well as I."

Felix became inscrutable. "Heyward's my friend."

"In picking you as a friend he showed that he didn't have to be an ass. But he's lived on that friendship too long."

He sighed. "We certainly have different spouses, then. Nobody has ever called Frances an ass."

"Ah, but you're begging my original question. Why, if she's

not an ass, does she unleash you to roam so freely in Butterfield Bay? Surely she doesn't think you're playing bridge right now at one of my mother's sedate afternoons?"

"No. She knows just where I am. And she probably has a good idea of whom I'm sitting by. Which may have something to do with a favor she asked of me today."

"Oh?"

He closed his lips the least bit grimly now. "She asked me not to go so often to Butterfield Bay. She suggested that I give it up altogether until next summer. You see, I'm right. She's hardly an ass."

I think the minutes that followed were the most wonderful in all my life. There was a strange completeness in our silent communication. I turned from Felix's steady stare to gaze down the long table and out the big window to the blue bay and the sailboats. I felt the sudden tears in my eyes. I noted the black and blue geometrical bridge by Joseph Stella on the whitewashed wall, and the big, ominous, evil heads of a Ben Shahn propaganda painting. I observed the rounded, pretty faces of the Truro sons and daughters, all so good, so idealistic, so naive, and fated, as I even then suspected, for such tragic lives. It had come, my moment. A great man was going to love me.

When, after lunch, our host gave me a knowing look, I did not return it. It angered me that Mark should think, cynical creature that he was, that he had been the architect of what was happening. He had had a whiff of it, that was all. He was not capable of envisioning the love of which Felix and I were going to be capable.

❖   ❖   ❖

If Seal Cove would not come to Butterfield Bay, then I would come to Seal. When Heyward returned from the city,

I told him that I was tired of the mundanity of our resort, that I yearned for the purer intellectual air that our neighbors to the north breathed. As I knew would be the case, I had no trouble with him. He agreed that it was a good idea, and that he had always wanted to see more of his friend Felix. But would he not bore Frances, he asked? I assured him that he underestimated himself and overestimated her. I promised that I would make everything all right. Then I turned my attention to you, Roger Cutter.

Yes, even that far back, when you couldn't have been much more than twenty-two, I knew that you played a role in Felix's life, though I didn't know quite what it was. Some people have said it was filial, that Felix was disappointed in the stupidity of his own son and, after the divorce, in the hostility of his daughter. But I doubt that he ever saw you with a father's eyes. Today, I suppose, people would seek a homosexual clue, but if Felix had any tendency in that direction, it certainly escaped me. No, I suspect that he felt about you the way a man feels about a faithful dog (you see, I am being just as frank as I threatened!), a rather surly dog that dislikes all the world but him. A man will always cherish something that he can own entirely. It makes him feel a bit like a god.

Anyway, I used you as my entrée into Seal Harbor. Once I had made a conquest of your wonderful old curmudgeon of a father — and that took but a day, as he was a pushover for women — it was only a step before Heyward and I were accepted as regulars at those ghastly evenings at the Troys' and on those tiresome mountain climbs that you were all so keen about. The things we do for love! But those mountains were indispensable to me: Frances's asthma kept her from climbing.

On one of those crowded walks — there must have been ten of us — Felix bounded ahead as usual, and I managed to keep up with him. It almost killed me, but I was rewarded with an hour alone in his company on the summit. We sat with our backs against a fine flat rock and gazed over an infinite sea. As always by now, in my brief times alone with Felix, I was possessed with a sense of intense happiness, part of which was the conviction that it was shared. It seemed a happiness curiously distinct from desire. I had no need to *do* anything, or even to say anything, in particular. Just being there was enough, and any chitchat would do. But that day he had something important to tell me.

"I've been offered a seat on the National Labor Relations Board. The call came in from the White House last night."

I did not quite know what this board was, but obviously it was something federal and very important, which was all that had to matter. "Oh, Felix! How very fine. Will you have to move to Washington?" I was already calculating what this would mean to me.

"If I took it. But I haven't. I turned it down."

"Because you thought it wouldn't lead to anything?"

"No. It might lead to the federal bench. I was told that."

"And wouldn't you like to be a judge? I think you'd look lovely in black robes."

"I have often thought that I should like to be a judge. An appellate judge. It is perhaps the nearest one can come to combining the philosopher with the man of action. Oh, yes, it has tempted me. It has even seemed the solution of a lifelong dilemma. Can a man swim and still comment on the swimmers? But there was something else in this offer. It was my chance to make peace with the New Deal. It was to be my forgiveness for voting for Alfred Landon. As a member of the NLRB I would be implementing the Labor Act."

"But you helped draft the Labor Act! I've heard you say so."

"And so I did. But I don't want to implement anything. I don't want to be on anyone's team. Frances says I'll end up a monk. But she's wrong. I won't fight God's battles, either."

"How has Frances taken this?"

"Oh, she's in a state! She says it's my last chance for redemption. She weeps. She tears her hair. Figuratively speaking, of course."

"How can she be so sure it's right for you?"

"Because she believes that those who are not for us are against us."

"Us?"

"The underdog. The great unwashed. Frances has always conceived it her function to keep me from wavering. When we married, you see, I was something of a socialist. She regards the least move to the right as motivated by evil things, whereas any move to the left, even too far, even beyond where *she* would go, she attributes to high ideals. Misguided ideals, maybe, when it comes to something like communism, but still high."

"How can she presume to dictate to you?"

"Because she conceives herself to be my guardian angel. And who knows? Perhaps she is."

"*I* know!" I sprang to my feet in a sudden ecstasy of release. "She has a bloody nerve! Instead of blessing her lucky stars that she's married to a genius, she hollers like a Bolshevik. Have you no guts? Are you going to put up with that?"

"No." Felix seemed vastly amused at my display of temper. "I told you, I declined the job."

"But you think she may have been right. You just said so. It makes me sick to see that woman trying to turn you into something you're not. Good God! As if she'd had the whole world to pick and choose from!"

"Gladys, Gladys! Take it easy."

"I won't take it easy! What sort of a moral code do we have that hands you over to a person like her, for life, because of some crazy sexual impulse that you felt two decades ago? It's all wrong! Look at Mrs. Roosevelt, married to the most charming and the greatest man of our time, and all she can think of is her boring causes. Does she appreciate him? Of course not! Small wonder that he had a fling with her secretary before his polio."

"But he needs Eleanor. They're a partnership. He'd never have been elected if there'd been a divorce."

"But *you*'re not running for office!"

Felix jumped up at this, and we stood for a moment staring at each other. He had turned very pale.

"Oh, of course, I hate your wife," I said with an angry shrug, turning abruptly away. "But only because she hates *me*. Don't deny it. I can tell. But I'd even forgive her that if she would only admit it's jealousy. But, oh, no. She's above a paltry female weakness like that, isn't she? I'll bet she tells you she dislikes me because I distract you from being the great man *she* would have you be!"

"Gladys, how do you know these things?"

"Because I know women. Which is more than you do, my dear."

"Perhaps I know more about one of them than you think." He had stepped close to me, and I felt his hands on my shoulders, turning me around, when we both saw Lila Nickerson's head emerging over a boulder, and he stepped back. In a few more minutes the rest of the party was upon us, and Felix and I had no further chance for private talk.

Lila arranged to walk down the mountain with me and took the occasion to deliver a discreet little sermon.

"You don't fool me, you know, Gladys. Not for a minute. I'm perfectly aware that behind that pose of the carefree butterfly of Butterfield Bay is a shrewdness second to none in Seal Cove. But perhaps there are one or two little things that may have escaped even your penetrating observation."

"Such as?"

"Such as the fact that everybody in Seal Cove is absolutely devoted to Frances Leitner. Including Felix."

"You think I have designs upon him?"

Lila did not look at me. She seemed intent on the rocks beneath her feet, to avoid stumbling. "I think you are engaging a great deal of his attention. I think it may be disturbing to Frances."

"Did I ask her not to come on this walk?"

"She has asthma. Walking makes her short of breath."

"Is it my fault that her husband won't stay home with her?"

"I think so."

"Lila Nickerson, you're being perfectly ridiculous. Wives don't *own* husbands — not husbands like Felix, anyway. He needs the stimulation of other people."

"Frances knows best, I think, what Felix needs. She has been the anchor that holds him down to earth. Felix, left to himself, is inclined to fly off on tangents. His head is always in the clouds. She knows that he must give so much to his law firm, so much to the bar, so much to his writing, so much to the public."

"And why does *she* know that so much better than he?"

Lila did not answer this. "What you don't realize, Gladys, is that for all our joking in Seal Cove, for all our parlor games and seeming lightheartedness, this little community is sincerely dedicated to making the world a better place for everyone. And none more sincerely so than Felix and Frances Leitner."

The nerve of the woman! To put herself in that class. As if she had ever cared about any human being but Lila Nickerson! But she had given me an idea so suddenly exciting that I felt my heart pound. For was not what Felix really needed the exact opposite of what his wife provided in such chilling profusion? Was it not the freedom to think great thoughts and to express them? Supposing *I* were in the seat of the censorious

Frances and able with my money to free him from the bondage of his law firm so that he was able to devote all of his genius to the discovery of the good life, the good society, the good world? Should anything be allowed to stand in the way of such a goal? What became *now* of a fatuously grinning Heyward, of a drearily sermonizing Frances? Were they to be allowed to dim the beacon light that Felix might hold up to a darkened planet? I was too thrilled at this answer to all my problems to be angry any further with an object as puny as Lila Nickerson.

"Well, you needn't worry about my sirenizing Felix," I said with apparent magnanimity. "Heyward is coming back from New York on Friday, and I'm inclined to think he's had a sufficient dose of Seal Cove. Poor darling, he takes you all at your face value and fancies he's way beyond his depth. I shall lead him back to the bridge tables of dear old Butterfield Bay. But don't think I'm retreating, Lila! Or that for one minute I agree with your theory about Frances's beneficent influence on her husband. I know a possessive woman when I see one. After all, I'm one myself! And I know that if I put Heyward under too severe an intellectual strain — or what the dear dodo *considers* an intellectual strain — he'll spend more and more time in New York. And *then* who knows what might happen? So you see, Lila, I shall be polishing my Culbertson in the interests of my own domestic bliss!"

With this I left her, but to show that I was not being subservient, I hurried ahead to where Felix was leading the group and accompanied him down the mountain.

"You'll be hearing from me," I told him, as we parted, with an enigmatic and (I trusted) bewitching smile. "I shall call you next week. I think I may have a message that will amuse you."

In Kent, a village ten miles inland, by a lovely lake, a rich woman friend of mine had a camp, which she used only two weeks out of the year and which she was delighted to lend me. It was from her lonely but charming cabin, decorated with light green curtains and dark green wicker furniture and hung with Picasso prints, that I telephoned Felix one morning in the solitary shack that he used for his writing. I invited him to a lunch of chicken salad sandwiches and a bottle of Moselle.

He agreed to come.

Manuscript of Felix Leitner's "My First Divorce," Written for Roger Cutter in 1965

IN THE SUMMER of 1938, at the age of forty-seven, I endured the greatest emotional crisis of my life. I use the superlative because I cannot conceive that, at the age I have now attained, any comparable experience could still be in store for me. What happened was simply this: the biological urge to mate created between myself and Gladys Satterlee a tension that subverted all of our other interests: intellectual, physical, spiritual, domestic. I recognized the force of the famous cry of Racine's tragic heroine: Venus, with all her force, attached to her prey!

I found myself at once exhilarated and profoundly depressed. I was ecstatically happy and at the same time achingly miserable. I had thought I had known passion, many times; I had certainly believed myself in love with Frances. But those earlier emotions, in contrast to what I now felt, seemed to bear the relation of a tranquil pastoral scene by Puvis de Chavannes to a flaming Tahitian landscape by Gauguin. Even as a young man, when I had reveled in the poetry of Byron and Shelley, I had never associated a woman with such acute pain. But now the mere idea that I might never possess Gladys Satterlee was like a drill on a tender tooth.

This tension between us, I should explain, was not only biological. If we were animals, we were still among the higher animals. Our physical union, when it ultimately came, acted to intensify the already existing union of our hearts. Never had I thought or written more clearly or cogently than in the first months of our affair; never had I felt stronger or more physically fit. I had the exciting sense that every talent with which, as a homo sapiens, I had been endowed, was being utilized to its highest degree. It made me feel like a god! But what kind of god? A god who meted out justice and mercy? A god who sanctified the solemn engagements that men and women made to each other in the ceremony called marriage? Hardly.

Until the Industrial Revolution our European forebears had lived in a society where the universe was deemed to have a purpose and where a deity judged men, rewarding them or condemning them according to an absolute standard of right and wrong. And the dethronement of the deity was followed by a long succession of political theories as to who was to judge men and by what standards: a king, a parliament, a congress, the people. But now we exist in a cold, mechanical universe where we are obliged to accept the lonely responsibility of each man for his own soul. I could not escape the bar of my conscience. I had to decide for myself how much I owed my friends, my children, my wife, my beloved.

I had first to review my duty to Frances. She had been a good and faithful spouse; she had given me, as the rather meaningless phrase put it, the best years of her life. It was not her fault that she no longer attracted me. Indeed, she had been a good sport about the cessation, a couple of years before, of our sexual relations, bravely putting the blame on her asthma in order to spare me the embarrassment of having to confess to a loss of desire. Whatever her physical need of me — and I was sure, poor woman, that it continued — she was willing to settle for what the French call a "white marriage" rather than risk alienating me altogether. Would she have countenanced an affair on my part? No. But she might have been ready to look the other way.

So far as Gladys was concerned, I could judge her joy by my own. If she, like me, felt that no punishment was too great a price to pay for the bliss of our physical union, I was under no duty to spare her the possible consequences. And our children, I argued to myself, her one and my two, had reached an age where they might be expected to absorb without undue damage the knowledge (assuming that such knowledge should have to come) that their parents had impulses that wandered beyond the neat and narrow park of matrimony. It was Heyward who continued to be my chief stumbling block. Surely I had a peculiar duty to Heyward. I had always allowed him to consider himself a more intimate friend than he actually was. Now I was stuck with his illusion.

There were two reasons for our special relationship. At Yale, he had represented many things that I had not had and envied him: athletic good looks, easy popularity, reputable money and social position. I had been touched by his frankly offered affection — unusual in the Yale of that day between a well-connected Gentile and an undistinguished Jew — but because I had feared that there might have been some element of social climbing behind my reciprocation, I had resolved that I should give Heyward every bit as much as he gave me. So it was that when I became a public figure and he remained a very private one — and when, to tell the truth, he lost the charm of youth and began to bore me — I took considerable pains to convince him that nothing had changed between us. The second reason was simpler. Heyward had always been sensitive and easy to hurt, and I had always dreaded hurting people.

But the presumption that informed the commencement of my affair with Gladys — that it should be kept secret to the world — was to be the guaranty of Heyward's continued serenity. It was also to be the guaranty of our reputations. I emphasize this last point because I still believed at that time that my duty to society at large obliged me to maintain the forms of marriage and the family. I had always allowed for divorce, but only in cases of serious incompatibility and after a prescribed waiting period. I did not believe that society would benefit from an absolute license in matters of sex, and now that we more or less have it, I still have doubts. So I planned to satisfy my passion without disturbing my family, to achieve my bliss without outraging convention. I would have my cake and eat it. No doubt millions of husbands have tried. Who knows how many have succeeded?

I was not destined, anyway, to be among the latter. From the beginning I worried about Gladys's indiscretions. Our setup, but for them, seemed foolproof. I had told Frances that I was planning a new book and needed to take long solitary walks on the mountains with my notebook. As this had been my custom with other books, it aroused no suspicion. Heyward had gone back to New York, and Gladys did not have to account for her time to anyone. If she were seen in the village of Kent buying groceries, she could say that she was redecorating her friend's camp. We used to meet there at noon and make love and then lunch by the lake. There was no other camp in the immediate area. We had the Maine woods and the shimmering water and the blue hills to ourselves. We were Adam and Eve in Paradise, and there were no snakes to bother us. Those days were the richest, the most heart-exploding, of my lifetime.

I have said there were no snakes, but if Eve's snake was really her ungovernable curiosity, perhaps Gladys's was her compulsion to embellish her surroundings. She had her alibi that she was decorating her friend's cabin, but that alibi was soon converted into truth. Every day she would arrive with something new: a cushion, a coverlet, flowers, silver, a teapot, a cocktail shaker. I would protest that we needed nothing but a "jug of wine" to adorn our wilderness, but I might as well have told a busy wren to abstain from building its nest. Sometimes I felt that Gladys actually enjoyed playing with fire. Some women cannot be content unless the world knows of their happiness. She must have had to struggle with the impulse to cry our love to the tree tops.

One day at noon I drove into camp to find an upholsterer's truck parked by Gladys's little Renault. She had asked a man from Kent to hang new curtains in the living room! I backed my car away quickly, turned it around and drove off, but I had seen a face in the window, and my initials were on my license plate. When I returned later in the afternoon, Gladys accused me of having made matters worse by my guilty flight. She was probably right, but who had gratuitously created the dangerous situation? We became so angry that we parted that day without the usual intimacies. It was the only time that this happened.

Who actually betrayed our hideaway we never learned, but only a week after the episode of the upholstery truck, when Gladys and I were in bed at noon, we heard the sound of a seemingly stuck automobile horn from the driveway. The horrid noise went on and on, blaring, declamatory, accusing, filling the forest air with its shrill note of human outrage. In my first dazed reaction, as I leapt from the bed, it seemed to me that everything behind the limits of the lake and the spruce trees, everything of man and woman, everything beside Gladys and myself, was unutterably low and vile. What fiend was sitting out there before the front door with a hand pressing down that horn?

Gladys pulled the covers over her head, and I hurried to the window to peek through the slats of the Venetian blind. There, only a few yards from the window, sat Heyward at the wheel of his open Bugatti runabout. He was staring right at the window; he might just have been able to make out my outline. But, of course, my car was fatally parked beside Gladys's at the front door.

Suddenly the horn stopped. "Hiya, lover boy!" I heard him shriek. And then, before I could even consider how I should try to handle the situation, he started up his motor and drove off in a spluttering roar.

*　　*　　*

Later that day, Gladys telephoned me from her house in Butterfield (she knew that Frances was away, visiting one of her sisters at Camden) to tell me that Heyward had gone to New York, leaving no message. But the next day she received a curt notice from a lawyer in New York to the effect that Mr. Satterlee had retained him to bring suit for divorce on grounds of adultery. I assured Gladys that she could count on me to the end, and, without explaining what I meant by this to her, or indeed to myself, I rang off, just as Frances entered the room. She had come back that morning, and it was at once evident from her gray face and glittering gray eyes that she knew all.

"What does Mrs. Satterlee say?" she demanded in a harsh voice. "Are you to come to her at once? Or may we have a talk first?"

"I had hoped, Frances, that you and I might face this thing without recriminations."

"That's what I've been doing for the past three years. Not recriminating. Where the hell has it gotten me?"

"Three years? I thought we were concerned with what's happened this summer."

"Oh, it's not just *her*. She's only a detail, if one can call the last straw a detail. I mean your whole attitude toward me, toward your work, toward . . . well, the whole world."

I began to suspect that Frances might have been drinking. She sometimes did, in times of great emotional tension.

"Can't we *ever* be particular? Even now, for God's sake?"

"It's like the NLRB job," she retorted, in some confusion. "You won't soil your hands with our grubby problems. You want to be above us all . . . way up on top of some mountain of yours. But you're not as detached and spiritual as you think you are! Because the only people who can join you on that mountain top are those who can afford their own private planes!"

"You're mixing your metaphors, Frances. Planes can't land on mountain tops."

"Damn it all, I'm not writing a column!" She actually stamped her foot. "You know well enough what I mean!"

"I know you've always believed that I've somehow 'sold out.' To whom and for what, I confess, has always mystified me."

"But you haven't sold out! You haven't had a penny for your soul! Do you think I think you could be bought? I'm not so naive. You *gave* yourself away! For a few swank dinners, for a dozen lunches at exclusive clubs, for a 'May I call you Felix, old man' from a Morgan partner . . . or for a roll in the hay with Milady Satterlee, you've joined the Pharisees!"

"Has it ever occurred to you that I'm not obligated to spend my life trying to be the man you *thought* you'd married?"

"Oh, but Felix you *were*!" she cried with a sudden wail.

"We must agree to disagree about that. I have a totally different conception of my function in life than you do." I decided, despite her obvious overwroughtness, that there was no avoiding the big issue. It had to come now. "And feeling as differently as we do about so many topics, don't you think . . ."

"What?"

"Well, doesn't it perhaps signify . . . or at least suggest . . . that we might do better to . . . go our separate ways?"

Frances walked slowly across the room and took a seat by a window. "So that's it," she said in a flat tone. "You want to be free to marry her."

"Why, as you said, do we have to talk about Gladys? Isn't the real issue between you and me? That I have ceased to be the man you admire and look up to? Why should there be recriminations? Why should I not lead my life as I like and you, yours? The children are old enough to accept it."

As I recreate this conversation, I can see that it sounds as if I was taking advantage of Frances's criticisms of my political and social attitudes; as if, by blowing these up to a much greater irritant in my life than they actually had been, I was using them as a reason for our separating. Certainly Frances interpreted what I said this way. I wonder if we can ever know all the sources of our motivations. Certainly I had been hurt by Frances's failure — nay, her willful refusal — to see my goal in life as I saw it.

"Oh, Felix, you have never ceased to be the man I admire and look up to!" she exclaimed bleakly. "And if it's really necessary to tolerate your new values, I shall most certainly try to tolerate them. I thought you needed the stimulus of dissent. I thought you even liked it. But if that's not the case, I can be quiet as a mouse. You'll see!"

"What I'd see would be you sitting on your tongue. Hanging on to it with all your might!"

"No, no, no." She became very disturbed at this. "You grossly underestimate me. I *have* considered it my duty, at certain times in the past, to act as a counterinfluence to people who I thought were doing you no good. But that doesn't mean that I don't love you and admire you, dearest, even if I think they've harmed you. You're *still* better than all the rest of us. You are, darling! And from now on I'm determined to accept you as you want to be. To stop being a nag." Here she came over to seize my hand pleadingly in both of hers. "Give me a chance, love!"

I turned away, stricken. I think I even jerked my hand away. All my plans were in ruins. "But, Frances, you must face something. You must face what has come between us. This terrible suit of Heyward Satterlee's. I can't leave Gladys to face that alone."

"How else can she face it?"

"With the man who is ready to marry her! Isn't that what I must do?"

"Are you out of your mind?" she almost shouted. "Since when has a man's adultery created an obligation to leave his wife?"

"I got her into this mess."

"I doubt that. But even supposing it were true, what of it? Has there ever been a society that held that a breach of contract creates a duty to the person for whose sake it was broken?"

Yes, Frances could talk that way, even at a moment of such emotional pitch. Anyone who cannot believe it never knew her.

"I didn't know that you went in so for codes."

"Since when have *you*?"

"But, my God, Frances, when I think of the agony I've caused that woman and how much she cares for me, and how little else she has in her life, and when I see you, usually so cool and calm and self-sufficient, so concentrated on your duty to the underdog, I can't help wondering if my place isn't with Gladys. At least she needs me, damn it all!"

She flew at me — no other word can describe it — and wound her short arms around my neck. Never had I realized before, except perhaps in the first months of our marriage, how deeply feminine she was. I shall not go into all the things she said. I cannot properly remember them or reconstruct them, but their gist was very clear. Frances wanted *me*, at any cost. She was perfectly willing to give up her ideas of my true career, to allow me to frequent any society that I chose, perhaps even to permit me Gladys on the side, if I would only remain at home as a husband and father, titular if I insisted, but at least there. It was a surrender, abject, groveling, utterly atypical of a great and noble woman and not further to be recounted here. I was ashamed for her and ashamed for myself.

Of course, I could not then and there deny her what she asked. I did not, I am quite sure, make any definite commitment, but I think I must have left her with the idea that the status quo ante had been restored — at least for the time being. I have been called weak, and I suppose I was, but I do not understand how any man with the faintest simulacrum of a heart could have told that wretched creature at that time that he was going to leave her. Could I have lashed her naked back with a whip? Could I have cut her face with a razor? It was unthinkable.

God! Why is it always considered hypocrisy for the deliverer of the stroke to cry out that it hurts him more than it does his victim? I am convinced that the breakup of our marriage hurt me at least as much as it hurt Frances. I even suspect that her refusal of a subsequent offer of marriage from a brilliant and important public servant was motivated in part by a desire, perhaps subconscious, to keep alive my feelings of guilt. But I always knew that the real weakness, the real cowardice, would have been to preserve a stale union to avoid a short pain, to abandon what I then believed to be a passionately loving woman for what I then considered an essentially possessive one, to turn my back on a life that offered the finest fruition of heart and mind. No, if I were ever going to be a man, I had to do what I now proceeded to do.

But how did I do it? Ay, there's the rub. How gloatingly our public seizes upon our poor means to scorn our larger end! I found that I simply could not face Frances and tell her that I was going to leave her. So I did what Professor Cutter angrily told all Seal Cove was my "invariable habit" to retreat, like an escaping squid, behind a cloud of black ink. In short, I took up my pen. I went down to New York where I holed up in a small hotel, giving my address to none but Gladys. From there I wrote to Frances, and to Heyward.

The latter returned my letter unopened with this note: "You have always believed you could do anything with the written word. You will find that in hell there are no readers." Heyward could never have thought that one up. I suspect that old Cutter had a hand in it. Frances, I was relieved to find, did not even write a note. She simply placed the matter in the hands of her lawyer who relieved me of every cent I had: savings, houses, book royalties, all, plus a whacking slice of my future income. She did it, the lawyer told me, to secure our children's future. I believe that she was perfectly sincere in this. At any rate, I was only too happy to pay up. I even thought it generous of her to allow me so to assuage some of my guilt.

I took a leave of absence from my firm. As my children would no longer speak to me (a state of affairs that lasted for two years), and as the furor among my friends and acquaintances reached a heat almost not to be credited in 1938, I decided to go abroad with Gladys until our divorces were final. We made a motor tour of the cathedrals of France.

Looking back, I think that this trip was the most serene period of my life. The agony of the great decision was behind us, and we were finding that we were able to live with the consequences. I knew that my children would have to come around in time, that Gladys and I would marry, and that the friends, however unforgiving, would ultimately at least tolerate the situation. In the meanwhile we had this enchanting interlude, this time suspended, with our love framed by the glorious facades of the cathedrals against the pale mist of a French autumn. We saw nobody, spoke to nobody. It was a Gothic Eden.

You may wonder why the soaring spires and blue glass of Chartres, why the craggy magnificence of Amiens, why the lacelike delicacy of Rheims, did not put me in mind of vows broken, of sacraments violated. But I had taken a strong stand about this. These churches were the moments of a civilization founded in the rule of a supervising God who dealt out awards and punishments. The people who lived under those towers had duties that we do not have today, but they also had rewards for which we should now look in vain. I had to live in my own time, under my own moral law. Each man must find it for himself. Once I had come to my decision, I was not to be thwarted by sentiment. It had never been easy to be a man. It was not in 1938. It is not today.

Roger Cutter (5)

FELIX has described the summer of his affair with Gladys as the happiest of his lifetime; I wonder if it was not the happiest of mine. He made me his confidant, and I thrilled with pride at the honor. I also think I felt some portion of his love. I had already, under his tutelage, come to face the fact that my joys, if any, were going to be vicarious, but that they need not be spurned for that reason. Felix had taught me that nothing in life was to be spurned.

My father was to accuse me at a later time of having derived actual pleasure from the Leitners' unhappy marriage because I could not marry myself, but this was not fair. He was never fair. I do not think that I derived any pleasure from the wreck of Frances's happiness; I simply reveled in Felix's. Then, too, I suppose, there was a part of me that could not help but feel that if a man has the exquisite possibility of complete sexual fulfillment, he is an ingrate, if not almost a sinner, in the cold eyes of a natural universe, not to avail himself of it. "Only God's free gifts abuse not," I hummed, perhaps heretically, to myself.

When Felix returned from his midday assignations with Gladys, he would be so bursting with energy that he would want to climb a mountain or go on a walk that was almost a run along the rocky coastline. As he was supposed to be ruminating about a book and gone for the day, he would give me meeting points on the Seal Cove trails where I would join him for these afternoon excursions. Indeed, I came to feel almost as much a part of his secret life as Gladys, and this, of course, was very pleasing to me.

On one of these walks, when we had paused to sit concealed behind a tree near a little mountain tarn, where an old bull moose was sometimes known to drink, Felix said something to me that I think he may have since forgotten.

"How is it all going to end, Roger? What is going to happen? Sometimes I think I am going to explode into tiny pieces and be scattered all over the Maine woods. It would be a solution."

"Only last Monday you said you had not thought 'of the morrow.' That the present was all in all."

"That was last Monday. I must be waking up."

"Go back to sleep. It's better."

"Ah, there youth speaks. If I only could! Do you know, there are moments when I actually wish that Heyward would discover us? When I want to see Gladys exposed and disgraced and hunted so that I, a Lancelot, could fly to her side and protect her?"

"You mean you want something to happen that will make it your duty to be her lover?"

"Instead of my duty not to be? I suppose that's it." For several moments after this he was so silent and still that I thought he might be waiting for the moose. I observed that it probably came only at dawn. "I don't give a damn about the old bull," he said with a chuckle. "He's probably off on a rendezvous himself. No, I was thinking what a smart mind-reader you are."

"I don't see why. Isn't it pretty obvious that you should be dreaming of a heaven where you *had* to marry Gladys?"

"It would be too much happiness," he muttered. "Then I really would explode."

This gave me what I needed. I had surprisingly little hesitation about it. It astounds me, as I look back, that I could have taken so much responsibility upon myself. Perhaps I lacked the imagination to foresee all the consequences. I had placed Felix in the position of the sun in my private universe, and what could I do but revolve around him?

My opportunity came on a Saturday night at the Troys' when I had a long chat with Lila Nickerson. She had sought me out and led me to a corner because she wanted to pump me about Felix. It was generally believed in Seal Cove that Lila had a "crush" on Felix, but it was considered a trivial, a harmless, even a rather amusing thing, about which her husband did not have to be in the least concerned, about which, indeed, it was even permissible gently to tease him. I had long suspected that it was something considerably stronger, and that Felix, any time he chose, might enjoy the privilege of decorating the temples of Aleck Nickerson with the same horns that now adorned those of Heyward Satterlee.

"Isn't it funny that we never see the Satterlees any more?" Lila asked.

"I believed Heyward has to be in New York a lot."

"Undoubtedly. A brain like his must be in great demand on Wall Street. But what about the divine Gladys? Surely she does not languish in torrid Manhattan?"

"I hope not, for her sake."

"You don't follow her comings and goings?"

"Why should I? Do you?"

"I know a little bird that does. I listen to its tweet-tweet."

"And what does the little bird tell you?"

"That she is meeting somewhere with our Felix."

"Happiness to their sheets, then!" I exclaimed. "What's it to me?"

Lila became pointed. "Gladys isn't the gal for Felix, Roger. You know that, don't you?"

"I don't even know that he needs a gal, as you so crudely put it. But if he does, why not Gladys?"

"She has no bean."

"Why should a man married to an intellectual like Frances need another? I should think it's just the opposite he'd be after."

"Oh, Frances!" Would anyone have guessed from her tone that Lila was speaking of her best friend? I sometimes feel today, looking back thirty-five years, that the women's liberation movement was needed to protect them, not from men, but from themselves. They could be very terrible to each other in the days when they still fought for mates. "Frances doesn't regard herself as a woman anymore. Look how she dresses! She's too busy reforming the world to care. Well, let her have the world! That should satisfy her. Felix needs a woman who can keep up with his intellectual flights."

"And who might that be?"

"Who do you think?"

I threw my hands up. "Poor Aleck! I'm glad I'm not a husband along this strip of Maine coast."

"Roger, be the man of the world I take you for!" Lila was totally one-tracked; nothing was going to deflect her from her chosen course. "Aleck is no responsibility of yours. Don't be stuffy. If anything *did* happen between Felix and myself, Aleck would take it like the perfect gentleman he is. You see how I trust you."

"Yes, but you take very little risk. If I were to quote you, not a soul in Seal would believe me."

"Pooh. People will believe anything, if it's bad enough. But tell me. Gladys and Felix are meeting. I know they must be meeting. How do they do it? Where do they go?"

"What good would it do you to know?"

"They are, then. I knew it!"

"If they are, it shouldn't take anyone as smart as you long to find out."

"How would you go about it?" she pursued eagerly.

"Well, they wouldn't dare go to the well-known hotels, would they? And the smaller ones are too crummy for Gladys."

"There's always the woods, I suppose."

"Not for anyone as urbane as Mrs. Satterlee. So it would have to be somebody's empty villa or cottage. Or even a camp." Now I pretended to reflect. "Owned by a relative or an understanding friend. Of course, Gladys knows everybody, so that doesn't help. Let's see if we can't narrow it further. It wouldn't be in Butterfield Bay. Everyone knows every house there."

"Or in Seal Cove. Same thing."

"Exactly. So what about . . ." I paused.

"Kent."

"Kent." I nodded and then shrugged with assumed indifference. "I suppose you could always try Kent."

"I could ask in the village," Lila said musingly. "Gladys would have been bound to buy things."

Of course, Lila did not accomplish what she intended to accomplish when she transmitted the fruits of her research to Gladys's husband. She had totally underestimated both the extent of Gladys's marital ambition and that of Heyward's jealousy. She thought that Heyward would simply make a blustering scene, and that Gladys, conventional at heart and terrified of scandal, would beg a speedily granted forgiveness, and that Seal Cove would then be emptied of their importunate presences, leaving the scene free for a new candidate for Felix's affections. But I had had a pretty shrewd suspicion that things would turn out just as they did.

To begin with, I knew Heyward Satterlee far better than Lila did. She regarded him as too trivial to be taken seriously. I understood his emotional dependence on Felix, for it was analogous to my own. Felix's friendship represented to Heyward the distinguishing aspect of a life otherwise banal, the proof that there could be in a poor stockbroker's soul something that a genius could, not only recognize, but value, like the deep red glow that the observer at last begins to make out in the somber grays and blacks of a Rothko canvas. Heyward could have forgiven Gladys any lover but Felix. For her to take his friend was not simply an act of adultery; it was a kind of murder.

And, secondly, I had had my talk with Felix. I knew how *he* would regard such a crisis. The reader may be shocked at the responsibility that I took upon my shoulders in dropping such a deadly hint to Lila. Looking back today, I am surprised myself that I had so little hesitation about it. I can explain it only as the single-mindedness of youth. Felix was to me the greatest man in the world. He would be happier, work better — be greater, in short — with Gladys than with Frances. Therefore, his acolyte should do what he could to accelerate the change. It hardly occurred to me that I might have any personal obligation to Frances or any duty to the institution of marriage.

What I did not anticipate was the storm that the scandal evoked and its long duration. Adultery following by divorce, after all, was sufficiently common in 1938. Some of the most respected persons of Butterfield Bay and of Seal Cove had been divorced and remarried. Indeed, Mrs. Livingston Polhemus, always described in the local gazette as the grande dame of the former community, had three living husbands. Why then the great pother over Felix and Gladys?

I think there were several reasons. First, there was the element of betrayal. People sympathized with Heyward more for being stabbed in the back by a friend than for losing a flighty wife. Second, there was the pathos of Frances's situation. She was as popular in Seal Cove as Heyward was in Butterfield.

Everybody excoriated Felix for not having had the "guts" to tell her to her face of his resolution to leave her. How could any but a fiend have so treated this plucky, generous little woman? How could any but the crudest worldling have deserted her for such a tinny social type as Gladys Satterlee?

And with this last question, we reach, I suggest, the real crux of the matter. There was always something about Felix Leitner that aroused a bitter little hostility in the hearts of his closest friends. I think that I was the sole exception to this, which, of course, in my own opinion, uniquely qualifies me to be his biographer, though others might take a precisely opposite view. I alone accepted the fact that I could never own Felix. I even accepted the fact that I could never own the smallest part of him.

People generally do not like a man who cannot be owned. They want him to belong to a family, to a creed, to a race, to a political party, to a dogma, to a summer community, to a team . . . to something. But Felix belonged to nothing but his concept of human liberty, which was in itself a kind of non-belonging. If liberals regarded his distaste for even a mild collectivism as a betrayal of his early socialist principles, conservatives deplored his continued espousal of the cause of the worker and the consumer against the giant corporation. If Jews resented the fact that he refused to call himself a Jew, Christians were not better pleased when he classified their faith as an "amiable anachronism." If Seal Cove found him a bit too well dressed, a touch too formal, Butterfield Bay found him on occasion too free in his talk, too little reverent of important things. Frances Leitner might have compromised with the Bill of Rights to raise the standard of living in city slums; Felix would have stubbornly held high the torch of liberty even if it illumined scenes of human suffering that its darkening might have at least temporarily ameliorated.

Yet all of this might have been permitted to Felix had he been willing to play the part of the wild-eyed anarchist or the surly curmudgeon, had he donned some respectably deviant garb that fashionable intellectual circles, left or right, could recognize. But Felix clung to the liberty of his own tastes. He *liked* to be well dressed and comfortably housed. He liked an ordered evening with good food, good wine, good talk. He had no use for loud voices or lost tempers. He abhorred violence. And he adopted — ah, here was the real trouble — a high moral tone in his conversation and in his writing, the tone of the civilized man who knows that he must find in himself, and not in God or in other men, the answer to the good life.

Felix, in brief, opened himself up to the charge of claiming to be superhuman. With what glee did the old friends proceed to bespatter what they called the "self-made idol" with every handful of mud within their reach! Of course, the storm abated in time, but never entirely. There would always be a relentless few to speak of him as the man who had betrayed his best friend and tried to explain it in a beautiful letter.

The ugliest scene that I witnessed occurred at the Lassiter Troys' New Year's party to welcome in what turned out to be a most unhappy year for the world: 1939. It was given at the Troys' big brownstone in the Murray Hill section, and all of the Seal Cove friends who wintered in New York were there. Felix and Gladys had been married in Maryland the week before. He had called me up when they arrived in the city to say that old Troy had asked them and that Gladys wanted to go. I advised against it, knowing that the Troys, kindly but both now very forgetful, had little awareness of how bitter the feeling was against the Leitners. But Gladys insisted, and they came. Frances was not to be there, so there was not *that* confrontation to fear.

But there was, alas, my father. When the Leitners appeared,

everybody was very polite, if distant, except Dad, who immediately stomped over to the bar exclaiming loudly that he needed "a stiff drink." He returned, however, an ominously dark whiskey in hand, to the little group in the center of which Felix was discussing the consequences of the Munich pact.

"You think Chamberlain did *right*?" Dad suddenly thundered. He had not deigned to greet Felix in any way.

"Not right, certainly, but perhaps what he had to do. If he uses the time he has gained to arm, the humiliation may turn out to have been worth it."

"To those, you mean, who can endure such humiliation?"

"If the British Empire can endure it, Professor Cutter, I daresay it is endurable." We all noted the apostrophe. Felix did not have to be reminded that he and Dad were no longer on a first name basis.

"Empires can fall, sir, as can individuals," my father continued irately. "An empire that grovels before a maniac does not deserve to be one. Nor will it be, long!"

"I think you may have occasion to see that the British can still fight for what they believe in."

"That will be an edifying spectacle! I have come near to being convinced that there are very few men left on this globe. Real men, that is."

"It may sometimes take a greater courage *not* to fight."

"Have you found that so, Leitner?" Dad now roared. "I shouldn't wonder. You were born with a yellow streak. And I miss my guess if you won't die with one!"

At this, poor Mother, who always kept an eye on Dad, came up to take him by the elbow and steer him to the coat closet. Very firmly, if silently, she took him home. He had had his say; he knew he had behaved outrageously, and he was now quite docile. But their departure left the party hopelessly chilled, and not all of Felix's diplomacy could warm it up again.

A worse scene, if possible, occurred that night when I came home. I reproached my father savagely for what he had done, and he exploded all over again. He accused me of having acted the pander throughout Felix's affair with Gladys, and the next morning I left the paternal roof forever. Dad and I eventually made up our quarrel, at least formally, for Mother's sake, but I never again lived at home. It was time, at any rate, for my departure. I had always essentially lived alone. In my own apartment I was able to face my isolation directly and make a virtue of it. Felix approved.

Passages from the Paris Journal of Fiona Satterlee, April 1946

APRIL 2. Mother and Felix arrive the day after tomorrow. They will be staying, of course, at the Ritz. They expect me for dinner on Tuesday night. There will be the usual assemblage of notables whose brains Mother will serve up to Felix to pick. He is writing a book on the future of Europe. Let us hope it has one.

I am oddly disturbed. I put the question: what did I expect? To have Paris all to myself? Did I think Mother would never come here? I suppose I simply hoped she would not come quite so soon, that I should have a little more time for my experiment in living alone. After all, I can hardly call myself independent after only two months.

Everything else has gone very well. I love my little studio. I love living in the Ile de la Cité. I paint in the morning. I've made a few nice friends. I've learned to drive my Ford all over Paris. And I find the French so wonderfully natural. They take my brace for granted. I feel less of a cripple that I ever did at home. I am getting to be fairly fluent in the language, too. I am a "person." Or at least I think I may be on my way to becoming one.

Of course, Mother has never really wanted me to be a person. She is too used to me the way I am — or the way I was. For twenty-five years I've been a fixture in her home, as familiar as the dining room cupboard, the unmarried and unmarriageable daughter, quiet, good-tempered, placid, yet just independent enough, just occasionally sharp enough to serve as a buffer against her loneliness when the brighter friends are not about. Oh, yes, my utility is clear enough. The great, charming lady likes to have a loyal attendant, like one of those confidantes in French classic drama who exist only to listen to the heroine's love problems and laud her depth of feeling. The very fact that I was occasionally prickly, even sometimes downright critical, gave my comments more value. Mother was far too clever to put up with a dunce.

That, I see now, was why she was so ungracious about my legacy from Grandma Dunne, though it was really very mean of her. After all, my little trust fund was only a token compared to the two million that *she* got. I suppose Grandma must have observed more than we realized. She probably saw that Mother was using me and resolved to make me independent of her. God bless you, Grandma! But I mustn't let myself become too critical of Mother. I must remember what Roger Cutter told me: people who turn themselves into carpets should expect to be trod on. And grown up children who are always beefing about their parents are the worst kind of bores.

April 3. Here I am still stewing about the impending visit. It is not only Mother. It is Felix. I must face that. The *real* reason I left home was Felix. I was getting too dependent on him. I was becoming too obsessed with the business of being one of his assistants. I had almost given up my painting. I was being sucked into the vortex of that whole whirling crazy life in Washington. Of course, I loved helping with the research. But I could never kid myself that I had contributed a single word, or even a single idea, to that sacred column. No sir! It was all Felix's genius, pure and simple! There was no room in that shiny palace for any but cleaning women. I could make telephone calls; I could verify facts; I could confirm appointments. That was all.

Well, what was so wrong with that? Mother has made a life for herself exploiting Felix's genius. But Mother preserves her individuality by being possessive, even, at times, by being disagreeable. I'm afraid she has lost much of her charm since she married Felix. Perhaps that is the price one pays for not being submerged by him. I was definitely going under. It is amazing how that man gets people to do things for him!

Will he try to make me come back? Not a chance, brother!

April 4. I met Mother and Felix at the boat train. She is more "great actressy" than ever, with too much luggage, too many porters, too much waving of arms and blowing of farewell kisses to fellow travelers. She was rather brief with me and deplored my hat. Obviously, I am still under a cloud for my defection. Felix was as charming as ever, the perfect stepfather, interested, kindly, making up for Mother's coolness. She was her usual grabby self with him. She brushed off a reporter with a sharp: "Come to the hotel. Mr. Leitner will have a release for you there. Can't you see he's tired?"

April 5. Mother and Felix gave a dinner for ten last night in a private dining room at the Ritz. I suppose it was a brilliant affair, all statesmen and diplomats, but I thought Mother rather spoiled it by calling for general conversation at table. That is her way of making Felix give a lecture. She can't bear to have people talk when she thinks they should be listening to him. He was obviously embarrassed by her tactics and showed his usual good manners by asking everybody's opinion on the topic of the day, which was the Nuremberg trials. But when the others learned that he disapproved of them, they wanted him to hold forth, and he had to.

I must write down all his comments before I go to bed. Otherwise, I'll never remember them in the morning.

"I cannot see what laws the Nazis have broken. It's all very well to talk about a conspiracy against mankind, but what law does such a conspiracy, assuming it to exist, violate? What it boils down to is that the court is going to make up a law and then hang the defendants for breaking it. I was taught that was something called ex post facto in my first week at law school!"

"You'd let them go scott free, then?" This from the British chargé.

"I think, if I'd been Harry Truman or Churchill, I'd never have let them be taken alive. I'd have simply told General Eisenhower, with a wink, how embarrassing it would be for us if they survived the surrender."

"But that would be murder!" This from the British chargé's wife.

"I admit it. But it wouldn't be judicial murder, which is something worse. Our century will be known as a lawless one, but not, God knows, for any lack of laws. We have legislated about everything under the sun, and now we're reaching up into the sky to pluck down a law to punish the Nazis with. We seem to think we can say, 'Let man be good,' and he *will* be good."

The British diplomat: "But doesn't it seem to you that Hitler and his gang went beyond anything in the past? Shouldn't civilization express its abomination of the gas chambers in some impressive, formal fashion?"

"What good will it do? You don't teach cannibals to stop eating each other by preaching to them. You do something about their food supply. The Nazis have shocked the world simply because modern systems of political control have enabled them to carry slaughter to a pitch not visualized before. But the Russians did a similar job on their recalcitrant peasants in the nineteen thirties. And just wait till India, China and

Africa get started! Then, as you say over here, *vous m'en direz des nouvelles!* Please don't think me cold-hearted. I only maintain that the Germans are not generically any different from the rest of us."

A murmur of remonstrance around the table.

"I may be a hopeless chauvinist, but I don't think Buchenwald could happen in England!"

"Gas chambers in Paris? Unthinkable!"

Felix: "Nothing is beyond the heart of man. In a generation the Nazi concentration camps will seem as remote as the Roman arenas. People never learn by example. The only way to keep them from slaughtering each other is to make it more profitable for them not to do so. Particularly now that the next Hitler will have an atom bomb. We shall no longer be free to destroy the ogre, or die in the attempt. No, we shall *have* to talk to him. We shall all have bombs, and we shall all have to talk! The United Nations may be a slim hope, but it's the only one."

Our British friend disagreed. He thinks the UN will only prove a debating society. He professed a nostalgia for the "good old days." He suggested a return to power politics.

Mother was at her worst. "Don't you have to have the power first?" This she considers supporting Felix!

Her crude reflection on the diminished status of His Majesty's empire created a strain around the table. Felix covered it as well as he could by making the conversation particular again.

After dinner, in the sitting room, Felix to my surprise came to sit by me. When Mother darted across the room to ask him which lady he wanted, he said he had one.

"I want to catch up with Fiona."

Mother, surprised, departed, but I knew she would be back. Felix gave me his whole attention in that wonderful way he has. We might have been alone in the room. This is what we said.

"You never really told me why you went to Paris. It couldn't have been just to paint. That you could have done at home."

"I'm making an experiment. I thought that if I changed everything in my life for a period — my friends, my home, my language, my habits — I might discover what there was left of the real me."

"But why Paris?"

"Because I speak French. I didn't want to take the time to learn a new language."

"That was your only reason? How utilitarian! Most people think of Paris as the city of light. The city of love."

"Im not looking for love, Felix."

"Why not?"

"You know perfectly well why not."

"Do the French? They are far too wise to think of love as something reserved for the physically perfect."

"I am quite aware that a withered leg should not exclude me from those delights." Oh, I was very direct! "That is a choice I made a long time back. I did not want to risk being pitied. You may say that is false pride. Very well. It is false pride. But there are some decisions one doesn't go back on."

"I see that." And I was sure that he did. Felix never wastes one's time. "Of course, there's still ninety-nine percent of life left. How do you find your mother?"

"Tense."

"It does show, doesn't it? She carries me around like a bottle of precious fluid, not one drop of which can be spilled. It's touching to have her care so, but it can be wearing."

"She always wanted a serious occupation. All those parties with Daddy were only a form of distraction. Now she's seen the light. Or should I say the Leitner?"

"Of course, she's helped me greatly in many ways." He was polite enough to ignore my sorry pun. "She's enabled me to devote all my days to writing. But there are times when I can't help feeling that my principal use is to be an ornament for her salon."

"Is that so bad? One can be a great writer and still be an ornament."

"I suppose one gets used to anything."

"Even marriage?"

"Maybe you're not missing so much in that state, Fiona. But this is a dangerous subject."

Then he asked me to be his guide and take him to a museum in the afternoon. We made an appointment to meet at the Carnavalet. Mother came over to break up our tête-à-tête.

I did not realize until I finished this entry that Felix and I had actually had an intimate talk. He makes intimacy as easy as formality!

April 6. Felix met me at the appointed hour of three. As always, he was on the minute. When I saw him step into the sunlight of the old courtyard of the museum, so tall and handsome, with his dark, perfectly fitting suit and walking cane, I had a sense of his great gift of making each chapter, even each paragraph, of life complete and interesting in itself.

Is that being disloyal to Daddy? I don't think so. I had never been "against" Felix in the famous family row. I had been sorry for Daddy, of course, but it had seemed to me that what was happening to him was a risk one took in the world of the able-bodied. To have had his two legs I should have gladly suffered what he insisted on calling his humiliation. Then, too, I was sure that Felix had been largely Mother's victim. I had more deplored him for weakness than condemned him for home breaking. After all, should not Mother's victims sympathize with each other? And after all, too, what did it matter?

What could my loyalty or disloyalty do for Daddy now? He has snuggled down for keeps in the deep, deep bed of his own self-pity. May he enjoy it, poor man.

The Carnavalet is my favorite museum in Paris. One usually has it to oneself. Wandering through the lovely rooms where Madame de Sévigné entertained her witty and congenial friends, gazing at the pathetic relics of the revolution, the copybooks of the poor Dauphin, the slippers of Marie Antoinette, the fatal cease-fire order of the king to the Swiss Guard, I have a thrilling sense, in that dim silence, of the muffled roar of an angry mob from the streets outside and the clangor of a tocsin.

Felix paid particular attention to the portraits of the revolutionary leaders. Here is what he talked about. (I am acting like his research assistant again. Already!)

"It was a fantastic time." This before a portrait of the beautiful Saint-Just. "And its leaders were fantastic men. For once in her history, France escaped the straitjacket of her fetish about *la gloire*. These men had a brilliant vision of a human society run by reason and equity. For this they were willing to make a clean sweep of the past. But they differed from the dreary socialists and communists of our time in that they were romantics. They loved art. They worshiped beauty. Saint-Just was a poet, if a very bad one. Of course they bogged down in blood. They were so excited about what they were doing that they persuaded themselves that only a few heads stood between them and Utopia. And then the good burghers of France saw their chance to get rid of them by branding them as monsters. *La gloire,* the friend of their pocketbooks, came back to rule the roost with Napoleon. But if it's blood you're worried about, compare the few thousand that died in the Terror with the millions who perished in the little Corsican's campaigns!"

"I'd hate to have been guillotined." My only comment!

"Would you rather have frozen to death in the retreat

from Moscow? Death in the Terror at least was stylish." And then this, before a portrait of Madame Elizabeth: "Do you know what the other ladies in the tumbrel did when they learned that they were to have the privilege of dying with the king's sister? They each made a deep *révérence* to her as they stepped out of the cart to the scaffold! What do you suppose the stinking, gaping mob made of that?"

April 8. Felix and I went to Versailles today. He was at his brightest, full of paradoxes, contrasting our government in Washington with the absolute monarchy of which this great palace is the symbol. He insists that President Truman, like Louis XVI, is the victim of red tape, that his seemingly vast prerogatives dwindle to helplessness before a bureaucracy based on tenure.

"The tragedy of the American president is that he is always being described as the most powerful man in the world. So, naturally, people expect him to solve all their problems. But can he halt one antitrust suit? Can he abate one tax? Can he fire one general? Can he remove one picketing student in front of the White House? No! He can only smile and smile and be a president. Of course, if he controls his party, like FDR, he has *that* power. But the White House, in itself, is very little."

At lunch, in the glass terrace of a restaurant near the gates of the palace, he startled me with this proposal:

"When you've found yourself, Fiona, and are ready to come home, why don't you come back to your mother and me? I promise that you'll be absolutely free. You'll have your own little apartment in our house, and we'll build you a studio. I assure you that I shall respect your desire for independence!"

I was horribly agitated.

"Why do you want me?"

"It's more than just wanting you. It's needing you. You're

always so sane and sound. You balance your mother. She's much better when you're in the house."

"You want me as a buffer against her."

"But only in everyone's best interest. I want her to have the benefit of you, and you to have the benefit of us. We do lead a fairly interesting life, you know, Fiona."

"But I don't want an interesting life!" I was almost in tears now. "I only want my own!"

He was obviously disappointed. "Well, then, I guess that's that."

I have been in a dither ever since, all day. Could it really be my duty to go back and live with them? Is it simply selfishness that makes me want to be on my own? Do I owe it to the world to make life pleasanter for a great man like Felix so that he may be more at ease to write his books and columns?

He reminds me of Thoreau. He pretends to need so little in in life: his brain and the world to observe. But just as Thoreau claimed that he was living off the land in his humble cabin by Walden Pond, whereas he was actually going home whenever he wanted a good meal or a comfortable bed, so Felix claims to live a life of austerity while he has servants and luxuries and people at his beck and call. And now he needs a poor stepdaughter to keep his wife out of his hair. No, it's too much. Really and truly, it's too much!

April 10. What a day! I called on Mother in her Ritz suite and found her "in all her states," as she literally translates the French phrase. She had just discovered, she told me, that Felix had not, as she had supposed, spent the day before yesterday at the American embassy.

"He must have been seeing somebody! Who do you suppose he can have been seeing? There's that French girl he had an affair with twenty-five years ago, but he told me she was dead. Who could it be?"

The unbelievable thing was that at least twenty minutes must have gone by before I realized that Felix had been with *me!* And then I was so paralyzed with astonishment that I could not tell her.

Good God, what can this mean?

The look of hate in Mother's eyes, directed not at me but at some imaginary woman, is still vivid to me tonight. I had never imagined that she could feel so strongly about anything. She is a dangerous woman, a terrible woman. She could kill me! What can I do about this ludicrous, hideous situation?

April 11. I have stayed home all day. Neither Mother nor Felix has telephoned. Perhaps if I do nothing, this whole madness will go away. What, after all, has really happened? I've been to a couple of museums with my stepfather! But why didn't he *tell* her that he had been out with me? Because, I suppose, she didn't ask him. She's watching him, spying on him, and he doesn't know, perhaps doesn't care. Why should *I*, then? Oh, Good Lord, I must be a poor thing. I am scared of literally everything.

April 12. Felix arrived at my door this morning to announce cheerfully that he was taking me to lunch. When I protested a bit hysterically that I couldn't possibly go, he explained that he had cleared up the misunderstanding with Mother, so the next thing I knew we were seated at a banquette at the Tour d'Argent, eating oysters and sipping a heavenly dry white wine. The relief was as stunning as the anxiety!

"What neither your mother nor I can understand is why you didn't tell her you were with me. Did you perhaps take a certain malicious glee in her discomfiture? I wouldn't blame you in the least. It was outrageous, her suspecting me like that!"

"Oh, Felix, I'm so ashamed! I don't know what I was thinking. It suddenly seemed as if life was just too much for me. I suppose I was scared." Was there ever such a ninny as I?

"Because Paris was suddenly hard and wicked. A place where my own mother would scratch out my eyes for her mate! Was *that* the world of grownups, of the able-bodied, that I had wanted? I guess I'd better get back to my childhood." Here I think I laughed bitterly at the pathetic collapse of my whole little European adventure. "I'd better go home with you and Mother, after all. And jump back into the old bed of my past and pull the covers over my head."

Felix was wonderful! He took my hand in his. "No, Fiona. You're going to stay in Paris. You're going to find out what it is to be Fiona Satterlee. And you're going to discover that Fiona Satterlee can be a most interesting person."

"Don't be so nice to me! You'll make me cry. What about you and Mother? Won't you need me?"

"Never mind about your mother. She's taken up quite enough of your life as it is. It's high time we concentrated on *you*. I want you to promise me that you will stay here and be *you*."

"I'll try."

"No, that's not enough. I want you to promise that you *will*."

"Very well, then, I promise." Here he raised his glass to touch it to mine, and we both drank. "But, Felix, will *you* be all right? Will your writing be enough?"

"You mean to make up for your mother?" Yes, he said it, he *said* it! Just that way. So matter-of-fact. There is nothing he can't face. "I have always been happy, Fiona. It takes very little, really, to be happy. When Henry Adams defined his ambition in the *Education*, he might have been speaking for me. It was about his history of the administrations of Jefferson and Madison." I looked up the quote in my copy tonight. Adams wanted "to satisfy himself as to whether, by stating, with the least possible comment, such facts as seemed sure, in such order as seemed rigorously consequent, he could fix, for a familiar moment, a necessary sequence of human events."

Felix says that if a man can do that, what more does he need?

Then he went on: "You hear a great deal of talk as to what is wrong and what is right in this world, but I think the only thing that rational men everywhere would agree upon is that it must be wrong to waste one's life. There are basically only two types of people: those who waste it and those who don't. The latter are all more or less the same sort. It doesn't really matter how much of life they don't waste, so long as it's a recognizable chunk. Join me in the good category, Fiona!"

Then we had more wine, and I looked out the windows at the Seine, at the spring, at April in Paris, and I was happy, very happy. Yes, Felix can give a person happiness. Oh, of course, he can take you over, smother you, but if you once let him see that you want to be free, want to live, like him, not just exist — if you let his extraordinary intellect encompass your problem — then he can bathe you in the sparkling stream of an understanding that is greater than any kindness.

I keep thinking tonight of what he said about our being equal: the non-wasters. It is very generous of him, but it is also true. It makes me determined to live up to my promise. Tonight I bless God for both of us!

Roger Cutter (6)

G EORGETOWN, in the District of Columbia, has always represented to me the outpost, perhaps the last bastion, of aristocracy in a capital dedicated to the popular, the democratic. It has been in this northwestern district of Washington that the rich, the diplomatic, the appointed (as opposed to the elected) members of our government have congregated, finding not only congeniality in taste and good manners, but also a certain sympathy with high ideals of government not always to be found in those favored by the popular vote. The houses of Georgetown, sometimes very small, sometimes, indeed, former negro shanties, have been rebuilt and repolished and redecorated until this portion of our national capital, multicolored, neat, vivid, sparkling, has come to suggest a brightly lit town square in a Restoration comedy.

Only the cognoscenti, in 1950, would have known how much wealth was represented by a simple, three-story, oblong brick house presenting only two windows to the street. Only they would have known that the tan cottage with Doric columns surrounded by half an acre of gardens represented one of the country's great fortunes. In dwellings such as these resided the richer cabinet officers, retired ambassadors, members of the big Washington law firms, and sometimes mere millionaires attracted by the glamor of the capital. There were also a few elected representatives of the people, but these were apt to be of famous political dynasties, such as the Tafts. Georgetown, with its intense, highly articulate and well ordered social life, might have been a patrician Roman suburb in the late empire under the shadow of Visigoth generals, or a legitimist Parisian faubourg in the reign of one of the Napoleons. It had brains and charm and even importance — but it was still not what it believed it was entitled to be.

As the second trial of Alger Hiss approached its verdict in New York, Georgetown cast nervous glances to the north. There was a tendency, even on the part of those who were by no means convinced of the defendant's innocence, to identify his cause with their own. After all, he was a Harvard man, a secretary of Justice Holmes, a high State Department official who had been with FDR at Yalta and, by all accounts, a gentleman and a charming one. Innocent or guilty, would his conviction not give the demagogues of Congress, growling at their gates, the chance to shriek that such conclaves as Georgetown were mere gilded cesspools of treason? Joseph McCarthy would not for another few months make his speech at Wheeling, West Virginia, denouncing the whole State Department as red, but smart observers were already aware of him. Did it not behoove the civilized to close ranks regardless of the truth or falsity of the Hiss charges?

Felix and Gladys Leitner had established in a yellow Georgian house on a prominent corner, and Gladys had filled it with gold-framed mirrors surmounted by eagles' heads, spindly-legged extra tables, marble-topped consoles and American eighteenth-century primitives. As usual, she had been recklessly extravagant; she was determined to be the first hostess of Georgetown, and by the time I arrived in Washington she had virtually succeeded. Felix's semiweekly column was syndicated in hundreds of newspapers; he was one of the most quoted journalists of the nation. President Truman had invited him on several occasions to the White House, and he was consulted by the secretaries of state and defense. At sixty he seemed to have achieved the summit of his ambition.

My own career had been less illustrious. I had published a volume of poetry and had had a one-act play produced by a university theater. I had worked for three different publishing houses, two magazines and a book club. I had resigned from the latter after a bitter argument over its selections policy, and at thirty-five I was out of a job, with a more or less deserved reputation of being a "floater," with a tendency to quit over what I termed compromises. I decided that it would be as well to disappear from the New York literary scene for a while, and where did I ever go, at loose ends, but to Felix? He gave me a part-time job as his research assistant, and I found a room only a few blocks away from his house. The job was all that I wanted, but Felix had limited it to a year. He always insisted that I had to lead "my own life." As if I had any!

It did not take me long to perceive that all was not well between him and Gladys. It might have seemed to some observers that the latter had all a woman could want: a famous, faithful, still handsome husband; a beautiful house; an unchallenged social position. But Gladys's temper was even shorter than when I had first known her, and she had developed the unlovable trait of habitual complaint, which contrasted unfavorably with Felix's continued air of benign equilibrium. Their relationship put me in mind of one of those inlets on the rocky Maine coast where the surf is sucked into a cavernous recess and makes a booming sound before being disgorged. Felix was the cavern; Gladys the ineffectual boom.

Her daughter, Fiona, was with them that winter. Her health

had taken a turn for the worse, and she had been urged to give up her apartment in New York and move in with the Leitners, where there were two maids to help her. The arrangement was only temporary. Fiona was planning to settle in Arizona. In the meantime she was a quiet, tactful but always observant guest. She and I had some revealing chats about her mother and Felix.

"Why can't your mother be happy?" I put it bluntly to her once. "Maybe she paid a high price for Felix, but now it's been paid, and her life is full of blessings. Why doesn't she try to enjoy them?"

"She may not have quite as many blessings as you think, Roger. Take yesterday's column about cronies in the White House."

"It was a masterpiece. The way Felix ran the gamut of favorites from Queen Victoria's Scotch gillie to her grand-daughter's Rasputin! It was devastating."

"Its devastation is just what I mean. Can you imagine its effect on the president? Truman, you know, is not only sensitive, he can be extremely vindictive. I should be very much surprised if Mother got another glimpse of the White House interior while *he's* in office. Unless she goes on the public tour."

"Oh, well." I shrugged. "You know about omelets and eggs."

"Of course I know. But the point is that Felix subjects Mother to a pretty steady diet of omelets. And she finds her life distressingly spattered with egg shells."

"She knew she was marrying a columnist. She took that risk."

"It's not just the columns. How do you think Washington's would-be number one hostess feels when she has put together the perfect dinner party to introduce, say, the chief justice to the secretary of defense, and finds her husband telling one that he's playing politics and the other that he's violated a treaty? Suddenly, she sees her dream evening a shambles, and red-faced, angry guests getting into their coats at nine o'clock!"

"Oh, come now, Fiona. That never happened!"

"*That* never happened, but plenty of other things have. Mother's like Katharina in *The Taming of the Shrew*. Succulent meals are spread before her only to be snatched away when she tries to take a bite."

"But how often? That's the point. Of course, Felix occasionally angers people. But usually things go off smoothly enough. Too smoothly, I sometimes think."

"But Mother never knows when it's going to blow! She has no security. That's the irony of her life. She could always count on Daddy, but he never attracted the lions. Now she has Felix, and he twists their tails. What she really wants, I suppose, is Daddy in Felix's shoes."

"But that's outrageous!" I exploded. "To want to turn a great man into a social puppet for her parties! And when I think how *she* used to criticize Frances for not letting Felix be what he was! Poor Frances. At least she had a noble goal."

"You've always been hard on women, Roger. You expect them to submerge themselves in their mates. But they have to do their own thing. Frances Leitner wanted to live for the poor and benighted. Mother wants to live for parties. You will say it's superficial of her. But Felix knew that when he took her away from Daddy."

"He did not! She was all for the life of the mind, *then*."

"Oh, that was just lovers' talk. Felix wasn't fooled by that for a minute, and you know it."

I collapsed. "You're so reasonable, Fiona. How do you manage always to be so reasonable?"

She did not answer me, but I suspected that, if she had, she would have said it was because of her art. Fiona had developed a small but definite reputation of her own. She had abandoned her earlier tempestuous themes and had settled, curiously enough, on exquisitely colored, highly accurate studies of birds and animals, which enjoyed a fashionable sale on Madison

Avenue to just the sort of people of whom Fiona, in earlier days at least, had seemed most strongly to disapprove. But now they supplied her with an additional income, assuring her independence, and she seemed satisfied.

What she had told me, anyway, prepared me to witness, with more sympathy for Gladys than I might otherwise have felt, the scene that occurred at the Aleck Nickersons' dinner party to welcome the Stuart Hamills to Washington.

Stuart Hamill had just been appointed a roving ambassador to discuss nuclear treaties with those nations that were in a position to develop such power in the foreseeable future. There had been a good deal of publicity given to the appointment, and Hamill was very much the man of the week, that week anyway, in the volatile capital. He was a Yale classmate of Felix's (and, of course, of Heyward Satterlee's) and had been, at least until the divorce, one of Felix's good friends. Hamill was a man who had seemed to prosper from the very cradle. He came of a wealthy Providence family, and he had risen rapidly to the senior partnership of one of that city's oldest and most respected law firms. He had served Rhode Island as both congressman and senator. He was a big, hearty, noisy man, whose style in dress and automobiles was as pronounced as his mild political liberalism was determined.

"Stuart does everything right," Felix once said of him. "His clothes are from Brooks Brothers, his sports equipment from Abercrombie and Fitch, and his opinions from the *New York Times* editorial pages. He is against all the bad things: fascism, communism, isolationism, laissez-fairism. He was a rich boy who was brought up with an iron sense of public duty. He is damned if he won't be good!"

"What's so wrong with that?" I asked.

"Simply that one of these days he may explode all over the room."

"You mean because it's his real nature to be a robber baron and grind the poor?"

"Not at all. He doesn't *have* a real nature. He hasn't been allowed to. But he has a strong ego and a hot temper, not to mention a first-class mind, and he must get weary of keeping them all under such tight control. Don't you sense that in the way his words jump out at you? Like a growling dog on a leash? Can't you hear his inner thoughts: 'Go to hell, if you think you're going to get me to admit I'm any better than you are, you poor sap! Damn it all, I'm a good guy, a good guy, a good guy!'"

"I'm afraid that's too imaginative for me."

"Well, wait."

Dorcas Hamill was a female counterpart of her husband. She was so soft and smiling and fragrant, with such faintly fading beauty, that she made one think of a fine old Chinese shawl. Yet it was draped, one also felt, over a hard substance. One suspected in Mrs. Hamill a character that might yield temporarily but would always snap back. She had borne children when doctors had warned she was risking her life; she had accompanied her husband on trips to distant lands when she had been told that her health would not stand it. She was passionately admired in Georgetown. "Dear, darling Dorcas" was considered the model of womanhood, one who combined the graciousness of a past era with the intrepidity of the modern female.

Only such a couple could have challenged the Leitners' social supremacy in Georgetown. It hardly surprised me that Aleck and Lila Nickerson should have offered the Hamills their first, big welcoming dinner party. Aleck was representing the *Times* in Washington now, and Lila and Gladys, out of their mutual need, had patched up a sort of friendship.

At cocktails, after all the guests had arrived, Lila talked

briefly with me. It might have been supposed that I was too obscure to merit such attention on so great an occasion, but Lila's need to denigrate Felix to his intimates transcended her natural snobbishness.

"Felix's nose is really out of joint tonight," she observed.

I glanced across the room to where Felix and Stuart Hamill — in a way that Washington ladies tolerated and New Yorkers would not have — were engaged, quite by themselves, in an animated discussion.

"Why out of joint? It doesn't look so from here."

"Oh, you know how Felix's back goes up whenever an old friend gets a position of real power."

"No, Lila, I don't."

"Come off it, Roger! I can almost smell his jealousy from here."

"Do you imply that Felix couldn't have a position in government if he chose?"

"Oh, if he chose. But he doesn't choose. He doesn't dare. He couldn't face the responsibility. He's always been that way. The divine umpire. The great onlooker who doesn't want to get his feet wet."

"I suppose there are always going to be people who sneer at political philosophers as non-doers. But it seems curious to find them in the family of the *New York Times*."

Lila did not notice criticism from pygmies. She brushed this aside. "Did you happen to see Lionel Straus's 'Letter from America' in the *Times Literary Supplement*?"

"I don't read Straus. He's a chronic liar and a self-made Cockney."

"He speaks of calling on the Leitners. He says he could hardly recognize his old friend Felix as the Duke of Georgetown. That the one-time socialist was now fussing over silver spoons and tea cups and boasting of his socialite friends!"

"The old bastard! I suppose you sent Felix a copy?"

"I thought he ought to know."

I was too irritated to talk to my hostess further, and I went over to Felix, who had just risen to greet Mrs. Hamill. I could tell by his mild stare that he questioned my interruption, but his manners were too good for a further hint. I told him bluntly that Lila had just informed me of the Straus column.

"How considerate of her," he said in his level tone. Then he turned to Mrs. Hamill. "Let me tell you how an old British friend has treated me. He comes to Washington to report on our national activities. He remains here for two days, a generous allowance you will admit. He has no time to call on me, but we meet briefly at the house of a common acquaintance. He also gives me five minutes on the telephone. From this exiguous communication he draws a picture of me at home, in which I appear as a debilitated Samson, shorn of my hair and manhood and sprawled amid the tea cups! You can imagine who my Delilah was."

"Oh, but, Felix, you must surely be used to that kind of thing!" Mrs. Hamill exclaimed warmly, clasping her hands! "You have to give envious mortals a chance to get rid of their excess bile. Look at you, my dear, so smooth and handsome. If I didn't know you'd been in Stuart's class at Yale I'd swear you were ten years younger. How is foolish Mr. Straus to believe that behind that cool facade is a furnace of hard work? He can't know what your friends know. Forgive him, Felix."

What a woman, this Dorcas Hamill! So charming was the appearance of her sincerity that it did not really matter whether or not it was true. A perfect work of art had to have validity in itself. I had been in the habit of criticizing Lila Nickerson for not being more grateful to providence for her brains and position, for allowing her spirit to be corroded by a hankering resentment that she was not beautiful and feminine, but when I contemplated the success of Dorcas I wondered if Lila were not justified. What were any gifts in a woman compared to those with which Dorcas was endowed? Even Felix, who had seemed more riled by the Straus episode than was his wont, was now mollified.

Perhaps Dorcas Hamill had a sense of trouble in the air already. Perhaps, like a good diplomat, she was trying to create an atmosphere of gentility that only a churl would break up. We had not proceeded through more than one course at the dinner table before Lila announced that we were to have general conversation. She then put a question to her guest of honor about the Russian government.

Hamill spoke well and convincingly, but he was inclined to lecture his audience. I noted the fixed stare on Felix's expressionless face as he listened. It meant that he was dissenting, for whenever he agreed with a speaker he would offer him the briefest of nods, or the slightest of smiles, but he would respond only to a direct question.

"It has become a platitude, I suppose," Hamill seemed now to be concluding, "to point out that the free world must win every election, but that Russia need win only one. Yet it puts the problem in a way that one is not apt to forget. When we say that eternal vigilance is the price of freedom, we are speaking only a literal truth. One blink, and we may be in the darkness forever."

As this marked a pause in what had been a considerable harangue about bolstering anti-Communist governments throughout the world, Lila asked Felix to comment.

"I think Stuart has put the matter very clearly," he began amiably enough, in that easy tone that took so wonderfully for granted the room's total attention. "But I'm afraid I cannot see the world situation in terms quite so simple. I see many gradations of communism, as I certainly see many gradations of capitalism. I do not foresee a world struggle of black against white, or perhaps I should say of red against white. I tend to be critical of any foreign policy that regards compromise as weakness. It seems to me that this may be the same dangerous point of view that was behind the demand for unconditional surrender in both wars."

"You would have made peace with Hitler, Felix?"

"I don't say that, Stuart. But I might have offered terms to any group in Germany that undertook to topple him."

"They would have been Nazis! There were no groups that weren't. How could you have trusted their word?"

"What country keeps its word when it's not to its advantage?"

"Britain! And, I'm proud to say, the USA!"

"Our history, until very recently, has been one of isolationism, where promises need not be given. As to Britain . . ."

And so it went. Hamill, who for all his efforts to be fair, was still a man who obviously detested contradiction, began to become heated, and his wife intervened to change the subject.

"I'm afraid I lean to Felix's persuasion," she said tactfully. "I've always been afraid of blacks and whites. I prefer softer shades. I suppose if I'd been a Roman I'd have asked Attila to dinner. Yet who knows what I might have accomplished? Isn't one of the Russian troubles that they have no attractive wives in their diplomatic corps?"

But Lila was determined to have her two lions fight it out, and she now asked for their opinions on the secretary of state's last statement on Russian aggression. Hamill promptly labeled it a "great" speech.

"But who was it aimed at?" Felix inquired. "The Russian people won't read it. Their leaders discount it and ask their intelligence people what Acheson really meant. Our allies shrug and look to the results. American fulminations tend to be aimed at Americans. Dean Acheson is trying to convince the

Republicans in the House and Senate that he's just as anti-Red as they are."

"And do you suggest he's *not?*" Hamill demanded, almost threateningly.

"My dear Stuart, of course, I know he is!" Felix explained, almost gaily. "*They* think he's not. They think the State Department is full of cookie-pushers and parlor pinks. Dean went to Groton; you went to Saint Paul's. Obviously, this only confirms the damning opinion of that most fatuous of all our patriots: the right-wing, middle-western congressman!"

Hamill was only half appeased by this. Clearly he did not care to be identified, even at a small dinner, with so sweeping a condemnation of any elected legislator. "Well, if that is so, is the secretary not right to make his position crystal clear?"

"I do not think so. I do not believe in addressing one audience, while you are really speaking to another. In Dean's case it is a kind of public muscle-flexing that is demeaning to him and confusing to others. I suspect, if there be a danger in schools like Groton and Saint Paul's, that it is precisely the opposite of what our western legislators supposes. It is not cookie-pushing; it is pugnacity. The violent games, the football, the intense team spirit, the sense of Christian gentlemen standing together against barbarians — I wonder if it doesn't all tend to make their graduates too aggressive, too belligerent. As if America were one team and the Soviet Union another, pitted against each other in a new kind of world series."

"Are you suggesting that the secretary of state and I are acting like schoolboys?" Hamill demanded, beginning to look black.

"Well, I remember, Stuart, in freshman year, that you actually wept when Harvard beat Yale!"

This may have been delivered in a good-natured tone, but the circumstances made it decidedly unpleasant. I had hardly ever known Felix to make an *ad hominem* argument in public. In private, yes — some of his most perspicacious observations were made as to the true motives underlying the actions of public figures. But when he spoke for the record — and even a small dinner party to him was a kind of record — he was usually detached and impersonal.

"I'll have you know, Felix, that I resent what you have just said! On my own behalf *and* on Mr. Acheson's!"

The "Mr." before the secretary's name was a nice little additional twist of the jabbing knife. It seemed to call into question Felix's prior use of the name "Dean." But Felix did not even blush. He simply looked serenely down the table at his adversary and blinked his eyes. After a minute of almost unendurable general embarrassment the conversation scurried desperately into smaller groups and finally settled in uneasy pairs.

There was no further confrontation between Hamill and Felix that night, but when I walked the three blocks afterward with Felix and Gladys to their house, the latter was ominously silent, and Felix's invitation to me to come in for a nightcap was almost in the nature of a plea for an ally.

"I don't in the least mind if Roger comes in," Gladys said coldy. "In fact, I should be rather glad to have him hear what I am going to say."

One might imagine that a person of tact would have absented himself, but when had I been that? I had no idea either of abandoning my friend to his enraged wife or of giving up my seat to an important scene in his drama. Felix and I sat in the living room, each with a brandy glass, while Gladys, smoking furiously, paced the floor.

"I know why you said what you did tonight, Felix. You may think I'm an empty-headed rattle, but I see what I see. For all your great brain and wisdom, you're petty and jealous. You can't stand Stuart Hamill's success!"

Felix's bland stare seemed to take her in and find her wanting. His silence drove her to fury.

"You *hate* Stuart Hamill! The way you hate his boss! Because they're above you. Yes, *above* you. I use antiquated social terms because they express so exactly what you're thinking!"

"You might spare Roger this final vulgarity."

"I'll spare Roger nothing! He loves it, anyway. You can't bear that men who were your social superiors when you were young are now running the world. Stuart Hamill was in Skull and Bones and on the football team at Yale, and now he's trying to save the world from blowing itself up. What were *you* doing then but scribbling for the *Yale Literary Magazine*, which nobody read? And what are you doing *now* but writing a silly column for old women to read while they sip their coffee?"

"Gladys, that's ridiculous!" I cried. "It's ridiculous and you know it!"

"Of course, it's ridiculous. I know what Felix is worth. I put it that way because I want *him* to recognize what goes on in his psyche. If he can ever learn that, it may help him to understand what he's doing to Stuart Hamill when he takes off at him that way at a dinner party. And if he can ever realize that, perhaps he'll stop!"

Felix now raised his hands in a gesture of helplessness. "Never have I been more impressed by the old adage that a little Freud is a dangerous thing."

"Well, it's helped me to understand a lot of things that have happened to *me*. For example, why you wanted me in the first place." Gladys ceased her pacing now and turned to her husband with what I thought was a rather stagy stamp of her foot. "You had to take me away from poor Heyward because he was a bigger guy on the Yale campus than you!"

Felix rose at this and came over to shake my hand. "The discussion has become inane. I am sorry to have exposed you to it. I'm going to bed. Good night, Roger."

*   *   *

It was never much fun for people to stay angry with Felix, because he would never acknowledge a feud and would greet you in the street just as politely as if nothing had happened. So in a few days' time Stuart Hamill had called to make up, and he and Felix were soon on as intimate terms as ever. Even Gladys seemed convinced that all was over, for she sent out invitations to a dinner party in honor of Ambassador Hamill and the lovely Dorcas, to which I, as an extra man, was invited.

It was a small dinner, only a dozen as I recall, and the first person I met in the living room was Lila Nickerson. She seemed very excited and motioned me over to the seat beside her.

"Haven't you heard?" she demanded.

"What?"

"The jury's in. Hiss has been convicted."

"He has!"

I knew that would be the end of any other conversation that night. When Hamill arrived, he made no effort to disguise his agitation, and the party again became an exchange between him and Felix, heated by the cocktails, which were rapidly, almost unconsciously, consumed.

"It's a national outrage!" Hamill exclaimed. "It's another Sacco-Vanzetti. I know the secretary feels as I do. I believe he's going to say something at his press conference."

"I hope he's not!" Felix retorted, his eyes widening into one of his rare expressions of alarm. "What on earth could he say?"

"Something about it's not affecting his friendship with Alger."

"But that would be taken as impugning the verdict."

"And if it were?"

"Aren't you forgetting the separation of powers? A high official of the administration has no business attacking the judiciary."

Hamill seemed to pull up a bit at this. "But it's not attacking the judiciary to say that a jury may have mistaken the facts. Surely, that must happen all the time. Can a man not state his mind?"

"A man, yes. A secretary of state, no. Mr. Acheson has no right to undermine his own authority and prestige by identifying himself with a man who, after two extensive trials, has been found guilty of perjury in denying that he was a traitor."

"I take it from that that you consider Hiss guilty!"

"I am not convinced. I think it quite possible."

"You believe a rat like Chambers? A known Communist? A proven liar? You take his word against a man who was trusted by everyone in the State Department?"

"A jury did. Why shouldn't I? And Chambers had no motive to destroy Hiss."

"There was a lot in all that that never came out."

"Well, I can't go into that. But I stick to my guns about the question of a statement. When a man takes public office he should give up the right of expressing his private opinion on matters outside his department. Particularly when such expression may give rise to the suspicion that he is allied with traitors."

"Do you mean, sir, that Mr. Acheson or myself could be suspected of actual treason?" Hamill glanced about the room, his face congealed as if ready either to explode in laughter or in wrath, as the situation might require.

"I most certainly do," Felix replied calmly. "The president himself may not be exempt in the hysteria that we're running into. The same thing happened after the First World War. It's something we'll simply have to live through."

"And you think we should take it lying down!" Hamill now thundered. "Where are your guts, Leitner?"

"I don't have to prove them, Hamill. The way you evidently think you have to prove yours."

"Dorcas, we're going home!"

The diminished party that sat down for dinner half an hour later was too dismal to be described. Gladys was grimly silent, and when the guests left, shortly after their coffee and brandy, I made no move to stay on with the Leitners. For once in my life I fled. No part of any account of Felix's life was going to be worth sitting through *that* scene.

*   *   *

The next thing that happened was Dean Acheson's famous statement at a press conference that he would not "turn his back on Alger Hiss." The uproar that followed this almost drowned out the statement made by Ambassador Hamill to a reporter as he boarded a plane at Idlewild on a mission to London. Mr. Hamill gave as his opinion that the jury had misconceived the facts of the case and that the verdict would be reversed on appeal. Indeed, no notice might have been taken of the remark had it not been for Felix Leitner's column two days later, which read in part as follows:

It is impossible not to feel some sympathy for Mr. Acheson's outbreak. He was goaded by reporters who were determined to make him repudiate Alger Hiss. In a moment of understandable temper he made a statement that simply affirmed his personal regard for a friend in grave trouble. Of course, he should have refrained from comment. Responsible public servants should be willing to forego the luxury of publishing their opinions in controversial matters unconnected with their departments, where such publication may jeopardize the success of their policies by undermining their public support. But Ambassador Hamill had no such excuse. No reporters hounded him. He thrust his opinion of the Hiss jury into an interview on quite other matters. Like the frog in Emily Dickinson's poem, he had to tell his name, the livelong day, to "an admiring bog." And far from limiting his statement to an expression of friendship, or even loyalty, he denounced the trial as a rank miscarriage of justice. Already the whole back of Red baiters is on his trail! How are foreign governments to know what credit to give to the words of an emissary so denounced at home? Mr. Hamill should resign his trust and learn the lesson that ministers of state lose nothing by the dignity of silence.

The effect of this in Georgetown may be imagined. As people were quick to point out, the Red baiters had *not* been on Stuart Hamill's trail until the publication of the column. It was Felix, they cried, and not the House Un-American Activities Committee, that had called Hamill's rash but largely unnoticed statement to the national attention. What was Leitner trying to do but destroy the ambassador? Ah, yes, there it *was*, what they had always suspected, they muttered and snarled, the envy of the Jew, the distrust of the person who has never been quite included, the malice of the academic against the man of action, the resentment of the boy who was not sent to a New England private school. Oh, yes, they had always known about *him!*

I had to go to New York at this time to help my now ancient, widowed mother move into a new apartment, and when I returned a few days later the storm was still raging. When I went to the Leitners to report for work, I found Felix alone in his study. He told me that Gladys had moved out.

"Moved out?" I asked, open-mouthed.

"She's gone to Lila's for a week. But she expects me out of here when she returns. The house, the contents, everything, of course, is hers."

"She's leaving you!"

"I think rather she expects me to leave her. I'll go to the Mayflower until I find an apartment."

"Felix!"

"It's all right, Roger, it really is." Seeing my distress he rose to put an arm briefly about my shoulders. Then he walked to the window and stood with his back to me. "It's been coming a long time, and perhaps it's just as well. Now I shan't be concerned every morning with what her reaction will be to what happened the night before. She has developed this obsession that everything I do is designed to pull her down. It seems to have been my fate to be married to women who think I want to torture them. It's only because they try to make their life in me. And if I don't fit, I'm repudiating them. I guess I wasn't made for marriage, Roger. Perhaps some day, when women have achieved a real equality with men — I mean an emotional equality, not just votes and jobs — marriage may be feasible for the individualist."

"I suppose what she really minds is your not minding the scenes she makes."

"But I *do* mind, Roger. You have no conception of how much I mind. Because I try to put an enamel layer over myself, I may seem immune. But Gladys's scenes and jibes are poison to me!" When he turned, I was shocked at the vivid red on his cheeks. I could not recall ever having seen such a color on his complexion before. "I want peace and quiet. God, I think I must hate her!"

In the weeks that followed, Felix went into seclusion at the Mayflower. He saw nobody but myself, and he told me more of his thoughts and emotions than he had ever done before.

He was sad, at times bitter, at times almost angry, but always firm and clear.

It was the principal difficulty in his life, he told me, that he had had to live in the great world. It was one thing to be a poet, a philosopher, a historian. Such a man could retire from the world, at least while he worked. He could seek a cloister and be alone with his books and thoughts. But a political commentator could not do this. He had to read, of course, but just as importantly he had to live in the world. He had to be acquainted with presidents, ambassadors, cabinet officers, legislators. There was no substitute for the personal interview, the direct impression, the unrecorded question and answer. Nor could it all be·done in offices. The social occasion was indispensable, with the relaxation that came with women and wine.

"Everyone in this world wants a friend, Roger. Most people, indeed, feel *entitled* to friendship. Even presidents want friends. With them, friendship may be a one way street, but they still want it. Nobody has ever really been able to accept the fact that I can have no friend but truth. It is absolutely essential for me to meet people, at parties, at lunches, over drinks. And once I've done it, they feel, even when they don't acknowledge it, that some kind of duty of loyalty, however slight, has been established. And so, inevitably, ultimately, they feel betrayed. The women, of course, are the worst. I don't suppose there really has ever been anyone who had understood me but you."

This must have been the happiest moment of my life. I glowed, I pulsated, with the fervor of my ultimate intimacy. But even then I had a little moment of doubt. A horrid little doubt. For if I had really succeeded at last in adjusting myself totally to Felix's needs, did I exist at all?

Roger Cutter (7)

FELIX never married again. I am sure that his two experiences had taught him that freedom was necessary to the career of the political journalist — at least as he conceived it. More and more now he turned to the ascetic life. He reduced his homes to a small Georgetown house run by an efficient black couple and a room for the summer in the Blaine Hotel in Butterfield Bay. His hours of work became absolutely regular. From nine until noon he read newspapers, press releases, magazines, congressional records, court opinions. He would then have lunch, never with more than one person, a key figure in whatever matter it was that he was investigating. The afternoons were devoted to writing his column, which appeared twice a week, or to further study. The evenings and weekends were given to more general reading. Social life was limited strictly to two dinner parties a week, and then he was always home by eleven. For exercise he walked his dogs, a pair of huskies, in Rock Creek Park.

Routine, he insisted, brought the only true liberation. If one did the same thing every day, one did not have to argue with people who tried to urge one toward variation. Felix would not even talk on the telephone, except on business. His secretary, Miss Farish, a loyal, industrious spinster, would take your message. A hostess would be asked whom Mr. Leitner was being invited to meet and what time dinner would actually be on the table. The rare weekend house guest would be told what hour to arrive, what hour to leave and during what periods Mr. Leitner was not to be disturbed. As Felix's fame grew and his years increased, everybody but the bitterest old friends came to accept his arbitrary ways. Indeed, his regularity, his austerity, even his famed coolness of manner began to seem to younger friends the appropriate characteristics of an internationally renowned seer.

If the need for concentration was not considered by some a quite adequate excuse for such rigidity of form, Felix's health could be pleaded in addition. After sixty he was afflicted with fibrillations of the heart which, although supposedly not dangerous, required a minimization of excitement and a maximization of orderliness. I think that Felix may have regarded this ailment in the cheerful light of an additional safeguard of his chosen schedule. It also protected him from women. Despite what people may have thought and said about Julie Pryor, she never achieved anything but an *amitié amoureuse*.

She told me this herself, and Julie was not a woman to mince such matters. She was (and still is) a ravishing blonde — blue-eyed, tall, willowy, with marvelous dresses that always seemed to pour over her slender but voluptuous figure. Her voice was high, affected, cultivated, absurdly affectionate, sweet. She went in for demonstrative gestures; she was a great kisser and hand-clasper, even a hugger. The word "darling" seemed always on her lips. Yet at the time of the episode that I shall describe in this chapter, Felix was seventy-five and she, sixty.

She had always been a man's woman. When young and poor, though of an old Philadelphia family, she had made two brief marriages to men of means more apparent than actual.

Her third husband had been a crook who had robbed her of what little she had gleaned from the first two, and she had found herself at forty, alone, childless, and perilously on the verge of sinking to shabby roles. As she once described this to me: "Friends with boring old husbands who wanted to distract attention from their own peccadilloes would ask me for the weekend, purring, 'Dearest Julie, nobody can keep Tom in a good humor like you.' And then they'd make me a present of last year's Dior or Givenchy!"

A lucky marriage to old Sam Pryor, the realtor, who died a year later and bequeathed her a legacy that was adequate for her support even after she had settled a lawsuit with his angry children, gave Julie the independence that she had long craved, and she turned from the pleasures of the bed to the pleasures of the political hostess. Her charming little Frenchified parlor in Georgetown was the perfect site for a salon, and I was naturally convinced that she was planning to make Felix its principal and permanent ornament. But she soon convinced me otherwise.

"I know what you're thinking, dear Roger, and I don't blame you at all. We women are a predatory lot. But you can put your mind at rest. I have no desire whatsoever to inveigle Felix into marriage. I have had four husbands, which already makes me a bit ridiculous. A fifth would turn me into a kind of monster, a Wife of Bath! And then consider what I should lose. Poor dear Sam Pryor wrote a will that cuts off my income if I remarry and sends it back to those ravenous brats of his. So I would bring Felix nothing! And what could he leave *me*? Such little principal as he still has is tied up for his children, and the income from the column would stop with his death. Which, however much we hate to think of it, could come any time."

Well, it certainly made sense. There was very little gain for Julie in becoming Mrs. Leitner. Furthermore, she would be taking on the responsibility for the time when Felix might become incapacitated or senile. Surely it was better for her simply to act as hostess at his small dinners, which she ably and charmingly did, and have her days free from the austere routine of Felix's household. Yes, I could see that she had made the wiser choice.

Julie and I thus became the team "in charge" of Felix Leitner. I had now achieved my ultimate ambition and had become his principal research assistant and general manager. It was too late for him to argue that I should make a life of my own: he had to accept the fact that I had no other life but his.

"What will you do when I die?" he asked me once.

"Write a book about you."

"That won't take the rest of your life."

"Then I'll write two!"

The years, as if responding to the smooth sails of Felix's well-regulated existence, sped by. He wrote no more books or articles; he seemed to have found his ultimate form of expression in the newspaper column. Like a poet who has spent a long lifetime on odes and epodes, on dramatic monologues and epic verse, and who at last falls back on the sonnet series as the perfect vehicle to drive his mind and heart in tandem, so did Felix now polish and repolish, cut and amplify, the jewel-like essays that, twice a week, conveyed his sense of a rash and giddy world to his adoring readers.

The columns were all the same length, almost to a word count. They usually feel into three sections: the statement of theme, a marvel of clarity and conciseness; the basic discussion, which contained the essential literary part, sometimes dramatic, sometimes rhetorical, sometimes almost poetic, a brief but exhaustive exercise in alternative arguments and points of view; and finally the conclusion, usually framed in a Leitner paradox. Felix dealt ordinarily with foreign affairs or government news, but he also noticed great events, such as the moon landing or the cure for polio, or the obituaries of famous men, and every six months he would compose a piece on what he once described to me with a dry smile as the "eternal verities." There was something of La Rochefoucauld in his method; as the great Frenchman strove to catch life in epigrams, so did Felix seek to hammer his columns into reflections of the essence of the political scene.

"I'm not such an ass as to think I even approach my goal," he told me once, "but I like to think that my columns, taken together, may provide a capsule history of the postnuclear age."

Felix had regarded the atom as the ultimate challenge to mankind. According to him, it had changed all our concepts of war and survival and required entirely new mental and emotional processes. Man could no longer afford the romantic luxury of fighting a vicious enemy to the death; a greater courage had to be found in compromise. The free states and the enslaved communities had to recognize that neither could predominate. There could be no more unconditional surrenders, no more . . . but I am not going to get into Felix's philosophy. That will be another book, a bigger one, my second. This one is addressed to his personality.

The years of Felix's life from the age of sixty to that of seventy-five, from 1950 to 1965, seemed to pass rapidly. They were not marked by important personal events, or even major trips or moves. There were no domestic embroilments. Felix's son, Frank, had finally found a moderate contentment running a gas station that Felix had purchased for him in New Mexico. Frank's problem had been the hardest that a brilliant parent can face: it had taken a psychiatrist to perceive that the boy was a near moron and pathetically ashamed of it. Felix's daughter during this same period was intensely occupied in New York with her rather tumultous marriage to the artist Stephen Cast. With his small court of two dogs and two domestics, with his secretary and Julie and me, Felix led a placid existence within the walls of routine. His life was a greenhouse where his genius flourished.

Oh, there were storms, of course, but they were the storms of journalism. They hardly penetrated the quiet house on Q Street. I remember Felix's chuckling over the screeches that greeted his description of Eisenhower's failure to defend General Marshall from Joe McCarthy's smear as "the most dastardly public ablution of the primary tactile organs since Pontius Pilate." I recall his evaluation of the Bay of Pigs as "a marine operation that brings to mind the genius of Philip II and Medina Sidonia." There were gaffes, to be sure, as when he promised his readers that the Soviets would never attempt to build a missile base in Cuba and that De Gaulle would not abandon Algeria. And there were triumphs, too, as when he solemnly warned Senator McCarthy, at the peak of that demagogue's career, that "the day will come when the United States senate, unlike its abject predecessor of Roman times, will rise from its vile posture of opportunistic groveling and redeem itself with a clarion censure of these lewd and reckless tactics."

And then old age surprised him. It was as if Father Time had been walking down Q Street on a quiet, mild spring morning, and met Felix with his dogs. I suddenly noted that there were lines on the clear cheeks and that the youthful face had somehow shriveled. Felix would pause more often now in his walks; he would sometimes stand still for a minute at a time. He was quieter at meals. But he listened just as sharply. There was no shortening of his hours of work, no drop in the quality of the famous column.

The last drama, if that be not too strong a word, was the arrival of Felicia in Washington at the end of 1965. She was now forty-five years old and the mother of two children, a son and a daughter, both college dropouts. She herself was a kind of dropout, for she had left her husband (at his own rudely voiced request) and had conceived as a bright new life for herself — a compensation, no doubt, for the mess that she had made of her old one — that of making a "wonderful home for Daddy."

Felicia had taken her mother's side so violently at the time of the divorce that it had been years before she and Felix had been reconciled, and the breach had never been entirely healed. I believe that it might have been, had Felix been fonder of her. But, to tell the truth, Felicia has always been a difficult person to love. She is bright and handsome and direct and honest; she has a generous heart, and she wants to love and be loved. But she is too big, in size, in tone, in gesture, in emotion. She is too violently partisan in all her conflicts, and she brings little imagination and no vestige of humor to aid her chosen team. In a word, she is exasperating.

She had adored Stephen Cast and had driven him almost mad. A sample of an argument she had with him once, when they were spending a weekend with Felix, will show what I mean.

Felix never much cared for modern art, particularly abstract, but he liked to preserve on open mind, and he was always interested in learning about any subject from a person who really knew about it. That particular weekend had been largely devoted to Stephen Cast's attempt to persuade him that representational painting no longer had a valid function in our century. Stephen was a big, burly, dark man, with the intense dedication and rough language commonly associated with painters, but he was quick to appreciate similar dedication, even in very different fields, and his respect for his father-in-law was not only apparent but deep. When I came in for cock-tails that Saturday evening, he was explaining to Felix a cubist water color which he had just given him and which was propped up on the mantelpiece for their better examination. It appeared to be made up of squares, some blue, some rusty red, some deep green, the colors spilling over the edges of their containing barriers and blending in blurbs. On top of the squares was a small blue-gray triangle.

"What should I be looking for?" Felix asked.

"Nothing. Just take it in. Absorb it."

"But that's what I find most difficult. I can't help having a reaction. I can't help saying to myself, What does it look like? What does it remind me of?"

"Well, there's no great harm in that," Cast said easily. "What *does* it remind you of?"

"Well, you may laugh, but it gives me the feeling of a moun-tain. It gives me a sense of my old summers in Seal Cove, when I used to go climbing. I see the gray of the rocks and the blue of the sea and the green of the forest. In fact, now that I begin to make it out, I quite like it. Yes! Thank you, Stephen. I shall call it *Seal Cove Summer — 1938.*"

I do not know if it was Felix's mentioning the summer of his affair with Gladys that upset Felicia, but she came into the argument now with a rumble.

"Daddy, that's not the way one approaches modern art at all! You mustn't be an old-fashioned representationalist looking for images in every square and squiggle. There's something rather pathetic about it, really — all that yearning for sunsets and landscapes and nudes and knights-in-armor in abstract canvases. Don't give in to it! You must learn to *feel*, without constantly objectivizing."

"I'm not sure about that at all," Felix retorted, slightly nettled by her condescension. "Take that series of landscapes Cézanne did of that mountain — what was it called?"

"Mont Sainte-Victoire," Cast supplied.

"That's it. Well, I remember a show in Paris where a great number of them were exhibited chronologically. The early ones were naturalistic — at least the way I use the term — and then came a group that I should call impressionistic. And finally there were some almost abstract ones. Very much like your painting here, Steve. In fact, if one hadn't seen the earlier studies, one might not have been sure they were of a mountain at all!"

"But, Daddy, Stephen wasn't *thinking* of a mountain when he painted it. He wasn't thinking of any sort of landscape at all."

"Oh, shut up, Felicia! How do you know what I was thinking about?"

"Well, you weren't, were you?"

"I don't think I was thinking of a mountain, no. Or even of trees or rocks. But there is some kind of organic origin to all my painting, and if that water color makes your father think of a mountain in Maine, it's a perfectly valid reaction."

"But, darling, you told me that you wanted people to *see* your pictures and not just paint what they want over them!"

"You're confusing two different things," Cast said impatiently. "I was talking about the kind of people who bring nothing to a painting but their own preconceptions. Your father has a totally different reaction. He is attempting to match his emotion to that of the artist. He is, in effect, seeking to complete the communication. That's what every painter wants. What difference does it make if he sees a mountain where I may have sensed only a particular shape? We each had a mountainous feeling."

"I don't see that at all! What is the difference between

Daddy seeing a mountain where you never intended one and that silly Mrs. Hicks, whom you made such cruel fun of, saying that the circles in your *Study in Black and White* reminded her of the cherubs in Murillo's *Ascension of the Virgin?*"

"Oh, Felicia, how can you compare your father with that idiotic Hicks woman? Try not to be more of an idiot than God made you!"

Felicia now fled from the room, in tears, an exit frequent for her in this last stage of her marriage, and Stephen announced that he would walk off his irritation by taking the dogs around the block. Felix, left alone with me, showed a certain callousness at his daughter's evident suffering.

"That was naughty of me," he admitted, but with a chuckle that belied his repentance. "I knew I'd put them at each other's throats, but I couldn't resist it."

"Resist what? I didn't notice that you said anything."

"I compared Steve with Cézanne. Indirectly, anyway. That was all I needed to get him on my side. Once Felicia attacked my point of view, she was destroying his compliment. So, presto! He had to jump on her."

"Felix, you fiend! You should be helping her."

Felix shrugged. "There's nothing to be done, my friend. That marriage is on the rocks."

Indeed it was. Only a few months after that weekend, Stephen told poor Felicia that he was through. In true artist fashion, he neither asked for a divorce, nor offered her the smallest support, nor took the least interest in what happened to the children. He simply holed up in his studio and went on with his painting. It rather shocked me that Felix described this reaction as "manly."

"You mean it's manly to leave one's family in the lurch?" I inquired.

"They're not left in the lurch. The children are old enough

· 260 ·

to support themselves, and Felicia has some money. No, what I mean is there's so much crap today about all the love and care and understanding a man owes his family, that I can't help applauding a male who sees the cultivation of his own artistic gift as his primary duty."

"Like a lion that nourishes itself by eating its own young?"

"Maybe that's better than pushing a perambulator!"

I knew that there was no arguing with Felix when he was in this mood. But for all his expressed independence of mind about family ties, he reversed himself when Felicia turned to him in her distress, and actually offered to take her into his house in Georgetown. Both Julie and I thought this was a very poor idea. Felix, however, evidently relishing the new vision of himself in the role of the good father, brushed our objections aside.

"Felicia needs me," he told us, rather loftily. "She has been humiliated by her husband, and to some extent by her children. She feels herself a failure. If it will save her pride to let her imagine that she is helping to sustain her doddering old father, shouldn't I go along with her fantasy? Who knows? It may turn out to be true!"

Felicia's son, an amiable, feckless lad, was living in a commune in California, but her daughter, Varina, was very much on the scene. She had reentered college, at New York University, but only to intensify her radical activities. She was big, like her mother, with long blonde hair parted in the middle, but she was much brighter and harder and more efficient. She had many causes, but currently she was absorbed in the fight against the Vietnamese war. Felicia embarrassed not only her father but I think her daughter, in the way she prostrated herself before the younger generation.

"I call them the generation of truth," she told Felix and me. "Never before have young people so resolutely challenged the hypocrisy and greed of the past. It is absolutely inspiring,

Daddy! They stand up to every once-accepted value and cry sternly: 'Prove yourself!' "

"But do they have to mix it up with drugs and beards and bad language?" Felix protested.

"Those things are simply badges of the movement. They are no more important than your tie or your collar or your habit of saying 'Good morning.' "

"That may be true of serious girls like Varina. But some of her friends seem to find the badges everything."

"I'm surprised, Daddy, that a man of your perception and intellectual curiosity should be so superficial."

"Well, my dear, that will be one of the blessings of your visit. That you will teach me otherwise. We must all learn to understand the young. Where else is the future?"

I was astonished at how mildly Felix reacted to what I regarded as Felicia's officiousness in seeking to take over the housekeeping in Q Street. She managed to be bossy and apologetic at the same time, overwhelming the couple with compliments and then suggesting changes in everything they did. Had they not been so devoted to their employer (and naturally conscious of what he might have provided for them in his will), they would have walked out. Felicia had evidently decided that I was a fixture and had to be accepted, but she tried to make me an ally against Julie.

"That woman is trying to marry my father. It's as plain as the nose on your face!"

I patiently supplied my arguments for not thinking this to be the case.

"Because she *said* so?" Felicia demanded scornfully. "And you believed her?"

"I did."

"Well, if she doesn't want to marry him, what does she want?"

"Simply to be his friend."

"And not . . . not his . . . ?"

"Mistress? No. She wants to be what Madame de Pompadour was to Louis XV when their affair was over: a charming and diverting companion. Fortunately, she doesn't have to procure girls for him, as the Pompadour did."

"Roger, please!"

"You brought the matter up, Felicia. Don't blame *me* for indelicacy."

After this colloquy I decided that Felicia might turn on me as well, so I decided to forestall her. I had a discussion with Felix about the advisability of setting her up in her own apartment. But he was still reluctant to take any definite step.

"If Felicia has made a mess of her life, it's partly my fault. Now that she has no mother to go to, she needs me. I can't fail her, Roger."

"But you don't have to let her live with you. You don't have to let her disrupt your household. You can be a perfectly good father short of that. You've spent a lifetime seeking the exact right working conditions for yourself. Why let her interfere with them? I think you owe it to the papers that publish you to keep her from messing up your life."

"You know as well as I, Roger, that I've always been accused of having a monstrous ego. Now here's a belated opportunity to do something for another human being, who happens to be my own child. I say, let's not let it slip!"

Well, as it turned out, I did not have to worry. All that was necessary was to supply Felicia with a noose and she would stick her neck in it. It was her daughter, Varina, who not only produced the rope but neatly tied the knot,

Varina had been delighted that her grandfather had so strongly opposed the commitment of ground troops to the fighting in Vietnam. She had been down to Washington to visit her mother and to quiz him, rather sternly I thought, about his position, to be sure that he was orthodox according to her "activist" principles. Although she could not induce him to support deserters or even draft evaders, she finally decided that his reluctance to do so was a holdover from "gentlemanly rules of conduct" that he was too old to shed. She invited him to address a students' antiwar rally to be held in New York in the gymnasium of a settlement house near Washington Square. Felix accepted despite my protest.

"They're all smelly and bearded," I warned him, "and they won't listen to anyone who deviates one inch from their sacred credo."

"Roger, middle age is making you an impossible Tory. It's like weight. You have to watch it. Of course I'm going. I think it will be a lark. I've been much too out of touch with young people these many years."

We flew up to New York for the rally, which was held on a Saturday afternoon, accompanied by Felicia, who, I think, was prouder of this invitation to her father than she had been of his Pulitzer Prize. The gymnasium, large and smelling of varnish, was packed, and Felix did not go up to the platform until several ragged students had made inane but much applauded inflammatory addresses. Felicia and I sat in the front row, and I spotted Varina, who, presumably from modesty at not wishing to stand out as the granddaughter of so famous a man, was over to the side, sitting with a particularly shaggy young man who was being constantly consulted by students who came up behind him and leaned down to whisper to him. He and Varina were evidently in charge of the afternoon's events.

When Felix at last rose to speak, he was as cool and clear and amiable as if he had been addressing a group of fashionable ladies at the Colony Club. He denounced President Johnson's escalation of the war; he denounced the domino theory of former Secretary of State Dulles; he excoriated the tendency to divide the world into Communists and anti-Communists, but he did it all as if he were delivering a fascinating lecture on some past conflagration, the Civil War, say, and the position of such neutral nations as France and England. The audience was interested but restive. They were accustomed to more fireworks.

It had been agreed that Felix would speak for only twenty minutes and that then the floor would be open for general discussion.

"I usually have a question planted in the audience to get things started," he concluded with a smile. "But I have a feeling today that everyone in this room has a question. Am I right?"

The hirsute young man by Varina was now whispering to her in a very animated fashion. He looked stern and suspicious. Finally, she nodded to him, as if to give him permission, and he rose to direct a question at Felix.

"Mr. Leitner, you have said that the United States made a 'tactical error' in committing ground troops to the fighting in Vietnam. Wasn't it more than an error? Wasn't it an immoral act?"

"Well, who was it who said: 'It's worse than a crime. It's a blunder'?"

There was some scattered laughter at this, but the young man did not join in it.

"What I want to know is whether *you* consider it immoral."

"In a sense, I do. It must be immoral to ask young men to die for idiotic reasons. It was the duty of our executive branch to make a more comprehensive study of the facts before it pressed for so drastic a remedy."

"You speak of asking young men to die. What about asking them to kill?"

"Doesn't it come to the same thing?"

"No. I understand that you think it's immoral for our government to kill American soldiers — or to allow them to be killed, under these circumstances. What I'm getting at is whether you think it's immoral for our government to kill *North Vietnamese* soldiers."

"Of course, I'm against senseless slaughter. For what do you take me?"

"I'm trying to answer that, Mr. Leitner. Let me put it another way. Do you think that it is immoral for American soldiers, acting under the orders of their government, to shoot and kill North Vietnamese soldiers, acting under the orders of their government?"

At last I saw his point and saw that Felix had seen it. The young man was hard and sure, the odious epitome of a generation that claimed a monopoly on virtue. But Felix, I noted to my dismay, was beginning to enjoy himself.

"No, I don't suppose I do."

"It is immoral, then, to ask a man to die in Vietnam, but not to kill there?"

"Yes. That may sound inconsistent, but I think I can show it is not. To ask a man to die in a hopeless cause, with no advantage to his country, is immoral. But if a man finds himself in South Vietnam, facing a cruel invader who wishes to enslave the state, I can hardly say that it is *immoral* of him to help the defenders, even to help them kill."

A slow, hostile murmur began to circulate throughout the auditorium.

"Then God, according to you, is on the side of the South Vietnamese?" cried the young man triumphantly.

"I don't know about God. How should I? But I certainly believe that right is on their side." The murmur was now becoming a tumult. "I have already stated my opinion," Felix continued, raising his voice to dominate, for a moment, the interference, "that the United States was justified in supplying South

Vietnam with air and naval assistance. Morally and politically justified! What would such military assistance be used for but against the armed forces of the invaders? Would it not result in the killing of at least some of them? And if that is the case, how could I possibly say that it would be immoral to shoot a North Vietnamese soldier?"

"Then the war itself is not immoral! It's only how we fight it!"

"Precisely."

"And you don't see the United States as an imperialist power spreading death and destruction to preserve its status in the Far East?"

"On the contrary, I see the United States as engaged in an insane act of international altruism. No great nation since the Crusades has ever expended so much blood and money fighting a war without hope of material gain. Future generations will marvel at it! If they don't merely laugh."

"Mr. Leitner, I see now what I must take you for. I denounce you as the archimperialist of our time!"

"My dear boy, don't be an ass. You're allowing yourself to reflect the most inane shibboleth of your generation." For a moment the audience was too surprised at this insult — so politely, so even amiably articulated — to be other than silent, and Felix was able to put in a few more words before pandemonium ensued. "You see evil only at home. You hate only Americans. You envision the world as threatened by Yankee militarists and Yankee financial pirates. But some day I'm afraid that you may awaken to face forces in Russia, forces in China, forces even in Africa, that will make Lyndon B. Johnson and Robert McNamara and all of their generals and all of the warmongers and all of the Communist-haters — nay, even the John Birch Society itself — seem like bright angels of love and mercy!"

Never shall I forget how Felix stood there amid the shrieks, the catcalls, the obscenities; smiling, nodding, raising his arms as if acknowledging an ovation. I made my way through the screeching mob to the dais and escorted him off it. As we came to the side door Varina rushed up with her hairy friend.

"Johnny warned me that you weren't really with us, Grandfather!" she cried in a harsh voice. "He warned me, and I didn't believe him. But he smoked you out!"

"Varina, you're a perfect ninny. You're worse than your mother. Nobody had to smoke me out. My opinions are available to all the world. Indeed, I'm very well paid for them."

"You have your thirty pieces of silver, Leitner," the young man, Johnny, sneered.

"The name is *Mr.* Leitner, and I'll thank you, sir, to get out of my way!"

I called to the chauffeur of our hired limousine to drive at once to our hotel, but Felix reminded me that we had left Felicia behind. He insisted that we wait, sitting placidly in the back seat while students surrounding the car jeered at us. But after a few minutes they tired of this and went away, and a rather bedraggled Felicia, who had been much jostled by the crowd, came up. I jumped out and pushed her into the car and told the driver to move away quickly.

"Oh, Daddy," Felicia exclaimed, bursting into sobs, "how could you? How *could* you?"

"Pull yourself together, Felicia."

"Do you think Varina will ever forgive you? Never! You've betrayed their cause. You've insulted their generation! You've made filth of their ideals and aspirations."

"Felicia, you're a greater ass than any of them. And it's worse for you, too, because you should know better."

"Don't be so high and mighty!" Felicia cried shrilly. "Do you think you're God? Yes, I suppose you do! All my life I've had to truckle to the idea that you knew everything. Well, you don't! You've missed the whole point of what's going in in 1965. The whole point!"

"Listen to me, my dear." Felix's voice was cold now, cold and steely. "All your life, like your mother, you've tried to see me as something I wasn't. You say you were made to truckle to the idea that I knew everything! Tommyrot! You resented everything about me from the beginning. You hated me for leaving your mother. You hated Gladys. You hated my success. More recently, you have tried to break up my friendship with Mrs. Pryor. You're even jealous of Roger here. Well, I'll tell you what. I'm an old man, and I am not going to have such little time as may be left me disturbed by your jealousy and possessiveness."

"Felix!" I warned him, for I saw the look of desperation in Felicia's countenance.

"When I return to Washington tomorrow," Felix continued inexorably, "I shall expect you to remain here. I shall, of course, pay your hotel expenses until you find a new home. We may continue to visit each other, but we shall most certainly not live together."

"Stop the car!" Felicia shrieked. "Let me out! I won't ride with you!"

The chauffeur pulled over to the curb, and Felicia sprang out of the car. I reached over to restrain her, but Felix, with surprising strength, pulled me back.

"Let her go, Roger," he said calmly.

For a long time, as we drove on uptown, we sat in silence. But when Felix spoke at last, his tone was almost matter-of-fact.

"Nobody could live with me, Roger. Nobody, that is, but yourself."

Roger Cutter (8)

JUST A WEEK AGO, at eight in the morning, Mrs. Corliss telephoned to say that the maid who had brought Felix his breakfast tray had been unable to awaken him. The end had been too long expected to bring anything but relief. Everything was ready. I made my telephone calls to Felicia, to Julia, to Gladys, and then to the *Washington Post* and the *New York Times*. Their obituaries had long been prepared. Only the date was necessary. I turned on my radio and television and waited.

Less than an hour later came the first news broadcast. Then the second. More followed, more and more, longer and longer, now with comments from dignitaries reached by telephone, now with stories plucked from newspaper morgues, until at noon a reporter on the TV screen announced the regrets of President Ford. My little drop of sorrow seemed to have swelled into an ocean of public lamentation. But it would burst soon enough, and I would be left alone again.

I did not go out. I turned off my telephone. I did not want to see anyone. I desired only to be left with my documents and papers about Felix. But this, of course, was impossible. Julie arrived and punched my doorbell. She and I had to do everything, make arrangements for the cremation, the service. For the next three days we seemed to live in a frenzy of irrelevant activity and ringing telephones.

The service was held in the National Cathedral. This was another of Felicia's eccentricities. She made her will — or should I say her whim? — much felt now. She said that so long as her father had had no religion, there was no harm in selecting any building that would comfortably shelter whatever multitudes should arrive. I thought fewer people would appear than she thought, but I was wrong, for the president came and, of course, then the church was packed. The prayers were innocuous — prayers usually are — but it irritated me that Felicia had insisted that we sing "A Mighty Fortress Is Our God." The whole thing seemed to have very little to do with Felix, and of course the Jewish friends and relations would say that it was the ultimate apostasy, that even in death Felix was trying to be a Wasp!

The long, laudatory obituaries, however, and the presence of so many of the mighty at the service had one good result. They briefly resurrected Felix, so that he seemed to stand before us again, as in raiment white and glistening. Then, as with a puff, he was gone again, restored to the nothing, the oblivion, in which the last two years had cast him. But as Easter brightens the darkness of the Passion, so did this momentary resurgence of Felix, young again and brilliant, provide me with what I hoped would become a permanent substitute for the sad memory of the sickroom and that vacant stare.

I took away my documents, and what I had written about them, for a solitary weekend in Julie's cottage at Virginia Beach, which she had kindly lent me. It was an experience as painful as I had long before, deep down, suspected and feared that it was going to be. All the doubts that I had obviously stifled about Felix, all the resentments that had almost strangled my unacknowledging mind during the tantrums of his last illness, now claimed their revenge. The Felix that arose from these pages refused to behave as he ought to have behaved. But, oh my God, if Felix wasn't Felix, what was I?

Had I loved him, or had I simply attached myself to him, like a pilot fish to a shark? And why did I use *that* image?

As soon as I got back to Washington I hurried to Julie's. She seemed to sense my perturbation, for she poured me a drink and simply waited, with an inquiring half smile, for me to tell her what was on my mind.

"Julie, tell me," I blurted out. "Were they right about him? All those people like Lila Nickerson and my father who said he was a monster?"

"A monster? Come now, dear."

"All right, not a monster. I'm being dramatic. But an egotist, a cold-hearted egotist, who wanted all the good things in life for himself. At least what he considered the good things: public glory and the joy of writing and a perfectly ordered home. At whatever cost to others, so long as their pain didn't show enough to spoil his fun!"

Julie was grave now. "Yes," she said. "He was that. Is it such a terrible thing to be?"

"But I've always denied it! I've always maintained that he was a man who had to subordinate everything and everybody in his life to his mission."

"And what was his mission?"

"Truth! He had to tell the world what it was! Politically and morally. Nothing could be allowed to get between him and that. He was like the saints, excused from the petty duties and loyalties of everyday living."

"Couldn't both theories be true? Couldn't he be a monster *and* a saint?"

"No! The issue has to be, Did he care more for truth or for the fame he derived in perceiving it? Did he love mankind or mankind as personified in Felix Leitner?"

"He was certainly very fond of Felix Leitner. But so am I of Julie Pryor. So are you of Roger Cutter."

"But I'm not!" I cried passionately. "That's just the point! Felix is more important to me than I am to myself. That's why I've got to be right! And now all these questions come boiling up. I suppose I've been repressing them all along. I suppose I've repressed my resentments, too. Maybe I even resented the way the poor man treated me when he was out of his mind."

"You wouldn't be human if you didn't."

"But he was a lunatic, Julie!"

"Lunatics can still hurt. What other kinds of questions keep boiling up?"

"Well, was he a free soul, or was he simply ashamed of his background? Was he the perfect democrat or . . . or was he the perfect snob?"

"He was certainly a snob."

"Julie!"

"He was, darling. Now listen to me. I don't share your theory about saints. I think they were all monsters, except perhaps Saint Francis of Assisi, and the tales about him were probably made up, anyway. But the point is that you have a very beautiful concept of Felix. Write it! What does it matter now what Felix actually was? How do you even know that he actually was anything at all? I should love to read a book about Felix as you see him. Or as you saw him, perhaps? You could call it your vision. Your vision of Felix Leitner."

"But that would be a novel!"

"Well, what's wrong with novels? After enough time goes by, they merge with fact. Would anyone care if I proved that Malory's King Arthur was nobler than the real one?"

For a moment I was actually intrigued by the idea. Then I brushed it off.

"That's ridiculous, Julie, Mallory probably thought his King

Arthur was absolutely true to life. One doesn't set about to create a legend."

"Why not?"

"One just doesn't, that's all."

Something, anyway, of vital importance to me, emerged from this discussion. After a long night of tossing on my bed and pacing the floor, I decided that, whatever should be my ultimate decision to write or not to write the book that would blend my raw materials into the portrait of a man who had dedicated every parcel of his being to the quest of truth, I owed something first to history. I had been Felix's disciple long enough to have developed a harder theory of truth and of my own obligation to it than any airy theory that Julie might play with. I might continue my private debate on the true character and personality of Felix Leitner as long as I chose, but it behooved me to assemble my documents and commentaries in some sensible chronological order and put them in a place of safekeeping available to future scholars who could make up their own minds about the questions that had troubled me. Very likely they would not care, but that was not the point. The point was to make the record.

And this I will do. When it is done I shall deposit my material with Felix's papers at Harvard. His shadow, then, will not be able to say that I tried to turn him into a puppet or to convert him into my own possession. My mission, whatever it was and whether or not it was one, will have been completed.

This decision made, I resolved to spend the day, not with the papers on Felix's life, but with his own work, his columns, and I took down from the shelf over my desk the morocco-bound copy of an anthology drawn from these.

It was an exquisite, immediate relief. For the words, the wonderful words, the crisp and pungent phrases, the sharp staccato sentences and their longer, subtler, mellifluous counterparts, now swarmed together in my dazzled mind to obliterate doubt, to overwhelm criticism. After a tumultuous grouping and regrouping, after a soaring up and a crashing down, they suddenly emerged, in even rows, in fantastic drill, like some beneficent, redeeming army marching into a stricken city after its occupiers had fled. And I seemed to make out that the prostrate town was the soul of Felix, over which women, good and bad, had fought and for which lawyers and statesmen had struggled, and which a fickle public had greeted with shrieks of praise and howls of derision. But now the words, the blessed words, redeemed all, saved all!

I heard the tramp on the cobblestones; I listened with a frenetic joy to the blaring martial music. I stumbled out of the cellar where I had been hiding from our oppressors and tore off my tattered shirt to wave it wildly and shout my welcome. The factions that had so long and cruelly held our ravaged city were no more. I was alone with Felix at last.